LAUGHING
DOWN THE

by

Eva Indigo

Bella
BOOKS

2013

Bella Books, Inc.
P.O. Box 10543
Tallahassee, FL 32302

First Bella Books Edition 2013

Editor: Katherine V. Forrest
Cover Designed by: Judith Fellows

ISBN: 978-1-59493-388-2

About the Author

Until now, Eva Indigo's writing has been somewhat closeted, even though she has not. By day, Eva Indigo teaches high school students about literature and writing, but by night she reads, writes, and runs—sometimes all at once.

In her recent history, she has helped to deliver lambs on the pasture; has developed a love of travel, thanks to her French wife; has earned a PhD in education out of curiosity; and has rescued several incredible companion animals. Ages ago, despite being very misplaced, she investigated the U.S. Army from the inside out as a member of the military police. After eight years, she found that she didn't like polishing boots, would never shoot anyone, and didn't understand what the war was all about anyway.

Now Eva splits her time between the woods around her cabin and her home in Minneapolis, unless she's fortunate enough to find herself running the hills of Ceyreste, France. It's in these places that she looks forward to un-closeting many more novels.

Spell for a Book Dedication

Light an indigo candle to honor another new beginning.
Scent your pages with cinnamon incense.
Sip something warm, sweet and mysterious.
Curl up in the corner of your couch.

This book is dedicated to
You
with the gentle moon held in your heart
and
deep magic flowing in your veins.

Acknowledgments

I must acknowledge and thank Catherine Friend, Katherine V. Forrest, and Cath Walker for their patient editing. I also thank Catherine Friend and Melissa Peteler for letting me farm-sit at Rising Moon Farm so that I could write surrounded by happy sheep. With unconditional love, I thank my wife, Florence. She is a self-proclaimed non-reader, yet she smiled as I followed her around the house reading my entire book aloud to her, and when I stopped, she asked for more. If I might be allowed to thank a place, I thank Bearheart Pond for feeding my writer's soul.

CHAPTER ONE

Laughing Half Moon

It was hard, but I did it. Right in the middle of a half moon pose, I managed a low rumble of a laugh. A few people in the laughter yoga class craned their necks to glance at me, but they didn't join in. Too shy?

Determined, I chuckled toward my navel during a very relaxing downward dog pose. No one joined me, but the magazine article said that people would chime in with their own laughter as the spirit moved them. Sometimes the first few laughs were infectious, and the whole room would rock with guffaws, trills and giggles. Other times the laughter might start slowly like a thunderstorm moving across the plains, a bolt of laughter here and there with quite a bit of time passing before the skies opened with the downpour of hilarity. From downward dog into chair pose and then into mountain pose, I let the chuckles continue as I arched my back and stared into the yoga studio's ceiling, wondering why the Y didn't paint it a more soothing shade. A stark white surface pocked with dark gray and black divots created the sky that covered us all as we flowed through the poses of my first laugh yoga class.

"Let your feet become one with the earth below you," the instructor advised through the microphone hooked over her right ear. "Dig deep into your world. Feel at one with yourself and everything that is around, beneath and above you," she said.

I laughed heartily to let her know I appreciated her words.

My attention was drawn to the young woman on my left as she let her arms fall to her sides, looked hard at me, scooped up her yoga mat and marched across the studio to unfurl her mat nearer the mirrors. It was important to feel your spot, I knew, and she must not have been feeling it next to me. No worries. I tightened my long dark ponytail and concentrated on my breath. At the direction of the instructor, I eased myself into the chair pose.

I started to think about last week's meeting with Dr. Browning, the psychiatrist I had consulted. Dr. Browning didn't think I was depressed, but what else could explain my recent experiences? My life had become lackluster. I suspected I *was* depressed. This diagnosis wouldn't be exciting, decadent or glamorous. It would be, in fact, just sort of…well, it would be just depressing, no pun intended; however, a proper diagnosis of depression would at least offer me a point from which to address the way I'd been skimming life's surface lately. Although Dr. Browning had said she wouldn't be sure until the screening had been evaluated, she said she believed I was experiencing the normal ups and downs of life. Why was I hoping for a dismal diagnosis?

I let out a giant guffaw straight from the depths of my belly, just like the laugh yoga article recommended. The way I'd been feeling lately was the reason I was here giving laugh yoga a go. Patrick, one of my oldest friends, had given me the article he'd come across in the *Star Tribune*. He'd recognized laugh yoga as something that was perfect for me. I was willing to trust him because he knew me better than almost anyone. He'd seen me through a long line of botched attempts at relationships and was still nursing me through this failure with my ex-girlfriend, Mickey. Patrick thought the laugh yoga might be more uplifting than anything Dr. Browning might prescribe. He had even gone out of his way to locate a class at the Y and buy me a new, deep green yoga mat. I hadn't the heart to tell Patrick that I already had a mat, but since it was collecting dust and probably housing a few families of mice in the garage, I welcomed the new mat as a happy beginning on my journey out of this funk that had enveloped me over the past year.

Patrick helped me become a Y member just yesterday. I was anti-gym but decided to give this a chance. I was surprised to find myself looking forward to the class this morning, so perhaps it was indeed just what I needed. Normally, because I have always disliked working out, it would have been doomed to go to the bottom of my to-do list. If someone told me that people-watching, eating Almond Joys and drinking red wine at Calhoun Beach counted as a workout, I'd never do it again. Seriously, the whole notion of working out took the fun right out of any activity. I was beginning to feel that way about my career as well.

Unfortunately, freelance writing had begun to resemble a job, work, rather than a career. The topics I was writing about seemed to pale in comparison to those I used to cover, even though there were no discernible differences between them. A few years ago the topics were fascinating. Now they were mundane. I was able to muster more enthusiasm to brush my teeth than to crank out an article. Perhaps I was burning out on writing. I let loose a loud haw-haw to chase this thought from my mind. This was really beginning to grow on me. I smiled more deeply as I heard another woman echo my laughter. Finally. I could already feel the benefit of laughing away bleak thoughts.

Did the instructor really just shush somebody? Or was that an almighty exhalation from a nearby yogi? At any rate, my mind focused on moving from warrior one to the triangle pose. I swiped at my sweat-soaked bangs and pulled down the elastic of the almost unnecessary shelf bra in my yoga top as I moved into the next pose. I pretended my next exuberant laugh was shooting straight out of my upstretched hand and aimed at the boring ceiling. I've read a bit about yoga and eked through enough yoga DVDs at home to know that the goal of yoga was to stop thinking mundane thoughts and focus only on breathing and the body. Okay, but banishing thoughts with laughter was proving to be good medicine. The next time I came for this class, I would concentrate solely on not thinking. I'd concentrate only on breathing and belly-laughing. It was weird that so far only the one woman had joined in, but that article had said that everyone should feel comfortable laughing at her own time. Perhaps this was an especially somber group today. It could be that they were all feeling the grim chill that had descended overnight. Whatever. I was feeling pretty good.

The instructor directed us into the smiling cow face pose. I wasn't familiar with that one, so I glanced over at my neighbor to my right. She was sitting up and folding her legs, one over the other like logs on the corner of a cabin. Ouch. I tried to copy her, stacking one knee over the other while sitting back on my sit bones. Good luck with this one.

"Let your face fall naturally, unclench your jaw and let ease flow through your eyes," the instructor crooned.

What? In this pose? I didn't think it was possible for ease to flow anywhere, let alone through my eyes. What did that mean anyway? I looked over at my neighbor who stared at me and then raised her eyebrows high. I raised my eyebrows back at her. Is this what "flowing ease" was? Or maybe this was the reason it was called smiling cow face. Made sense. It did feel good to raise my brows high, but my legs wouldn't do what they were supposed to do. I unclenched my jaw, but kept my eyebrows raised, so that I at least had that part of the pose correct. After a few more excruciating seconds of smiling cow face, the instructor directed us into child's pose—one that I was especially good at—and had us stay with our foreheads pressed to our mats for several moments. While I was communing, head down, with my yoga mat, I slowed my breathing and let out one more long, soft laugh. All this laughter soothed and energized me at the same time—incredible because it had been some time since I had felt energetic. As I eased myself back into the corpse pose, I realized the feeling was a welcome change.

"Namaste," the instructor said, and rose and bowed at us.

What? Was the class over already? The instructor sounded like she was eager to be somewhere else. We had gone through all the well-known poses, ending with a series of relaxation postures…was it really over? Why had only one other person laughed? I looked around the dim studio while the other yogis busied themselves with rolling up mats, putting on socks and shoes and drinking water. No one looked around in bewilderment like I did. In fact, everyone looked down except one woman who looked across the studio toward me. I couldn't be sure if she was looking at me, so I smiled, still feeling the warmth of all my laughter. Her expression didn't change at all. I watched as she tucked her black chin-length hair behind her ear. She had rolled her mat and slung its cord over one shoulder, holding the cord taut across her chest with one hand. Her other arm was bent at a ninety-degree angle in front of her. She was standing stock-still. Waiting, I guessed, for her friend who eventually took the woman's free arm and walked with her toward the studio door. They bent their heads together to discuss something that made them both smile. I looked down at my mat as they walked past me; I didn't want to be thought rude for staring.

In the locker room, the stinging glow left by the hot shower encouraged me to bundle up before facing the gray November chill. I hummed a bit of a Kings of Leon song as I packed my limp gym clothes into my bag and donned the usual—a smart black pencil skirt, an amber long-sleeved T-shirt and an amber bead necklace. I dried off on a butt-sized length of locker room bench and then sat to pull on chunky, woolen knee-high socks and my black cowboy boots. Most days this was my chosen uniform for living. Though the colors of the shirt and beads often changed, the skirt and cowboy boots were almost a given. To finish the ritual of dressing, I anointed each wrist with lavender oil. I didn't look in the mirror as I left because my hair rarely acted up. I knew what I'd see if I did look in the mirror. Elbow-length straight brown hair with eyebrow grazing bangs, brown almond-shaped eyes, wide cheekbones, decently rosy lips and a smattering of big freckles. The freckles were the only things that gave away the fact that I was Irish as well as Japanese.

As I left the Y, I said goodbye to the girl behind the desk and pulled my cell phone from the outer pocket of my gym bag to check the time. Ten thirty. I tucked it back in the pocket, just to have to yank it out again as it began an incessant buzzing, informing me I had six texts waiting for me. Five were from Patrick and the other was from my younger sister, Falina. I turned the ringtone back on and read the texts in order starting with the earliest.

"Shoot canceled! Will c u at the club for yoga!" That was Patrick at eight-oh-four a.m. Patrick was a photographer.

"Let's meet prior?" Patrick again, eight-ten a.m. Since it was Saturday morning, I had silenced my phone in order to sleep in before the nine o'clock class. I didn't even think to check the phone prior to class. Patrick must have decided not to go to yoga since I never returned the text.

"Waiting at 9th St entrance," wrote Patrick at eight forty-five.

What the hell? Ninth Street? The Y was on Blaisdell Avenue, just a few blocks from my home. Ninth Street would be…oh my Goddess. Ninth Street would mean Patrick was at the Downtown YMCA. I was at the Uptown Y.

"Going in. C u inside?" Patrick at eight-fifty.

"LOL! What a riot. I LOVE laugh yoga. Missed you!" Patrick ten minutes ago.

An uncomfortable heat rose up my neck and splashed across my cheeks. I squeezed my eyes shut. Oh. My. Goddess. I clenched my teeth as tightly as I was clenching my eyes. Was I going to be sick, right here on the sidewalk? I heard the whoosh-click of the Y's door behind me and forced myself to breathe in and open my eyes. Two people made conversation as they walked away from the club's door, away from me—thank the stars. I jammed my phone into my gym bag pocket without reading the text from Falina and ran nearly all the way home.

I threw my heavy front door open with a force that threatened to shatter the wavy lead glass in its windows, then slammed it shut. Nothing shattered; nothing, that is, except my pride. I whipped my gym bag into the corner of the front room and launched a full-body attack on my favorite piece of furniture. Face-down on the vintage fainting couch, with my forehead pressed to the red crushed velvet, I began to replay the non-laugh yoga class that I had, in my stupidity, tried to turn into a laugh yoga session. What the hell must everyone have thought of me? Why didn't anyone tell me to stop? Did they all think I was crazy? What else could they possibly think? How was I ever going to show my face there again?

U2 belted out "It's a Beautiful Day" from the pocket of my gym bag letting me know someone, probably Patrick, wanted to talk to me, but I couldn't bring myself to get up and answer the call. I wasn't crying, but I was close to it and didn't feel like keeping things in check for someone on the other end of the phone if the tears did come. The instructor's "Ssshhh…" echoed in my ears. That had been meant for me—or for the poor soul who'd laughed once with me. Or maybe she had been laughing at me! I let out a huge, shuddery sigh.

I gave in. I had a long cry, wetting the crushed velvet. Perhaps it would be cathartic. Maybe then I'd move on or at least pry myself from the cushions once the tears subsided, but the tears went on for much longer than I expected. I hated that I'd been crying more often lately. I hated that I'd ruined a nice Saturday morning for a bunch of people, but even more, I hated feeling embarrassed. I was also beginning to hate my ringtone as the phone rang again and Bono reminded me how un-beautiful my day had become in comparison to his.

Some time later, I pushed myself up off the fainting couch—how aptly named today—and wiped my eyes and nose with the amber sleeve of my T-shirt. There was a face-sized, dark-red splotch on my couch now. Had anyone else ever had a huge crying jag in that same spot? With vintage furniture, you just never knew. I tried to shake off those shuddering after-cry breaths that made me feel like I was bouncing down a few ladder rungs. I looked around the room and took in the pile of last week's newspapers, the three mostly empty mismatched coffee cups on the end table, the various papers and pencils scattered about the room and now my abandoned gym bag in the corner. Tidying up—that's what would make me feel better.

Ever since I had bought the Victorian house ten years ago, nothing made my world seem more right than making the old place feel tidy, warm and colorful. Mickey, my ex, had been a neat-freak, and since she had moved out I had rediscovered my enjoyment of the natural ebb and flow of clutter and cleanliness. This, however, was the first time I had felt like cleaning in a couple of weeks. Things were out of control since I had not been able to motivate myself to organize the evidence of life strewn across the house.

With the classic soundtrack of *Dirty Dancing* coursing through the surround sound, I began creating piles of the notes and mail: these go upstairs to my office, these go into the recycling bin and these go into the homeless pile to be re-sorted later. Before attacking the piles, I prepared a floor wash. Since I identified more with Paganism than any other religion, part of my practice was using herbs from my windowsill garden for healing and charms as well as for eating. Floor washes could be used to ask the Goddess or Mother Earth for help through any number of situations, and I needed help clearing away this funk and negativity. As I picked lavender and sweet basil from the needy windowsill garden, I boiled salt water on the stovetop. Like the rest of the house, the herb plants had been a bit neglected lately. I pinched back the basil and apologized to the rest of the garden. I promised to look after them better than I had been. Just as the water began to boil, I poured it over the herbs I'd picked for the floor wash. I'd let it steep for an hour before straining and using it. The scent was calming, so I breathed deeply over the bowl before addressing the paperwork piles I'd created.

With my arms full of the office-bound debris, I headed up the narrow staircase, noting on the landing halfway up that the window needed cleaning. I'd catch that on the way down. I pushed open the door to my office and felt the familiar dread when I entered the room. There was nothing wrong with the room itself; in fact, it was one of my favorites with its built-in dark wood bookshelves, the oversized window that faced the park across the street, the light wood floor, the heavy desk that sat right in the middle of the room like an invitation, and the dark green swivel chair parked at the desk. It was exactly the room I envisioned as I was going through my master's degree program for journalism. It was still my ideal place from which to conduct my career, even if the career was no longer ideal. I sighed and set the load of papers and notebooks on the desk. I planted my butt and spun around a few times before stopping the spiraling with my foot against the windowsill.

Despite the gray cold and the post-Halloween sugar hangover most youngsters would be suffering today, a few kids played soccer in the middle of the park, a couple of preteen girls jumped rope and an even younger boy attempted to make some shots at the basketball hoop. I toyed with the amber beads at my neck. The little boy failed time and time again.

I'd dashed right by the park but hadn't noticed anyone as I fled the laugh yoga crime scene. Now one of the jump rope girls put down her rope, scooted the little boy closer toward the basket and showed him how to hold the ball. She took a shot and made it. The little boy held up his hand to high-five her and then retrieved the ball to try it for himself. I pushed my foot hard against the sill so that I didn't have to witness his imminent failure. I spun the chair toward the desk and its new pile. Ugh. Watching the kid fail would be better than dealing with that, so I spun back in time to see the ball shimmy through the hoop. It didn't even hit the rim; it was all net. How do you like that? I attacked the pile of papers.

Book of Shadows
Spell for Dispelling Embarrassment

Cast the circle.
"Blessed be Creatures of Light."
Light white candles in brass holders to bring protection
and love.
"Thank you, paper and pen, for allowing me to cast my
negative energy onto you
as I write, thereby freeing myself from the shadows I
have created."
Greet and honor the four directions and the universal
elements.
"I'm writing to Mother Earth, God, and Goddess to
request relief from the embarrassing laugh-non-laugh
yoga class.
I may have ruined some people's morning,
and I definitely made my own morning uncomfortable,
regardless of how comfortable it was before I knew I was
in the wrong place.
I'm asking for assistance in being able to forget about
this little incident.
Thank you."
Written on paper from my desk. Washed in salt water
until the words run together.
Soaked in same salt water until softened. Torn into
shreds.
"Embarrassment, like this paper, will be shredded.
To ease and comfort, am I now headed."
Thank the four directions and the universal elements.
"Blessed be Creatures of Light."
Extinguish candles.
Open the circle.

CHAPTER TWO

All Samhain's Silent Supper

"You said I needed a few big, deep laughs, but all I got was a melodramatic crying spree on the fainting couch!" I said.

"Yeah, but don't you feel better?" Patrick asked.

We were sitting on the floor with our elbows on the low oak coffee table in his and Trisha's living room. Their house was a welcoming arts and crafts bungalow in a friendly neighborhood in south Minneapolis. An abundance of rich colors, gleaming wood and charm surrounded us. I felt at ease here. I listened to the stone fireplace crackle and sizzle as the logs yielded to the flames and heat. I thought about Patrick's question.

"Yes and no," I answered. "Honestly, I liked the laugh yoga—I was so into it that I didn't even realize it wasn't laugh yoga!" I laughed. "But now, looking back, I feel stupid."

"Oh, Allura," Patrick said. He pushed up the sleeves of his gray fleece pullover and patted my arm. I noticed his ears stretch backward under his coppery red hair as he tried not to laugh. "Maybe later we can try it again in the right class," he pressed his lips together, "but for now, I'd just avoid that YMCA."

"Definitely," I said.

"It was cool though," he continued, "I thought there'd be actual yoga, the kind you need a mat for, but there wasn't. It was more of an internal yoga thing."

"Mm-hmm…"

He patted my arm again and said, "You'll like it."

Trisha, dressed head to toe in stylish, soft, pale blue denim, entered and set down a tray containing a decanter of red wine, five glasses, a hunk of creamy white cheese and two or three dozen crackers on a plate, two little knives and a king-sized Almond Joy bar. Ah, these were my people. Knowing that the Almond Joy bar was for me, I gave Trisha a look of gratitude. She smiled, the corners of her blue eyes crinkling up like half-closed paper fans. I love Trisha's face. She has the quintessential pale blond look that just screams Scandinavia. She was glacial ice—in appearance only—whereas Patrick was a glowing ember with his red hair, freckles and strawberry blond eyebrows.

"As soon as Veronica arrives, we'll start the Silent Supper," Trisha said. Veronica was a floor manager at a dialysis clinic and was often required to work long hours.

Most Pagans held their Samhain celebrations to honor the dead on October thirty-first, but since Patrick was a devout Catholic, he and I had started a set of traditions decades ago that allowed us both to feel like we were doing the right thing. We used the traditional silent Samhain supper to honor the dead on the November first Catholic holiday of All Saints' Day. It worked well for Patrick and me; for Veronica, however, it worked a little less well, but she partook each year in our celebrations. Veronica is what I call a hard-core Pagan, whereas I am what I like to refer to as a soft-core Pagan. Call me wishy-washy, but I just think that there is more than one path to the well-being of the soul.

Over the years, Patrick, Veronica and I had culled a hybrid spirituality. We celebrated Solschristice, which was Yule alongside Christmas; Eastara, which was Ostara combined with Easter; and All Samhain, which was Samhain on All Saints' Day. Recently we'd created Spring Equipassion, which was the Equinox woven into Passion week. Patrick and I had decided in high school that all of these rituals and celebrations had likely originated from the same early practices anyway. As we started to get to know Veronica at university, she began to water down her Pagan ways with our hybrid ones. Trisha, not being given to one religion or path of spirituality, was always a graceful participant in our celebrations. Of course, she had only entered the picture a few years ago and probably knew she'd never change our eclectic ways.

Veronica gusted into the house without knocking. Above her tightly laced Victorian boots, her inky black swing coat swirled. Her dark hair had a row of sister knots, or "sistah knots" when she said it, that framed her face while the rest of her hair sprang delightfully out in all directions. She was just into her forties, but with her chubby cheeks, she looked much younger. The flames roared more brightly in the fireplace from the torrent of fresh air, so Veronica's entrance was accompanied by the satisfying scent of burning pinewood. Veronica had gift bags, a backpack and a heavy cloak thrown over one arm and a bouquet of homegrown, dried flowers in the other. She must have cut down what was left of her impressive garden in preparation for the winter. I jumped up to unburden at least one of her arms. Patrick did the same. I went for the flowers, and he went for the backpack and the cloak. Veronica, with gift bags still dangling, gave us both hugs and called hello to Trisha who had returned to the kitchen. I placed the dried flowers in the glass vase that stood on the tiny table by the front door. The vase was always there, always ready, for Veronica never arrived without something from her garden.

"Happy All Sah-veeeeen, Veronica!" Trisha called.

Veronica tossed her coat over the banister. She wore a low-cut dark green blouse that showed off her deep, soft cleavage. An even darker green velvet skirt with black lace edging and her tiny black ankle boots finished the outfit. She and I smiled at each other over Trisha's careful pronunciation.

Veronica called back, "Thank you, my dear!"

"What's in the bags?" Patrick asked, setting the backpack on the floor and draping the cloak over the back of a chair. He returned to Veronica's side and started peering into the folds of black tissue paper that filled the intriguing silver bags.

"Never mind, nosy!" Veronica jerked the bags out of Patrick's reach. Her brown eyes were shiny with secret knowledge. She loved surprising us with what she called her little giftees. "See if you can find some patience in one of those wineglasses," Veronica said.

"Harrumph. I'll find *something* in here," Patrick said, holding out an empty glass and inspecting it by the light cast from the collection of candles on the fireplace hearth, "but I doubt it will be patience."

He filled it with wine and passed it to me, then handed another to Veronica. She found a space for herself on the floor as Patrick filled the remaining three glasses, called to Trisha and passed one to her after she set a stack of five small white plates on the coffee table. Trisha settled in on the floor beside me. She leaned against the couch, tucked a strand of her flaxen hair behind one ear and inhaled deeply over her wine.

"Ahh," she breathed out.

"Everybody ready?" Veronica asked.

We nodded and looked at each other to make sure there was nothing else that needed to be said before we honored those who had passed before us with our silent supper. I was more than ready this year. Having to listen to Patrick tell Veronica about the laugh yoga mishap this morning was not high on my list of fun evening activities, so I was relieved to be entering at least an hour of silence. If the story came up after dinner, well, so be it. For now, I welcomed the communal solitude.

"Wait!" Trisha hopped up, dashed to the mp3 deck and turned the volume up. "There's nothing worse," she said, "than listening to chewing during these silent suppers." She arranged herself on the floor next to me again. "That's okay, isn't it? To have music at dinner, I mean. It's not silent, but—"

"Of course it is," said Veronica, nodding. Her lingering glance touched all of us. I knew she was going through some of the ritual in her head, rather than in actuality, in order to not weird out Patrick. She cleared her throat and sat taller, kneeling with her heels tucked beneath her beside the low table. "Okay," she continued, raising her wineglass toward the middle of the coffee table, "tonight, in silence, under the light of the waxing moon and with the warmth of the creatures of fire, do we honor those who have come and gone before us. Let us do what we can to walk respectfully in their steps and be open to their words tonight if they need to reconnect themselves with us to offer guidance. We give thanks for another wonderfully abundant harvest, and we give thanks for the beginning of the end of yet another incredible year. God, Goddess, Mother Earth, let us sense you in every way possible as we honor our ancestors."

With this, she set down her glass, carefully sliced a bit of cheese from the hunk and placed it on one of the small plates. She put two crackers on the plate beside the cheese and set the plate in the center of the table. She moved the unclaimed, fifth glass of wine beside the plate and grasped her wineglass again by its stem. She clinked its rim first to the glass in the middle of the table and then to each of ours. We each clinked our own glasses to the center wineglass and then to each other's. "So mote it be and amen," Veronica said.

"So mote it be, amen," we all replied with gusto, our smiles the last act of communication for the next hour. Patrick dipped his head at Trisha and gave her a wink, which she returned.

I loved being with them. I was so grateful that nothing had changed between Patrick and me when Mickey and I had broken up. Or when Mickey dumped me, I should say. Trisha and Mickey were like Bert and Ernie from *Sesame Street*, total opposites, but great friends. They'd known each other long before they met Patrick and me. They had gone to the same all-girls' Catholic school as children and had been friends since the sixth grade. Mickey had been the one to introduce Patrick and Trisha a few years ago, thinking that they'd hit it off. They had, and the rest was a delicious history.

They were married a year after they met and were, in my eyes, the perfect couple. It was the kiss of death to think of them like that, but there it was. I couldn't handpick a better mate for Patrick. Trisha was smart, independent, beautiful and gutsy, and

Patrick deserved the best of the best, as far as I was concerned. I had told Patrick several dozen times that if Trisha were gay, I'd steal her right out from under him. He had told me each time that if Trisha were gay she would never be under him in the first instance. He makes a good point. I smiled, raised my glass, inhaled the dark aroma and took a large sip of the merlot. I let it have its way with each taste bud as it journeyed over my tongue.

Our first All Samhain with Veronica, all those years ago, had for some reason made me nervous. Now, taking my second sip of wine, I thought of that night. I must have been drinking double-time in order to ease my nerves because before the dinner had ended, I had made eye contact with Patrick, who had then looked at Veronica, who, when I looked over at her, had been staring at me. This absurd eye contact triangle had struck me as infinitely funny, so I had burst out in a big, tipsy laugh, much like I had this morning at yoga. I cringed.

At the time, Veronica had also started laughing. Then Patrick had choked on some bread as he had tried not to laugh with us. Soon he couldn't even breathe. Veronica, who paled despite being so dark complexioned, had reached out and whacked Patrick hard on the back. Eyes wide, Veronica had stopped laughing, and so had I. The whack had catapulted the bread wad out of Patrick's throat and right onto the plate that was set to feed and honor the dead. We all stared at that soft little bread ball that had attempted murder, and Veronica had started to cry. Patrick and I had comforted her. I remembered him saying that the dead would not be upset that we ruined their dinner, which had made Veronica begin to cry harder and, at the same time, begin to laugh again.

"No," she had wept, "I was scared you were going to die!" Her face had been shiny with tears and laughter. We never quite regained our composure that night. That seemed so long ago now, long before Mickey had joined us in our celebrations.

Thinking of that now, I kept my gaze on the dishes at the center of the table. They were the only plate and glass that were not emptying as the dinner went on. Would Patrick empty the plate and glass after Veronica and I left for the night? Or would

Trisha? All these years of celebrating Samhain and I never thought about this before. Odd.

I had also never thought about how we looked like a group of poster children for a multispiritual, multiracial ad campaign. Veronica's brown eyes and brown skin were set aglow by the pale whiteness of Trisha and the golden ruddiness of Patrick. Trisha's long, flaxen hair stood in ethereal contrast to my own long, dark straight hair. And that helped showcase the wonderful spring of Veronica's brown hair and the fiery sheen of Patrick's red hair. I was pretty certain that everyone's round-shaped eyes highlighted my own almond-shaped ones. And then, too, we ran the gamut of sexual orientation…from straight to lesbian with bases covered in between. Somewhere, a human rights campaign was smiling down on our gathering. Granted, our poster was missing people of Latin and Native American descents, but we did have the Asian, Northwestern European and African angles covered. Funny how these things come together sometimes.

After an hour of silence, Veronica cleared her throat. I never broke the silence because I could never think of anything important enough to say to bring attention away from those who had gone before us to those of us who were still here. Plus, I didn't trust myself not to crack a joke.

"Blessed be the beings whose spirits may have stopped by for a visit tonight. Blessed be the Goddess, God, and Mother Earth," Veronica said. I expected more, but she rose, collected the gift bags and deposited one in each of our laps. She then went over to the heavy green cloak she'd brought and draped it across my outstretched legs.

"This is for you—you'll need it to go with what you learn from the book inside the bag," she said to me. "And you two won't need cloaks—or much else for that matter—to go with what you'll learn from your books." She smiled devilishly at Trisha and Patrick.

The cloak's weight pressed my legs to the floor. Its crushed pale green velvet exterior and dark green satin lining thrilled my palms as I ran my hands through its luxurious folds.

"Thank you, Veronica," I exhaled, "it's beautiful."

Veronica's smile was warm and full.

From my gift bag I pulled a book called *Drawing Down the Moon* by Margot Adler. Drawing Down the Moon was a ritual for bringing the energy of the Goddess into yourself. I realized that it was exactly the ritual I needed to snap out of this funk. I had seen this book before but had never read it.

"Thank you, Veronica," I said. How did I ever find such wonderful people?

"You're welcome," she said, ducking her head a bit. I thought I saw a blush warm her brown cheeks, but it was hard to tell in the candlelight.

I laughed when Patrick held his gift aloft, his smile huge and his eyes alight. His new book was a travel guide to the clothing optional beaches in Europe. He and Trisha were planning a trip for next summer. Trisha's book was called *Sky-Clad*, evidently also about nudity.

"Well, I sense a theme here," Trisha said, laughing.

"I'm going to have to put in a few more hours at the gym, I guess," Patrick sighed, patting his imaginary beer belly.

"As if," I snorted. Trisha rolled her eyes.

For the next hour or so, we looked over Trisha and Patrick's new books. I was saving mine for later when I could truly savor the ideas within it. Patrick dog-eared pages in his book as he found beaches that caught his or Trisha's eye. At the end of the evening as we were saying our goodbyes, I realized I still hadn't read the text from my sister.

CHAPTER THREE

The Assignments

The daisy-shaped clock on the sky-blue wall ticked as loudly as a time bomb. Dr. Browning shuffled through the papers in my file. Mine, I noticed with some relief, was the thinnest among the files stacked on her desk. I looked at Dr. Browning's forehead, furrowed behind her clunky black-framed glasses, wondering what she'd add to her earlier informal diagnosis. She wore a white cotton blouse with poufy short sleeves. I counted the blue star-shaped buttons that ran down the front of her shirt until my view was interrupted by her desktop. Seven. Even though I couldn't see her legs now that she was seated, I knew she had on a full, dark blue skirt that was edged in white cotton lace. And despite the chill of autumn, her bare legs ended in strappy, white high-heeled sandals. Her style, I thought, was too young for her forty-some years. I was almost forty and wouldn't feel comfortable in poufy short sleeves. Tick, tick, tick, tick. She took out a page of her handwritten notes, placed it on the desk, drew a red ink circle around a word or two and then proceeded to make hasty underlining marks on down the page. Tick, tick.

She nodded three times before looking up at me. Her dark hair swung forward with each nod.

"Adjustment Disorder, with a specifically depressed mood, is what I had assumed we'd be dealing with here," Dr. Browning said, "but there is nothing in the results to lead me to that conclusion. You are not depressed. You have nothing to worry about, other than dealing with the normal variability of day-to-day life." Tick, tick…pfezzzzz…a dud, thank the Goddess. Wait, if I wasn't depressed, why did I feel like I had lost my edges and was slipping through life?

"Nothing to worry about?" I asked.

"Nothing."

"How do I get back to feeling normal?"

"Tell me more," she responded, peering at me through her heavy glasses.

I hated it when people use statements that are so stereotypical of their profession. I sighed.

"I feel like my highs aren't as high and my lows aren't as low as they used to be."

"You want low lows?" she asked, looking at me with that direct I'm-going-to-sort-you-out look.

"No…of course not," I said. I sat back, folded my arms and then toyed with the garnet beads around my neck as if this would buy me time to think. "But I do want high highs again. I don't want to feel as if I've already lived the best parts of my life. That would just be so…so sad."

Dr. Browning laughed and said, "I see." She made an additional underline on the notes from our last meeting, the only meeting where we had actually talked. The second time I'd come to her cheerful office, I'd filled out a Minnesota Multiphasic Personality Inventory to determine where I was emotionally. I didn't even see Dr. Browning that time, as her assistant had led me into a small pink-walled room and had shown me how to fill out the test. But before the test appointment, I had already told Dr. Browning about what I had been experiencing for the past five months.

Mickey and I had broken up a little over a year ago, but she hadn't moved out until this past July. I didn't know if it was her absence and the deafening silence in the house or if it was the gloomy pall cast over my work by humdrum writing assignments, but something had me down. Perhaps I had been feeling down for longer and only since Mickey's absence had I had time to notice. I didn't know how to be certain about it, whatever it was. Maybe it was a combination of bad projects and loneliness, or maybe it was something completely unrelated, something like the onset of menopause or maybe a brain tumor that was putting too much pressure on the joy receptors in my brain.

Whatever the case, Falina, Patrick and Veronica had each spoken separately to me regarding my emotional state. Each said it wasn't like me to be so flat. I had to agree. Come to think of it, I had noticed other things as well. My skirts were hanging a bit baggier around my hips because I didn't really have the high taste bud needs that I usually did, and I wasn't getting excited about my social engagements. In fact, I had even skipped a few events. I wasn't sleeping well. I'd been living an uninspired life lately, not feeling much of anything one way or another.

The test had been interesting. It had statements that I was supposed to rate as being like me or not like me to varying degrees. Most statements were straightforward and dull, but every now and then there would be a zinger, like "I like to swear when I get mad." I wanted to respond, "Fuck yes," but that option was not offered. And I would have felt guilty using the word in such a happily decorated place. Another test item stated, "I have met problems so full of possibilities that I have been unable to make up my mind about them." What a beautifully crafted sentence. I answered that that statement was very like me.

"What I notice from my notes," Dr. Browning said, still looking at me like she was going to say something that would just knock this funk out of me, "is that you have experienced a loss in your relationship. Then you experienced a loss in your home and therefore your work environment, since you work from home. First when you and your partner decided not to pursue a love relationship and then again when she moved out of your house."

"Yes," I said, probably quite unnecessarily.

"Then you began experiencing a series of mini-losses as you discovered that many of the friends you and Mickey shared did not know how to handle the end of your relationship," she continued.

I nodded, not having viewed what happened with my and Mickey's friends as losses, but now as I heard Dr. Browning's words I realized that loss was exactly what I felt. I hated having to wonder which friends or acquaintances would still act the same and which would be different, weird or distant. I really hated the quietness of the house. Not even the combined efforts of the TV, mp3 player and the dishwasher could fill up the house the way Mickey had. Not that she was an unusually noisy person, but when she was there, I always knew she was there.

"You are not depressed," Dr. Browning said. "You'll likely be feeling normal soon without medication, but I do have a few other things I'd like you to try before our next meeting."

* * *

So it was not depression. This was good. No one wants to hear she's depressed. It's not happy; it's not celebrated. No one would ever buy tickets to a show called *Depression: The Musical*. I laughed out loud as I imagined the stage and the actors in a musical about depression. Everyone wearing cement shoes, having faces as long as Melpomene—the Greek muse of tragedy—dragging their knuckles on the ground as they moped across the stage and basically had a miserable time. I watched the cracks of the sidewalk pass under my boots as I walked home from Dr. Browning's. The cement was littered with brilliant fallen leaves collected into mounds, and before I could trudge through them, the wind lifted and shifted these mounds like East Coast sand dunes. I kicked at one of the larger leaf dunes. Surprised at its lightness, I almost fell over at the lack of resistance.

What else would *Depression: The Musical* be like? It could be a tragedy where everyone offs themselves in the end, or it could be a satire perhaps, where the main character winds up losing all her friends due to the almighty sadness she drags around with her. Yes, that would be the heart of the musical, a tangible bag of sadness thrown over the heroine's shoulder. The bag would wear her down slowly, slowly, ever so slowly until…until what? I didn't know and didn't have to wonder; I was not depressed. I didn't have to star in *Depression: The Musical.* Give me a show like *Hilarity Ensues: A Musical Joy Ride!* I'd gladly star in that one.

According to Dr. Browning, I was experiencing the normal variability of life. According to me, I was experiencing an insipid period I'd refer to as The Funk. She said this could wear me down unless I attacked it head on, and she suggested a list of tasks that might bring back my edges. She prescribed taking a class of some sort that had nothing to do with anything I'd ever done in my life, adopting the homeliest animal at the Humane Society, attending social functions that I'd rather skip and watching some old TV shows from my teen years while reflecting on events I perceived as crises during the time the shows originally aired. It was an odd list that felt long despite its only having four items, but I was ready to give them a go.

The cool damp tobacco smell of autumn wrapped itself around me and then vanished. I sighed and took another swipe at a pile of leaves. This time, however, I kicked more gently, and the leaves fanned out in front of me and fell like pillow fight feathers.

Wouldn't yoga class count for one of Dr. Browning's assignments? Before last week, I had never taken a yoga class. I had only done yoga with DVDs in my living room at home. Dr. Browning wanted me to try something brand new, so technically it should count. Part of me wanted to nitpick every one of her assignments, but each one made sense based on the information she had drawn out of me. This new class assignment made sense. But if I used the yoga class as my new class, I'd have to tell her about it, and I still hadn't come to terms with the ass I'd made of myself in the non-laugh yoga class. Talking about it might be the very event that would push me out of The Funk and into a full-blown depression. So, no, then. I'd find another type of class.

Maybe a cooking class over on Grand Avenue or a creative writing class at the Loft, a literary center for writers, would do. A cooking class might help me bring back my appetite, but a creative writing class might give me the outlet that I craved. My column for *The Indelible* had grown bleaker and bleaker. All I wanted to do these days when writing it was burst out in humorous, irreverent quips that were the class clowns of my mind. The topics I found myself covering were so mundane that all I could do to stay even peripherally interested was to create cynical, sarcastic barbs in response to what I was writing.

Maybe a change in publication would do me well. *The Indelible* was a well-respected, well-established magazine whose full name was *The Indelible: The Final Word in Writing*. But if it were really the final word, wouldn't there have been only one installment? That had always bothered me. But at any rate, my column focused albeit loosely on technology for writers. So for the last few weeks, as I considered looking for an alternative magazine, I wondered whether I just needed a change of topic, something other than about writing…but I hadn't tackled any unsolicited articles to send out to other publications. Instead, I was mired in the sticky, unsavory here and now.

I barely remembered to take a left on Thirty-Seventh to avoid the crazy-looking cat that was no doubt plotting my death every time I walked by him as he perched on the porch railing. Safely on the sidewalk of Pleasant Avenue, I kicked another mound of leaves just as a murder of crows burst from the trees above me. For a moment their inkiness blotted out the weak sunlight and the flock became as one before scattering. I watched them seek new perches. As they cawed, one glossy ebony feather floated down to the sidewalk and landed inches in front of my boot. I bent down to pick up the feather and twirled it between my finger and my thumb. Its iridescence came from some unknown source, since it wasn't the watery November sunlight being reflected off the tiny, separate fronds.

The crows stopped their raucous protesting. They eyed me, but not suspiciously. I eyed them back then offered them a thank you, silently so as not to rile them up again. I tucked the feather into my woven shoulder bag. A century or two ago, witches were often depicted with a crow nearby. The crow would be investigating a mystical token or poking at a shiny trinket with his beak, but the viewer would always know that the crow was doting on the witch. What would it be like to have a crow for your companion animal? Or for your familiar?

Lots of cultures had familiars. Pagans usually believed their familiars were real live animals that they connected with on psychic and emotional levels. Back in the day, familiars were thought to be animals taken over by fairies or demons who would carry out the bidding of their witches. In some Native American cultures, familiars weren't real animals at all but rather spirits who offered guidance and protection. I saw them as friendly animals to learn from, so having a crow as a familiar would teach a person to be resourceful and curious. That wouldn't be so bad.

Because it was the middle of a school day, the park across the street from my house was empty save for a shaggy beige dog leading around a lone walker. It was hard to say if it was a man or a woman with the amount of outerwear the person had on. The park became a different place at various times of day and through the range of seasons. In a few hours the park would be alive with shouts, balls and discarded jackets. But right now, it was quiet.

I turned my back on the peace of the park as I strode into my front yard. As I took the porch steps two at a time and entered the warm foyer, a sense of home made me forget about the crow's feather for a while.

CHAPTER FOUR

Sibling Bribery

"Why are you calling and not texting?" Falina asked later that evening.

I curled my feet under me on the fainting couch and cupped my cell phone to my ear. "I'm lazy," I answered, "and I didn't want to have to explain why I didn't read your text when it came in."

"Yeah, why didn't you read it? That was days ago!" Falina said.

"Uhm, long story. So, what did you mean when you texted that Mom and Dad finally did it?"

"Really?" Falina spouted. "You really think you're going to get off without telling me the story now? Nice attempt at changing the subject—really highlights your evasion tactics."

"What evasion tactics?" I tried for a light tone of innocence, but I had raised my little sister too well. She was a savvy one.

"Nice," she said, "real nice try. You can tell me your story first. Then I'll tell you about Mom and Dad, or you can not tell me your story and live in ignorance."

"Or I could hang up and call Mom," I offered.

"Oh, come on!" Falina cried, "Just tell me! You always text back immediately! And here it is, what, twenty-four-plus hours! What's up? Did you lose your phone in an embarrassing place?"

I shifted my phone to the other ear and reached around behind myself to see what was making me uncomfortable. Behind the throw pillows on the fainting couch I discovered my big leather-bound Book of Shadows. A Book of Shadows could be compared to a prayer book or a cookbook. Some Pagans, Wiccans, and other witches used the books to write down their intentions, rituals and spells. Many people also recorded the outcome of their spells, but I rarely remembered to go back in and do that. My Book of Shadows had started out as a blank journal, but now it was over half-filled with handwritten charms and spells that I'd tried over the years. I set it on the table in front of me, reconfigured the throw pillows and got comfortable again. Did I really have to tell Falina about the whole fiasco?

"Okay, no," I caved. "I decided to try a laugh yoga class after Patrick had told me about it, so I joined the Y."

"Laugh yoga?" Falina asked.

"It's supposed to stimulate your core and get you breathing more deeply. So anyway, I showed up at the class and it wound up not being laugh yoga. That's all."

"That doesn't really explain why you didn't text back to me," Falina pointed out.

"Well…" Painful as it was, I told her what happened.

Falina was laughing on her end of the call. I actually smiled, hearing her laughter. Falina had that hiccupy, sometimes silent laughter, so I always pictured a wave ebbing and flowing when she really got going. I knew her pretty, pale face would be luminous with her eyes screwed up tight and her mouth thrown wide open. I listened to the soundtrack of her amusement and began to feel a little bit better.

"I guess I single-handedly dispelled the myth that all Asians are good at yoga, so there is that," I said. My self-induced smile was rueful.

"Well," Falina said as soon as she got herself under control, "you know what they say: there's nothing like a good old Tupperware party to help you forget your worries!"

"Who, exactly, says *that*?" I felt better, but not better enough to attend a Tupperware party with her.

"I do," she said, "I'm throwing one at a teacher's house near Lake Calhoun, and I think you'll enjoy it. It'll certainly take your mind off yoga," she coaxed.

Falina had sold Tupperware for years. She was good at it, with a whole bunch of people selling Tupperware underneath her—her "crew" she called them, but I'd never been to one of her parties. That suddenly seemed peculiar to me, but at the same time I wasn't sure if she had ever read one of my articles. How could we be so close yet not have any firsthand experience with what the other did on a day-to-day basis? I remembered Dr. Browning's advice about saying yes to social events that presented themselves to me. Damn it.

"Okay, tell me about Mom and Dad while I make up my mind about your party," I bartered.

With a mixture of disbelief and awe in her voice, Falina told me their news. My eyebrows rose higher than they did when I had been trying to assume the smiling cow face yoga pose. I told Falina I'd go to her Tupperware party as I tried to digest the news she had just delivered about Benji and Elly Satou, our Mom and Dad.

Book of Shadows
Spell for Finding My Familiar

Three days after the New Moon cast the circle.
Set out a dish of dirt collected from a footprint
and a bowl of clear, clean water.
Burn juniper incense.
"Blessed be Creatures of Light."
Light white candles in brass holders to bring protection
and love.
Missing image of Familiar due to indecision—use the
earth's offerings, whatever is around me now—this
pinecone will do.
Greet and honor the four directions and the universal
elements.
"I'm writing to Mother Earth, God, and Goddess to
request assistance
in finding my Familiar.
I have no idea how to recognize my Familiar, therefore
I have no specifics in my request, other than to humbly
request that my Familiar be an animal other than a cat."
Written on birch paper fallen from front yard tree.
Placed in amulet and worn until Familiar comes home
with me.
Thank the four directions and the universal elements.
"Blessed be Creatures of Light."
Extinguish candles.
Open the circle.

CHAPTER FIVE

Pink, Naked Belly Needs a Home

"Take the neediest animal—the one who practically throws himself at you," Veronica said as she opened the door to the din of the dogs' wing at the Humane Society.

"The neediest one?" I asked. "Why? So he can die in my possession two months from now?" The barks, bawls and brays were already crushing my heart, and we hadn't even reached the first kennel.

"He won't die in your possession." Veronica sounded exasperated. She took off her swing coat and held it over one arm revealing a simple dark blue dress made less simple by a black satin corset elaborately laced up her back. The garment showcased her ample cleavage. "He'll be so happy to have you as his new owner that he won't even be able to contemplate dying. And because it's one of your assignments from your shrink." Veronica made air quotes around the words "assignments" and "shrink."

I had told her about my short to-do list from Dr. Browning. Veronica was anti-therapist, not trusting that people's best interests were well-served by someone who charged by the hour, but the list of tasks did appeal to her, especially this task of adopting a companion. Bringing home a pet to help me feel better adjusted to the hole left by Mickey's and some of our communal friends' departures was not one of my favorites. Joining a new class, practicing saying "yes," and watching old TV shows, now those assignments were reasonable.

"Excellent corset, and we'll see," I said, pointing at her outfit and then kneeling down to look into the eyes of a small, tail-wagging hybrid of a dog.

"Thanks, and just go with the one that grabs your heart the hardest. You'll know him when you see him," Veronica assured me.

"It won't be a dog, but we can look," I said to Veronica. "Hi, little guy," I cooed. The dog sat his little beige butt resolutely on the floor of his kennel. "Whatcha doin?" I asked. What a dumb question. He was doing the only thing he could do in his little kennel and that was to wait. Wait for someone to notice him, pick him out and take him home. I made the mistake of looking at his next-kennel-door neighbor. He was a big golden retriever who literally smiled at me between giddy barks. I tipped my head toward his kennel because either he had two wagging tails or he had a kennel mate.

Kennel mate it was. He shared space with a medium-sized black dog that didn't want to make eye contact with me. So I looked back at the grinning golden. When I did, I felt the eyes of his kennel mate on me. So I looked back, but he looked away again. His tail wagged faster when I looked at him, though. He must have been playing hard-to-get. Good tactic, I told him in my head. But a dog was not the right companion animal for me.

I had thought a good deal about it all and knew my familiar would have to be an animal that matched my own Japanese-Irish temperament. Dogs were too outgoing and dependent. I needed a familiar who could do his own thing while I wrote, didn't need to be let in and out, yet who would bring some life to my home. What kind of animal would *that* be? I ran my fingers over the amulet in my skirt's pocket, wondering.

I heard a raspy scrambling behind me and when I looked over my shoulder, I was greeted with the sight of not one but two scruffy-faced Jack Russell mixes. How did two dogs, from what I'm guessing was the same litter, wind up at the Humane Society? They were chasing each other in tight circles. Every now and then, they'd slow down enough for the tawny and white blur to become two separate dogs with well-defined spots. One kept his eyes on me even as he raced after his scrappy little buddy. He sent his metal water dish flying. I was shocked to hear the metallic clatter over all the yapping and howling in the clean, cement-walled corridor. The new puddle stopped the race as both dogs nosed around in the water, investigating. Aw Goddess, what was I doing here? How did people ever just choose one single dog to adopt? I turned back to the beige dog in front of me. He was still sitting, waiting for me to bring my attention back to him.

"Okay, little guy, good luck here," I told him, making up my mind. "Somebody is going to come and take you home soon." As I stood up to walk down to the kennel that Veronica was peering into, the beige dog raised one paw and seemed to caress the air in front of him, as if he had been taught to shake by his previous owner. Had it not been for the wire between us, I would have shaken his paw. Sadness pooled in my throat and pressed from behind my eyes. I couldn't take this.

"We're going to the cats now, right?" Veronica asked as we left the din of the dog section behind and found ourselves in the main foyer of the Humane Society again.

"I don't know..." I said. Cats had made me nervous for as long as I could remember. They were beautiful. I'd give them that. And they were very intelligent—which was part of the problem. I wasn't keen on having a cat lurking around the house doing little cat things like sending a milk cap back and forth across the kitchen floor, planning a hostile takeover or batting at the curtain tassels. I knew proper witches had cats, but the lack of one was not the first thing to make me improper, that was for certain.

"Come on," Veronica said, "let's at least have a look. Just looking won't hurt anything. You never know, maybe you'll make a connection with a needy kitty."

"Veronica, that's the thing, no cat is needy," I explained. "Cats don't actually need us. They just need our things, our homes, litter boxes, food, whatever. In fact, they don't really even need those things; they're just icing on the tuna-flavored cakes that the cats feast on as they plan to take over the world." I was thinking of the mystery cat that pooped in my garden beds. I despised being outside, digging or weeding in the productive plot of earth behind my house, feeling the sun warm my back and my toes curl into the soil as I knelt and then, whammo, finding a cat turd right next to the carrots.

"Perhaps you haven't met the right cat," Veronica said.

She lived with cats that she believed were the right cats, but I was on to them. I was not fooled by the way they wove their bodies in and out between my feet as I visited their home where they deemed it permissible to let Veronica live. I knew what they were doing as they pushed their fuzzy cheeks along the surfaces of my cowboy boots.

They wanted me to think that they were welcoming me, but I knew better. They were scenting my ankles so that territorial feral cats might be more likely to attack me on my walk home. When they looked at me through their half-closed, please-think-I'm-dozing-and-not-thinking-about-the-way-the-meat-of-your-thigh-might-taste eyes, I could hear Dr. Evil laughing.

I had to content myself with the fact that even though they were highly intelligent, they didn't have opposable thumbs. So taking over the world would be just *that* much harder for them. A cat would not be my first choice in an adoption.

"We can walk through, but I don't think a cat is a good idea for me." I gave in to the idea of visiting the Humane Society's cat house, but knew they'd all still be there when I finished my tour.

We walked, stopping a few times to read the names on their placards. I had to humor Veronica so that she wouldn't think I didn't at least contemplate bringing a tiny terrorist into my home, but none of the cats made me feel as if my adopting them were a matter of life and death. Soon enough we were exiting the cat section through a corridor that led to the foyer. I was empty-hearted, which surprised me.

"Well, we tried," I said over my shoulder to Veronica, trying not to show any disappointment.

"Watch it!" Veronica cried. The air whooshed in front of me. I stopped as a huge cage rolled toward me.

"Oh!" I yelped. An echoing "Oh!" came from the cage.

"Excuse me, hon!" another voice said, "I almost ran right over you, didn't I?" The cage was so big and had so many wild, colorful things hanging in it that I couldn't make out the owner of the voice.

"Sorry," I said, "I wasn't watching where I was going." The woman parked the cage in front of me and peered around it, grinning at me. She had unruly brown curls and root beer brown eyes. She looked like Sigourney Weaver.

"Easy to get distracted here," she said.

I looked for whatever might be in the cage. Was it a monkey's house? Did the Humane Society ever get monkeys? I doubted it—weren't they every little kid's dream pet? I could remember more than half a dozen of my own grade school friends who confessed to wanting monkeys when we were kids. I never saw the appeal. Granted, a pet monkey would be better than a cat. I toyed with the beads at my neck as I leaned forward to search the cage. Monkeys didn't talk, so the echoing "Oh!" was likely the work of a big bird. I looked for beautiful, glossy plumage amidst the hanging toys.

"Where are you, little fella?" I asked quietly.

"Lilfella," something responded from the bottom of the cage. Upon seeing the owner of the voice, I recoiled in a way that still embarrasses me. He was a raw pink, plucked-bellied large bird. He was adorned with a black and red-banded tail, a few black feathers on his head and not much in between.

"Oh!" I said.

"Oh!" the bird echoed.

"Is he talking?" The woman pushing the cage sounded surprised. Her face was suddenly right next to mine as she scrutinized the homely bird. In another second, Veronica joined us. We all stared at the poor thing on the bottom of the cage, and he tipped his beak up to stare right back at us.

"He hasn't said anything since he got here," the woman whispered.

"What happened to him? Did he get burned?" I asked.

"No," the woman answered, "his owner died, so his sister looked after the bird, but surrendered him to us after he plucked his feathers out. She couldn't bear the sight of him like this and didn't know what to do. He's been here for several months."

"Oh!" I now sounded like a parrot, but it was the only thing I could think to say.

"Oh!" the big, ugly bird replied.

"Why, he's talking to you!" the woman cried.

I was humbled and honored, and my knees were getting kind of wobbly, so I repeated my greeting because it was the first thing that I could muster.

"Hi, little fella," I said, even though he was not little at all.

"Hi lilfella," he said, looking me in the eye. He made me smile and then made me do something that would have been really out of character for me a year ago, but that was sort of becoming a bit of a habit these days. He made me start to cry. Hot tears scouted out paths down my checks and then dripped off my chin onto the shiny floor.

"It's okay," Veronica said, patting my back, "it's okay."

The woman stared. She was smiling about the bird's words yet looking concerned for me all in the same face.

"His name is Dwight."

I snuffled back a few ounces of tears and snot and said, "Hi Dwight!"

"Hi lilfella," he said. He bobbed his head up and down a few times, lifting his meager black crest feathers up as he did, so now I was crying and laughing at the same time as Veronica's hand made warm circles between my shoulder blades. His rough, dark pink belly brought to mind the crow's feather from a few days ago. I pictured it taped to his naked tummy and smiled at this imagined picture.

"Actually," said the woman, "his name is Dwight Night, Jr."

"After his owner?" I asked.

"No, his owner's name was Sheldon. Sheldon worked at the Como Park zoo, which is how he met Dwight, I think. Dwight's a red-tailed black cockatoo. They're not as common as other cockatoos, as far as pets go. I'm guessing Sheldon got him from a zoo connection or something."

"Is he adoptable?" Veronica asked.

I held my breath. I hoped, really hoped, that the answer was yes.

"Yes," the woman said.

Dwight Night, Jr., Veronica and the woman all watched my face, waiting.

Book of Shadows
Spell to Welcome My New Familiar

Cast circle around myself and Dwight.
Light golden candles in Dwight-proof chimney.
Burn frankincense and diviner's sage in metal bowl.
"Goddess, God, and Mother Earth,
I request affection, companionship and connection with
my new familiar."
Offer a dish of veggie bits and bowl of water to assure
Dwight of support.
Relax, share breath.
"Thank you, Dwight, for being.
Thank you, Goddess, for bringing me Dwight.
Blessed be Creatures of Light."
Snuff candles.

Book Of Shadows
Cleansing Spell for Dwight

Cast circle around myself and Dwight.
"Blessed be Creatures of Light."
Light winter-white candles.
Burn myrrh incense.
Rub Dwight from talon to top of head with egg.
"I request, from the Goddess, protection, cleansing and
renewal for Dwight."
"Blessed be Creatures of Light."
Snuff candle.
"Thank you, egg, for absorbing negative energy."
Flush egg down the toilet.

CHAPTER SIX

Boxes of Childhood

"Hold it, hold it!" my dad called out from somewhere under his end of the blue corduroy couch he and Alaina were hefting into the moving truck. I couldn't see his face, but the fog his breath made in the cold air rose above the arm of the couch. Alaina, my older sister, struggled to get a better grip and braced her shoulder against the couch's armrest.

"Seriously Allura," Alaina said as the hood of her olive green parka fell over her eyes. "Could you lend a hand?"

I set down the box of record albums and helped Alaina hoist up her end of the couch.

Of my two sisters, Alaina was by far the less giddy. Falina was like a kitten on speed, but Alaina was more like a rainfall. You knew it was a good thing, sometimes you welcomed it, but often it could be a bit of a downer. It was not what one would expect because Alaina had the bright, good-natured looks of our Irish-American mother. They had the same luminous red hair, the same ivory skin smattered with thousands of tiny freckles and the same light blue eyes. Both Mom and Alaina were sturdily built, whereas Falina and I were on the slight side. Falina had much more of a dark, mysterious look, which fit her personality about as well as Alaina's bright, cheerful good looks fit Alaina—which was not at all. Falina was an open book, happy to share whatever she was or had with anyone who was around. Falina looked very Japanese like Dad with her full, high cheeks, delicate chin, bee-stung lips and button nose.

I looked like a hybrid with my brown hair, almond-shaped eyes and big, scattered freckles. I had hated my teeth as a kid because they were sort of bucky, but I changed my mind after watching Beverly D'Angelo in the *National Lampoon's Christmas Vacation* movie. I found her irresistible and sexy, so I began liking my somewhat prominent front teeth. I had convinced myself that I was the Japanese-Irish version of Beverly D'Angelo. Growing up with a beauty queen on either side of me wasn't easy, but over the years enough people had told me I was cute that I had to start to believe it. So I was content with my looks.

"Okay, go!" hollered my dad, his thinning, silvery hair and black eyebrows now visible above the opposite end of the couch as we trudged up the wide ramp into the back of the truck.

I could feel one of my woolen socks sinking beneath the arch of my foot in my boot. It was making me uncomfortable, but to fix it would force Alaina to bear the entire weight of our end of the couch, so I waited until we had the couch set in place.

"Where're Mom and Falina going?" I asked as Falina's ancient Volkswagen Beetle tootled away from the curb in front of my childhood home, which Mom and Dad had recently put on the market. I pulled off my mittens and leaned over to pull my sock out of the nether regions of my boot. My parents had decided to sell the house, donate almost everything they owned to Goodwill, buy an RV and hit the road in a grand tour of casinos and national parks. This had been the news that Falina had held hostage in trade for my laugh yoga story. Mom's arm waved out the open car door window.

"I don't know for sure," answered Dad, waving back at her from the open back of the moving truck. He pulled up the green hoodie of his sweatshirt to ward off the chill. "Are they already going to the women's shelter?" His question came out in a puff of frost.

Mom decided that the boxes of high-quality professional clothing and the kitchen appliances that wouldn't fit in the RV should go to the shelter, but the boxes were still sitting on the front steps.

"I don't think so," I answered, putting my mittens back on my chilled hands.

"They're going," Alaina grunted, blowing her red bangs out of her eyes, "to get coffee for us all. Someone packed the coffeemaker too soon." We all looked toward the boxes on the front steps.

"Ah." Dad smiled. "Good idea."

He and I wore the matching hooded "Satou University" sweatshirts that Mom had ordered all of us a few years ago. There was no real Satou University that I knew of. Mom had found an online company that would create a university based on your last name. I smiled to note that he had cut his at the neckline just as I had. I had ditched my usual pencil skirt for jeans in honor of moving day, but not my cowboy boots.

Two crows cawed above us in the bare maple tree branches, reminding me I was the new companion of a half-naked, seven-year-old cockatoo. It had been a week since Dwight had moved in with me, and I was solidly in love with him. Stupid, insignificant events and nuances reminded me of him. The crows' bobbing heads made me picture Dwight bobbing his own head at my small talk. The bird seemed to approve of everything I did or said. Barbara, the woman who had been pushing Dwight's cage at the Humane Society, thought I must remind Dwight of someone he knew and liked, maybe his old owner. I had never thought of myself as a bird person, but here I was, inexplicably bound to a strange, homely bird.

"Girls." Dad looked somber. Oh no. A joke was on its way. No doubt it would be a death joke. "Girls, I heard a good one the other day." He put his hands up to his mouth, blew on them, rubbed them together, stuffed them in his hoodie pocket and then asked, "Where do gravediggers get their coffee?" He smiled and his eyes wrinkled into tight crescent moons.

"Dad, really," Alaina scoffed. "They get their coffee at the burial grounds." She pulled a death face, her tongue lolling out and her eyes rolled back in her head. I laughed at her and for Dad's sake. That was one of the lamer jokes I'd heard Dad tell.

"Dad, I hate to be the one to tell you, but you're slipping," I teased.

Alaina and I continued loading the truck with smaller pieces of furniture and boxes of books, games and other bits of our childhood. Our exhalations created little puffs of fog as we paced from the truck to the house and back to the truck. I expected to be melancholy about this whole moving day, but now that it was here, I was content. It was even encouraging that it was happening. I liked the idea of Mom and Dad still having the gumption and energy to start a new leg of their journey together. The whole idea gave me a refreshing sense of hope. After some small talk about how glad we both were that the snow hadn't started to fly, Alaina and I worked without speaking until it was break time.

Falina pulled her car up to the curb and jumped out to race around and help Mom with the tray of coffees and bag of what I assumed to be bagels. Mom climbed from the orange Beetle, folded her seat forward and tugged out another bulging paper bag from the local grocery store.

"Come and get it while the getting's good!" Mom called, smacking the grocery bag several times like she was herding children on the playground. And like children on a playground, Dad and I dropped what we were doing and followed her into the house. Alaina came in at a more relaxed pace. We were all eating and drinking at the kitchen counter when Falina couldn't hold it in any longer.

"Guess who we ran into!" she exploded, right at me.

"Uhm…" I said, "I don't know, who?" My shoulders inched protectively toward my ears.

"Falina." Mom's tone oozed caution like a salve that might heal any upcoming wounds.

"Oh," Falina faltered.

Because "Oh!" had been Dwight's first word to me, I relaxed. It had to be my ex they'd run into. They wouldn't tiptoe around running into anyone else like that. I willed my shoulders to settle down.

"No, it's okay, tell me." And it was okay, or at least it was more okay than it would have been a couple of weeks ago.

"Really?" Falina asked, still looking apologetic and almost embarrassed that she had brought it up in the first place.

"Really. Let me guess. You ran into Mickey." I said it for her.

"Uhm, yeah," she said. "Yeah, at the bagel shop."

"That's cool," I said, wondering what had changed. Mickey hated bread. For years Mickey had refused to even go into a bagel shop with me. She said the smell of bread dough made her nauseated. She set foot in a Subway sandwich shop only once before vowing never again to go into another one. I loved the warm smell of Subway. I should have known then that we'd never last.

"Yeah," Falina said.

"Did you say hi?" I asked, not wanting Falina to feel bad for bringing it up.

"Yes, I did, but Mom…" Falina said, looking at Mom with a smile on her face again, "Mom ignored her."

"You didn't!" I laughed. "Why?"

"I just don't have anything to say to her, that's all," Mom said.

"Humph." Dad's laugh came out of his nose in a small huff because his mouth was full of orange.

"What?" Mom asked, trying to look indignant.

Dad finished chewing and then laughed properly. "Last time this came up, you had plenty you were going to say to her!" He was looking at Mom with his brow furrowed and black eyebrows raised.

"Yes, but that was with you as the only witness," Mom retorted and then pried the lid off her coffee and blew on it. She took a sip, swallowed with a grimace and said, "No need to go getting myself arrested right before our RV adventure." She blew on her coffee again and asked, "How can this still be so damn hot?"

"What?" Dad asked with a sad smile, "Your anger or your coffee?"

"Touché," Mom laughed.

What was it about being with your family that made you feel young? My parents hadn't aged at all. If I closed my eyes, I could have been a teenager with them bantering on about one thing or another. I was lucky, I guess. Here I was, middle-aged, feeling young and protected by my family. The subject of Mickey was dropped. I was relieved no one brought up the idea that I search for a new partner although they were keen on seeing me happy with someone. Countless times I'd tried to convince them I was happy alone. But was I? Maybe. Alaina and Falina were both happily single. Why should I have to pair off with someone? Alone, I was at least spared the potential of being hurt or left. But with a partner, I'd be able to talk about how it felt to say goodbye to the home in which I grew up and marvel over my sweet family.

We finished taking our break. The remains of our collective childhoods were safely delivered to Goodwill, and we saw our parents off as they embarked on the next chapter of their lives.

Book of Shadows
Spells for Home Goodbye and Relocation Protection

Nearing the Full Moon, cast the circle in childhood
bedroom. Scatter salt and water.
"Blessed be Creatures of Light."
Light white candle on paper plate; allow dripping wax to
create a secure base for candle.
Greet and honor the four directions and the universal
elements.
Letter is written in myrrh-scented dove's blood ink and
anointed with honey.
"I'm writing to Mother Earth, God, and Goddess in
gratitude for the memories I will carry with me from my
childhood home. Thank you for the security of family,
home and time. I will not forget the abundant gifts that
presented themselves to me in this house.
I hope the same amount of happiness is experienced here
by the next inhabitants."
This letter gets burned by candle's flame, released.
(Never again burn letter over paper plate—almost was
the forever kind of goodbye.
And it's hard to sell a pile of ashes that used to be a
home.)
Create protection in relocation letter using dragon's
blood ink.
"God, Goddess, Mother Earth, please be with my Mom
and Dad as they set out on their next adventure in life.
Guide, guard and humor them as they continue their
life's story."
This letter gets folded into tight triangle, emblazoned
with sigil for protection
and hidden alongside small chunk of comfrey root in
Mom and Dad's new RV.
Thank the four directions and the universal elements.
"Blessed be Creatures of Light."
Extinguish candle.
Open the circle.

CHAPTER SEVEN

The Stalker

"Hi, lilfella!" Dwight called out as I closed the front door. This was the only thing he had said to me since he had moved in, but each time it made my heart feel too big for my ribcage.

"Hi, Dwight!" I hollered up the staircase toward my office where his huge cage now occupied a good deal of space. Dwight didn't say anything back to me, so I sat down on the fainting couch and pulled off my cowboy boots. These I left by the front door and padded up the staircase in my socks. I ran the short distance down the hall to the open door of my office and slid, like Tom Cruise in *Risky Business*, to a halt just outside the door. Dwight's feather crest perked right up, and he bobbed his head in approval.

"Hi there, big fella!" I said. "Whatcha doin'?" Dwight didn't answer, but he continued to bob his head, so I figured he was happy enough. Our first couple of days together had been spent just looking at each other and being near one another, like the Internet articles advised. The time had been filled with my making small talk in a soothing voice—again, Internet recommendation—and Dwight just listening.

I had called the Humane Society several times to get advice about various things on which I had found conflicting online advice. Each time, the person on the other end of the line spent as much time as I needed to get all my questions answered and each time the person ended the call with a sincere thank you for adopting Dwight. Apparently he had been a favorite of the employees and volunteers at the Humane Society. It sounded like a few people there had started to think no one would ever adopt Dwight because he was such a mess. It did hurt me to look at his raw, plucked belly, but the Internet sources and the Humane Society people seemed to think that Dwight would let his feathers grow back in if we developed a bond.

After the first couple of quiet days had passed, I found myself doing physical things that might amuse him. I did little dances for him. He bobbed his head. I did karate for him. He bobbed his head again. I read passages from my writing. He bobbed his head. I acted out snippets of *Romeo and Juliet*, with voices and actions. Dwight bobbed his head. He was a bird of few gestures.

A couple days ago, I had made four or five trips into the house with grocery bags, my gym bag and some odds and ends that I had kept from my parents' moving day. It was then that I discovered that Dwight thought it was a good idea to say hi to me each time I opened the front door. So after I had put things away, I came in and out of the front door several more times so that we could practice calling hi back and forth from my spot at the front door to his spot in the office. My joy, with each one of Dwight's "Hi lilfellas," felt as if it were going to expand and explode in the air in front of me. I felt stupid, coming in and out of the front door like a village idiot, but I couldn't stop myself.

The last time I shut the door, I tiptoed up the steps to see him, but he must have heard me coming because he was looking right at me as I peered into the room. He bobbed his head. I bobbed mine. I grabbed the beautiful green velvet cloak Veronica had given me on Samhain, threw it over my shoulders and spread my arms out so the cloak made wings. I pretended to fly around the office. Dwight spread out his wings and pretended to fly. My heart felt too full, and I had to hold back a rush of emotion. I was so very glad he was here.

I wrapped the cloak around me and collapsed into my desk chair, laughing, and rocked myself to the left, to the right and back to the left. It was soothing, and Dwight copied my movements even though he had no chair in which to swivel. The cloak was warm. I felt so comfortable and cozy that I began to wonder if The Funk had left me. When was the last time I felt detached and edgeless like I was just sliding through life? I couldn't remember. I smiled.

"Life is good, Dwight, life is good," I said as I wheeled myself over to the window. I looked out over the playground and ball fields. The park was almost empty. A few kids played on the jungle gym while an adult stood nearby texting and looking up occasionally. Another person walked her Pomeranian on the far side of the park. A flash of black silk caught my eye. A black squirrel? I knew we had black squirrels, but this was bigger. It stopped in the exact middle of the park, turned around twice and sat down on the ground. It was a cat. And it looked up at me, through the window, as if it knew I was watching. I shuddered and felt my lips tighten. It was looking right at me.

We stared at each other for what seemed like a long time before the cat stood up, stretched low in the front and high in the back and started sauntering toward my house. This must be the fellow who pooped in my gardens. I drew back from the window but did not stop watching. I couldn't; it was as if I were watching a slow-motion car wreck. I didn't want to look at the sly thing, but I couldn't look away. When the cat got to the edge of the park, directly across the street from my house, he stopped and sat down again. He never took his eyes from mine. He was now close enough for me to see that he had very pretty golden eyes. Pretty eyes or not, I wanted him to stop looking at me. I was becoming unnerved. He was close enough for me to see the tufts of black hair that sprang from behind his ears. He was black from head almost to toe—but he had one white toe in the middle of both back paws. These white toes gave me the feeling he was flipping me off. They appeared to be the cat equivalent of a middle finger.

"Well, fuck you, too," I whispered and then snapped my head around to look at Dwight. It wouldn't do to have him whispering obscenities. He was watching me, but he said nothing. Dwight leaned over as far as he could without tumbling from his perch. He attempted to peek out the window, but he couldn't lean far enough to see out.

"That's okay, buddy, you're not missing anything."

CHAPTER EIGHT

Slurry

The mound, slick and smooth and cupped in my hands, began to tremble. I reduced the pressure of my foot slightly to slow the spinning wheel, and the clay started to right itself. I had enrolled in an open studio class where I could pay by the visit, which was a grand idea because then I could visit whenever I wanted to rather than being bound by a class schedule. I think it might defeat one of Dr. Browning's reasons for having me take a class, which was probably to make new friends, but it was a start, right?

I dribbled a small handful of water into the shallow depression atop what was to be my first ever thrown pot. I gave the foot pedal a light push to get the wheel back up to speed. That, however, was not the thing to do.

Gravity failed me and pure centrifugal force took over. Before I could stop it, the entire mound of clay slid off the wheel, careened through the air and smacked into the back of a very large young man.

"Oh!" he yelped, grabbing his lower back with a hand that was covered with a reddish clay. Conversations ceased as people looked up. He whipped around, his shaggy blond hair making him look like a large surfer. He looked at my face and then looked down at the mass of clay on the floor.

"I'm sorry." I tried to stand up, but my apron caught the edge of the potter's wheel and dashed the wheel and its tray's contents to the floor. "Ooooh," I breathed as the slurry ebbed over the cement floor. It oozed out around the soles of my feet and headed for a few frameless canvases that leaned against the wall. I scrambled for the canvases to save them when my feet went out from under me. I landed on my ass in the slurry. All the conversations in the studio halted now. Then the big guy who took the clay kidney punch started to laugh.

"Wow, way to distract attention from your original accident!" He offered me his enormous clay-covered hand and levered me to my feet. "Are you okay?" he asked.

Everyone except one black-haired woman near the back of the studio was peering at me or at the mess I had created. But even the woman who wasn't looking seemed to be listening for my answer. I decided to make the most of a bad situation.

I threw my arms in the air, arched my back like a gymnast who had just stuck her landing and yelled, "I'm okay!" That cracked me up, so I laughed heartily. Many people joined me. Their laughter was a bit less raucous than my own. The big guy and two artsy-looking women helped me to clean up the spilled slurry and to right the upended pottery wheel.

"You know," one of the women said, "you shouldn't feel bad. That same thing happened to me once."

"Really?"

"Uhm, no," she said with a gentle smile. "It didn't. But it could happen to any of us, so don't feel bad, okay?"

I really didn't feel too bad about it since it could have been so much worse. The guy could have been a prick about getting nailed in the kidney, or I could have cracked my head wide open and bled to death in a pool of bloody, watery clay. I also could have broken the potter's wheel, which was kind of a lightweight, cheap one anyway, but it seemed to be in fine order. So I was going to say okay, but the other woman helping us to clean up beat me to speaking.

"No, I don't think that could have happened to any of us," she said. "Man, it was like a scene from a movie!" Her pink, orange and mousy brown dreadlocks wiggled as she exclaimed, "It's like you practiced for all that to go wrong, you know?"

When I replayed the events in my mind, I realized they were kind of awe-inspiring, in the kind of way that you don't necessarily want to be involved with but would rather just appreciate from a distance.

"Yeah, I did practice that, but after a few hours' worth of rehearsals, I felt ready for all of you, my adoring fans." I laughed. Over a bucket, I wrung out the cloth with which I had been wiping splattered slurry from the walls. I dabbed at a few last splotches and stood back to see if I had missed any.

"I think you got them all," the guy said as he looked at the wall with me.

"Thanks for helping me clean up," I said to all three of them. People were so nice. I looked at each of them, tried to imprint their faces into my memory in case I ever ran in to them again. If I did, I'd try extra hard not to be dangerous or messy. They each grinned and nodded and said it was no problem. So I said thanks again and wandered over to the vat of mixed clay.

I tried hand-building rather than the wheel for the remainder of the class. I pried out a couple handfuls of clay, found a space at one of the tables and started gingerly. I replayed the whole thing in my head. It was hard not to start laughing. Everyone had seen. Well, not everyone. There was that black-haired woman near the drying racks who had not looked. I looked over at her now. I could see over the top of her shoulder that she was building a sculpture that had many planes, some covered with sharp-looking spikey bits, some smooth as glass and some with striations like muscles in anatomy class. I couldn't see her whole face, but the half of her profile that was visible made me think I knew her from somewhere. She wore a dusty canvas apron over a stylish red and white striped boat-neck shirt. The shirt looked expensive, but perhaps it was the cleanly cut edges of her chin-length hair. I watched her a minute longer, taking in the grace of her hand movements, the prettiness of her cheekbone and the way her hair was tucked behind her ear.

The clay was drying out under my hands, so I began pressing my thumb into the center of the ball until my right thumb was buried in the middle of it. The grit of the clay worked its way under my thumbnail. This, for some reason, was reassuring. I tried to remember what the instructor had said about rolling and pinching the pot while forming the walls. I wasn't sure if I was supposed to push or to pull at the edges, so I chose to pull with minute gentle tugs that were more like squeezes than pulls. Slowly, a fat, squat pot began to emerge. I liked this—less could go wrong here than with the wheel, that was for sure. I continued to work the pot around in my left hand, squeezing up the edges with my right.

Finally, the pot had walls thin enough to not be embarrassed by and thick enough to not collapse in on themselves. I set the pot on the table before me and admired it. I might use it for Dwight's food bowl once it was fired and glazed. It appeared to be about the right size. I could picture his glossy black head dipping into the bowl for various… glossy black head…I glanced back at the black-haired woman and groaned. Was she the woman who had been looking my direction after the non-laugh yoga class? Really? Yes. It was the same woman. What were the odds? We had these two huge Twin Cities—Minneapolis and St. Paul—to live in, and she had to witness what might be the two most embarrassing moments of my life. It wasn't fair.

CHAPTER NINE

In Ad Equate

Ugh. I pushed back from my desk and my chair wheels caught on the area rug so abruptly that my ride stopped and nearly threw me like an angry horse. I shoved my desk with my foot so that I spun in two lazy circles before coming to rest facing Dwight's cage. I couldn't bear to write another word about how Sentesto's would revolutionize standardized test-taking for students across the nation. Maybe it was that my palms sweated at just the mention of standardized tests, or maybe it was that this column was starting to feel like a commercial and that seemed like the worst feel a column could have. Try this, buy this, it will enhance your life to the point of ecstasy. That is until the next great product comes out and is covered in my column, which, I know, I know, might easily be confused with a commercial. Had I sold out?

"Dwight?" I asked, "Have I sold out?"

I was tired of feeling like someone had used sandpaper to rub off all my edges. Without those edges, I had no way of getting caught by life—I was just slipping through now, unnoticed, ineffective and unaffected. I felt bland, off-white and boring like a slow-motion bullet with no edges to catch on anything, better yet, a stop-action motionless, ineffective bullet. No, not a bullet; a bullet had a target. I was without a target. I wanted my edges back.

I pulled my head up from my arms. I wanted my edges back even if it meant being hurt or not liking what I saw. Anything would be better than this uninspired feeling of not being caught by life.

Book of Shadows
Spell to Banish Negative Energy

Waning Moon
Cast the circle.
Set out bowl of earth from windowsill herbs combined
with black pepper,
cinnamon, salt, ground ginger and cayenne powder.
Set out bowl of clear, clean water.
Burn chicory and waft it about to banish negative energy.
"Blessed be Creatures of Light."
Light gray candles in copper holders to bring healing and
love.
Greet and honor the four directions and the universal
elements.
"As the moon diminishes, so too will this feeling
of living an uninspired life. By the time the moon recharges
herself and begins to fatten up, so will my feelings of joy,
inspiration and delight."
Thank the four directions and the universal elements.
"Blessed be Creatures of Light."
Extinguish candles.
Open the circle.

CHAPTER TEN

Burp This

"No, there's no more burping," Falina said and demonstrated the new snapping action rather than the old burping action. "See?" she asked as she held the bright orange bowl aloft. The lid was indeed intact, virtually airtight.

There were murmurs of approval and several women wrote down the name of the bowl set on their order forms. I wrote, "These women are hysterically sweet," and "Fal, you do a great job," on my order form. I was at one of Falina's famous Tupperware parties. The wine and laughter were flowing freely, and the other attendees were Tupperware junkies.

"Is there anything left to burp?" asked a woman in a tight ski sweater. I had to admit, these were not the types of women I had imagined when Falina invited me along. I never would have said yes, not having a need to buy Tupperware at cost since Falina had always been happy to hook me up with my favorite plasticware at her discounted price, but I had remembered Dr. Browning's therapy assignment of saying "yes" to social events and then following through on my commitments.

So here I was, along for the ride. The party was being held in a beautiful house near Lake of the Isles in Minneapolis. This was the type of house that should be owned by a ritzy, stay-at-home mother of three East Coast university-attending sons. Instead, the owner was an edgy, chain-smoking, high school teacher with a penchant for hitting on me, even though she was straight. When we were introduced, Camille gave me a wink and a Cheshire grin and then asked me to call her Cami. She sported a thin, pale gray clinging cable-knit sweater and darker gray French terry yoga pants. On most people the outfit would never have worked, but on Cami it came together like champagne and strawberries. She wore no jewelry, but with those glittery hazel eyes, she didn't need any. Her hair was tawny, parted close to the middle and just gracing the tops of her shoulders.

"You want to burp something?" Falina asked the wearer of the tight ski sweater. She turned to the big oak table where she had artfully arranged a mountain of brightly colored Tupperware and drew out a radiant white and orange bowl. This didn't look like old-school Tupperware, the kind a person would have to "burp" to get a good seal with the lid, but Falina said, "burp this," and handed the bowl to the woman. Conversation stopped around the room as everyone watched the ski sweater woman. She set the bowl and the lid on the stone-topped coffee table before her, cleared her throat, flipped her hair over the shoulders of her ski sweater, rubbed her hands together as if conjuring up some serious burp-power, placed the lid atop the bowl, eased its outer edges to the lip of the bowl and, with something of a flourish, "burped" it.

I laughed out loud as a mighty cheer went up from the rest of the women in the room. A few clinked wineglasses, and I even witnessed an exchange of high-fives. These women were funny. Were they really that excited about the product, or did they just enjoy having something to laugh over together? Did it really matter? Falina did excellent business with Tupperware. She had never needed another job. She thrived on providing a good product—one with a lifetime warranty—and bringing people together in social settings. Some of the stories she had shared were almost unbelievable. Did people really get that excited over plastic? But now, seeing the cheer for the burp, I got it.

I had expected a bunch of crotchety, traditional women who'd be knitting as they listened to Falina's spiel on how the new set of Vent-n-Serves could go from the freezer, to the microwave, to the dinner table, to the dishwasher, just like that! But these women were funny. Two were frightfully non-traditional with severe uptown piercings, stretchings and spikes. These two were by far the most serious about their Tupperware shopping. They had been at the demonstration table when I arrived, holding up Modular Mates and discussing which size would best accommodate flour and which would be appropriate for rice. Did they really eat rice and flour like everyone else? And did the rice ever get stuck in their labret piercing holes that held silver studs beneath their bottom lips? But they were shockingly cute. They put the Modular Mates back into their proper places in the Tupperware display and practically fell over each other as they raced for their seats when Falina got the demonstration under way.

Through the huge plate glass window behind the Tupperware display on the dining room table, a bit of black dashing across the yard caught my eye. I felt my lips purse and my eyebrows knit together. Was that the cat? I tried to smooth out my forehead, which made me think of the smiling cow pose episode. How could it be the cat? It couldn't be. I was simply too far from home. I drew my attention back into the room while I fingered the garnet beads at my neck.

I heard the oohs, ahhs and thank yous as Falina passed out the Citrus Peelers, the piece I used the most because oranges were an easy dietary staple. Recently I'd discovered the non-business end of it was perfect for dislodging clay from under my nails after pottery class. Still, I was dumbfounded when everyone at this party got so revved up over this little freebie Tupperware tool. Were we, as a collective group of human beings, really that starved for a communal experience? I'd have to ask Falina later to see if all Tupperware partiers were this excited or if it was just this group.

Cami plunked herself down next to me. She twirled her Citrus Peeler like high school boys twirled cigarettes. In her other hand she held a glass of wine.

"Whatcha writing?" she asked me, looking at my order form. She smiled and said, "Yes, we are hysterically sweet, and yes, Falina does do a good job. Sorry, I'm used to spying on my students' writing. Are you having fun?"

"It's okay and yes I am," I answered. She had the sparkliest eyes, all green and brown, that I had ever seen.

"Good, good," she said and took a sip of her wine.

For a split second I had the impression that she might raise the Citrus Peeler to her lips to take a drag. Instead she pressed its flat end to her bottom lip, tapped it there several times and then asked me, "You're a freelance writer, right?"

"Well, yes, but I also do a column for a writers' magazine," I answered, reaching over the stone coffee table for my own wineglass. Why did I feel compelled to drink every time I saw someone else drinking? It wasn't only with wine, either. It didn't matter if it were coffee, water, tea or whatever. Compulsive? Easily swayed by suggestion? I made a mental note to try not to drink next time Cami took a drink.

"Have you been doing that for a long time?" Cami was full of questions.

"About five years I guess," I answered, hoping my math was correct. I had started the column right about the time the IntelliBoard had come out on the market.

"Hm," Cami said, clearly contemplating a question.

"Do you have an IntelliBoard in your classroom?" I asked her before she could continue her interview.

"Yes, why?" she answered, eyebrows drawn up over her glittery eyes.

She took a sip of her wine, and I did the same. Damn! Creature of habit, I was.

"My very first column covered ways IntelliBoards might be used in the classroom," I said, thinking about how lame that sounded. "It was more exciting when it was new, I guess," I said, setting my wineglass back on the coffee table. The glass rung out musically as it touched the stone top of the table. Whoa, real crystal.

"Everything is more exciting when it's new," Cami said, laughing a little. She tapped her bottom lip again with the Citrus Peeler. She had nice lips, and I started wondering if she was trying to draw my attention to them. "Babies, cars, dogs, classes full of ninth graders, eyeglasses, boyfriends...they are all wonderful fun when they're new, and then, well, one day you wake up and go, 'Oh! You are not nearly as much fun as you used to be!' and that's how it goes," she said. She took a sip; I took a sip. Damn! Double damn.

"Hiking boots," I said.

"What?" she asked, holding her wineglass balanced on her right knee.

Maybe this copycat behavior of mine explained The Funk. Was I only mimicking others as I moved through this world? Was I not living an original life? Was I out of fresh ideas and actions? Possibly. Not wanting to miss the fun of the party, I tucked these questions away for future rumination. I was going to turn the tables on this next sip. I'd take one first and see if she followed suit. I took a sip; she took a sip. Haha! I wasn't the only lemming here. I felt better.

"Hiking boots," I repeated, "they're no fun when they're new."

"No," she agreed and shook her head slowly, frowning as if we were discussing a dearly departed friend. "Hiking boots are definitely not fun when they are new."

Falina called us all together for a game. I shuddered. I silently willed Falina not to foul up a perfectly good party with games. Don't do it, don't do it, don't do it. I got up and wandered back over to the display table, trying to look interested in a colander as I examined how far I could see through the tiny holes. I faced it toward the window for better lighting. I did not want to play Tupperware games. Falina was about to kill a very enjoyable time.

Surprisingly, I could see well through the colander holes. I held the plastic tool like a spyglass viewing various shrubs and tall dry grasses in Cami's yard, just hoping Falina would change her mind about the game. The base of one shrub, an evergreen, was shuddering. I moved the colander away from my face and scowled as a black cat emerged. He looked just like the cat who'd been ambushing me. But I couldn't be sure until he came all the way out of the shrub. I groaned out loud. I spied his little white and black feet, his little defiant flipping off toes. How had he gotten here?

"Okay, everyone, here's how the first one goes!" Falina called out.

She hadn't changed her mind. When she said the *first* one, I groaned out loud again. I reclaimed my seat by Cami.

"Oh, c'mon, you'll love these!" Cami said, sitting up straight and kind of bouncing on the wide ottoman beside me. "I actually use Falina's games in the classroom. They're fun!"

Cami was right, of course. Falina had us laughing our heads off over ridiculous things that we made up according to her rules. For one of the games, we had to introduce ourselves and then using the first letter of our first name, tell where we'd like to go, wearing only one article of clothing, with one other person, using one mode of transportation and tell what our first activity would be there.

So Cami wound up going to Cairo, wearing only a camisole, with a call girl, riding a camel, for some cavorting on the coastline. I had to go to Asia, wearing only an apron, with an anonymous admirer (I got extra credit for that answer, which meant I scored a tiny Shape-o-Ball keychain,) riding my own airplane, for an afternoon of adventure.

There were some pretty funny ones, but I was glad I didn't have to go after the pierced, spiked girl whose name was Bailey, because she was going to go to the bra store in butt-less chaps, with her brazen best friend named Bettie Page. Her plan was that she and Bettie would ride her boyfriend to the bra store where she and Bettie would spend a bunch of time busting out black lace B-cups with their beautiful, bared breasts. The place fell apart with hoots and cheers for Bailey's plan. Falina decided that Bailey had definitely earned an entire set of microwave-safe luncheon plates, and these she marched over to the proud recipient. Bailey held the green translucent plates aloft as she took bow after bow, with her spikey hair never once losing its points. Maybe this was why she had been so serious when I had first arrived—she was planning her show-stealing answer to this introductory game.

By the end of the party, my cheeks ached from all the laughing. I stood by the table at which Falina had been helping people fill out order forms, wanting to ask her about the next party. Some sort of rice-making bowl held my attention as I waited while one of the other attendees was making plans with Falina to start her own Tupperware business. I eavesdropped into my sister's life a bit and heard the woman telling her how she had considered this after every single Tupperware party she had ever been to and now that she had been laid off, she knew it was time. I knew this was good for Falina's business and important to the woman, Liz, who was going to Lima wearing nothing but a leather jacket, so I pulled out my phone to text Falina my question. That way I wouldn't forget and Falina could answer when she had more time. I looked up after texting, and Cami was standing right in front of me looking like she had another question of her own.

"Thank you for letting me come to your party," I said to her.

"You are more than welcome," she said. "Say, may I ask a really big favor?"

"Yes?" my answer sounded more like another question. I wondered what she was going to ask. I hoped she wasn't going to flirt with me again. I had been warned about straight women who wanted to "explore" the pathways of their sexuality and about the lesbians who got caught up in relationships that were going absolutely nowhere with these travelers. I wasn't sure I could say no to Cami's sparkly eyes and pretty lips, which she was now pursing and moving slightly from one side of her mouth to the other as she thought, perhaps, about how to phrase her question. I tried to focus on something else but then found my gaze drawn to her pale gray sweater as it clung to her athletic shoulders and abdomen. I looked away.

"Well, we don't have any money for things like this," she began.

Oh Goddess, was she going to try to pay me for my services? To that I could certainly say no. That would just be wrong. If I had a wineglass in my hand, I would most assuredly be the first one to take a sip.

"But I'd really appreciate it if you would come speak to my English Eleven class about being a writer," she finished.

Oh. Not what I had thought. Not at all what I had thought. Whew. I was relieved, but honestly somewhat disappointed, too. She was attractive, but I wasn't genuinely attracted to her. Even so, it felt like a long time since I'd had a good go at physical contact with anyone. I had to force myself to stop twisting the garnet beads at my neck.

"I'd love to," I said.

So we made plans to meet and discuss what things her students would be interested in hearing about and which dates would work best for both of us. To talk about the job would be cool, even though doing the job, right now, was a shade less than cool. Maybe sharing the best parts of writing with the kids would bring back some of my energy and passion for the whole business. I planned to go straight home and start outlining my presentation.

CHAPTER ELEVEN

Hilarity Ensues

"Tell me," Dr. Browning said, setting up her question from her chair directly across her desk from me, "what is your favorite phrase to write?" Today she wore a blue and white striped sailor's dress, still with the strappy white sandals and bare legs despite the cold. The intense gaze from behind her big, black-framed glasses hadn't changed either. I knew my favorite phrase, but I didn't really want to share it with her. I had thought we were just about to close things up. Tick, tick, tick... The daisy-shaped clock on her wall had a second hand with a bumblebee attached to its end. The bee seemed to be flying very slowly. Before this question I had reported to her that I was, surprisingly, making progress with the assignments. She had laughed to the point of tears over a few Dwight stories, she had chuckled—only after I started laughing—during the first pottery class story and she had smiled during the Tupperware party story. I felt like a junkie taking a hit every time I made her laugh, like a comedienne who brought the house down, and I liked the feeling. I didn't have to think at all about my favorite phrase to write. It had been the same phrase for as long as I could remember, but what would she make of it?

"Hilarity ensues," I said. I made the jazz hands motion as I said it so that she could get the additional impact of the phrase.

"Hilarity ensues," she echoed, smiling and making a note in my file, which hadn't really grown much. It was still the thinnest of the pile. I didn't find the same sense of relief that I had the first time I noticed its underfed look. I looked hard at the stack of files and sent good energy to each of the other patients. Dr. Browning watched me.

"Hilarity ensues," I re-echoed her because I couldn't think of what else to say. I nodded.

"I am not surprised," she said. She removed her eyeglasses and rubbed the bridge of her nose. "You enjoy creating laughter for people."

I hadn't even told her about laugh yoga.

"Yeah, I guess I do," I said. I did; it was true. All I wanted to do in my column these days was make people laugh, not inform them of new writing technologies. I did just receive an assignment that actually excited me, introducing the new OutWrite technology for blind writers. For some reason that I couldn't specifically grasp, I knew this article would be more worthwhile than my usual topics which centered on home file organization, plot line creation, music download and storage, or business solutions.

This OutWrite technology seemed different. Perhaps that was because I was a writer and could not bear to think of not being able to write. Even though I wasn't feeling a great deal of love for my recent assignments, I did always feel love for putting words together on paper. Always. As I shared this news with Dr. Browning, she listened, made notes and then put down her pen and closed my file. She smiled and nodded at me as if she knew something I didn't. Maybe she did.

CHAPTER TWELVE

A Bang-Up Job

"Oh no! What did you tell him?" I laughed into the phone and asked Falina this as she described an awkward date moment caused by the fact that Brian, the guy she had recently started seeing, had his shirt buttoned one button out of alignment for most of the night. She had only noticed after they had sat across from each other for a couple of hours over dinner. She was uncertain then as to whether or not to point it out to him that his shirt was mis-buttoned. As it turned out, he came back from the restroom mad that she had not said anything. He had noticed it in the mirror. And while she was secretly pleased, she said, because she felt safe in assuming that if he had looked in the mirror it was because he was there washing his hands, she still felt horrible for not saying something earlier.

"I told him that I hadn't noticed, but while he had been in the bathroom, I had purposefully mis-buttoned my own shirt, so that if he was going to be hurt by the fact that I hadn't noticed, he could at least see that my shirt had been messed up, too. And then he could decide if he wanted to still be hurt or not," she explained.

"Because he wouldn't have noticed that your shirt was mis-buttoned, because it really hadn't been." I chuckled, picturing the whole scene. "I cut my bangs this morning by myself because I could barely see out from under them, and I did a really horseshit job. They have never been so crooked," I told Falina. "Wonder if I had a date tonight if she would take the time to disappear into the bathroom and come out with crooked bangs to save me from embarrassment." I laughed at my own question and spun around in my chair to watch Dwight as Falina started talking again. Dwight mimicked my laugh perfectly and loudly. I made big eyes at him as I halfway listened to Falina. He made big eyes back at me.

"It wasn't to ease his embarrassment as much as to prove a point. Either way, I think he saw through my coverup, but he didn't seem as put out by the time we left. He never said anything about my shirt, but I have to imagine he noticed, for all the staring at my chest he does—which is really starting to piss me off," Falina continued.

I laughed even though it wasn't appropriate.

"Hahaha!" Dwight repeated. I loved it. I felt like a comedienne whose audience adores her. It made me think of what Dr. Browning had told me about my needing to make people laugh. It was so true.

After Falina and I finished our call, I went through a short, soggy stack of mail that contained three ads, a postcard, two bills and an envelope that had my neighbor's address on it. I'd return it later. The postcard, looking terribly old-fashioned and a bit bedraggled from its short stay in my leaky mailbox, bore a picture of a palm tree and a pool. The pool was devoid of swimmers, yet across the top of the postcard was emblazoned "Everglades National Park! Wish you were here!" Wish I were at this empty pool? How odd. I'm sure Everglades National Park had scary alligators or tropical beaches, or some other incredible natural wonder to show off on the front of its postcards. That pool could have been anywhere. Well, it could have been anywhere palm trees grew. Nice choice, Mom and Dad.

I flipped the card over to be greeted by my mom's pretty

handwriting spelling out my full name above my address: Allura Tuki Satou. Tuki. Mom loved my middle name, but I thought it made me sound like a porn star. It meant "moon" in Japanese. My mom and dad both thought it appropriate because of the huge, golden full moon that had hung over them the night they drove to the hospital where my mom delivered me into the world, but its Japanese meaning only strengthened the porn star theme. What do porn stars do to the camera? They moon it. And who sends postcards anymore, anyway? Could they not get an Internet connection in the national parks? Email would be more practical. At any rate, I sighed and read the postcard.

Allura, how are you doing up there in the cold? It is wonderfully warm here. Your father and I have not even had to turn on the heater in the RV. By the way, we have named the RV Gladys. We are her Pips. It feels like we are on a honeymoon; can you tell? The pool on the front of this is not even in the park, as far as we can tell. That cracked us up. How random. Hi from Dad.

Love Mom and Dad.

Well, that almost explained the mystery of the empty pool. She did sound as if she and Dad might be experiencing a honeymoon. My parents had always been happy with each other and within themselves, but over the past few years they had both seemed tired and dulled by life. I was glad they had made this decision to travel the states. It almost made me wish I had a new partner to share life with. But then I mentally ticked off all the things that could go wrong between lovers, set down the postcard and went downstairs to make dinner for one.

CHAPTER THIRTEEN

Locker Room Proposal

I felt the woman's presence behind me. Even so, when she grabbed my elbow as I was leaving the locker room at the Y it startled me, so I spun around faster than I would have had I known she was topless. She held a towel up in front of herself to cover up from the navel down, but her bare breasts jiggled from my yanking my arm free.

"Wait, sorry, wait," she said, pulling the towel higher to cover her breasts and then looking down at exactly how much of her lower half was bared by this action. She lowered the towel a little, but this left just enough breast and just enough upper thigh uncovered so as to be almost suggestive. "Uhm...wait here, okay?" she requested.

"Sure," I said, not knowing where to look or what to do with myself as she dashed back to her locker, her butt bare. I investigated a sign-up sheet for a Holiday 5K that was being run around Lake Nokomis, counted the twelve names that had committed to traipsing around on what would probably be a very chilly morning and wondered what I'd look at next if the woman didn't come back soon. There was never really a safe place to rest your eyes if you were a lesbian in a locker room full of straight women. I had never eyed anyone up in the locker room, and I certainly didn't want to start now. Perhaps it was my own stereotype that straight women thought all lesbians wanted them, that we were not as selective as they were about their men, but that we simply lusted after all women. It was probably also my own stereotype that they were all straight here in the locker room. But still, I avoided looking at anything other than the inanimate. I could describe the carpet and the wood patterns of the locker doors in intimate detail to anyone who asked, since that was where I usually rested my eyes as I was dressing or undressing.

"Hey, I'm sorry," the woman said as she approached me with an embarrassed grin.

"That's okay," I said.

She had thrown on a blue sweatshirt with the orange initials W.H.S. on it and a pair of black warm-up pants. Her hair was wet from her shower. If I knew her, I didn't recognize her. Maybe it was the wet hair's fault.

"This is going to sound really stupid," she began, "but I have a friend who has asked me to do her a favor if I were to ever see you here again. And here you are."

She was right. It did sound stupid, but I was intrigued. She looked at my bangs, probably wondering what the hell happened. It was the first time I had come back to the Uptown Y after the laugh yoga incident, and I was hoping she wasn't one of the witnesses.

"Okay…" I said, not really knowing what else to say.

"So I was at a yoga class and so were you," she said.

Argh. Of course she was.

"And so was my friend," she continued, "and she was also at some pottery class that you were in—a studio class that ended last week?"

"Okay…" I said, still at a loss for words.

"So, do you know who I'm talking about?" she asked.

"The woman with the black hair down to here?" I asked, holding my hand like I was going to deliver a little karate chop to my carotid artery. I was hoping she said yes to that because if there were more than one person who had witnessed both of my most charming moments, I was going to ask the Goddess for my money back on this life.

"Yes, that's Shiloh," the woman said.

Oh, thank you for small mercies, Goddess.

"And I am Collette," she said, holding out her hand.

"Hi, I'm Allura," I said, feeling relieved to muster up something other than "okay."

"Allura, hi," she said. "Right, so Shiloh..." She looked around.

I looked around too, for what, I don't know, but I did look around. I was getting nervous.

"Shiloh wanted me to ask you three things," she said.

"Okay." I was back to that brilliant one-word comment again. But what else could I say?

"Shiloh's first question..." Collette held out one index finger. "Her first question...don't be offended, okay? For obvious reasons, don't be offended if your answer is no," she said and looked at me with a combination of concern and apology and curiosity. I recognized that look. It crossed most people's faces just before they asked if I was a lesbian.

"I can make this easier for you, I think. Yes, I am a lesbian," I said, raising my hand to reassure her that I wasn't offended. Two women brushed past us, one after the other, on their way out of the locker room, so Collette and I both sidled closer to the wall.

"How did you know I was going to ask that?" she asked, her eyes growing large.

"I just did," I said. "When you've been asked that before, you start to recognize how people look when they are going to ask."

"Oh. I guess I wouldn't know," she said. "Not that there's anything..."

I lightly touched the back of her hand. "It's okay," I said. "What are the other two questions your friend wants answered?" I patted her hands and then took my own hand away again. This was awkward—the whole thing—but I was getting a kick out of it, not the kind of kick that happens at someone else's expense, but the kind that comes from a very unusual conversation you'll replay in your head, laugh about and share with others over drinks.

"Well, she also wants to know if you're single," she said.

"I am." Was she going to ask me out? Why else would she have her friend ask me these questions? I hadn't dated anyone since Mickey. The exciting little cranial kick I had been getting out of the conversation turned into an exciting little kick in the gut. I braced myself against the wall. Dating. Ugh. I didn't like the sound of the word, let alone all the emotion and preparation that went into the actual...what was dating? An event, a performance, an action? However it could be categorized, I did not look forward to it. I'm pretty certain that to Collette I must have looked like an opossum who was preparing to play dead. From what I remembered, though, of the black-haired woman, of Shiloh, she was sexy and cute with a presence that I had indeed noticed.

Collette watched my face carefully, as if she were reconsidering her willingness to ask me the third question.

"Is sh...she," I stuttered, "is Shiloh going to ask me out?"

Collette still watched my face.

"Yes, I think that was her intent," she said. "If the answers to the first two were yes and yes, then her third question was do you want to do something sometime. If yes, do you want her number so you can call?" She started talking hard and fast to make up for my obvious discomfort. Could she tell I was panicking? I stood up straight and pointed out that she had now asked me four, not three, questions. She laughed and said I was funny.

"This is exactly the reason Shiloh wanted to ask you out. She thought you were funny in yoga and funny in pottery class," Collette explained, chuckling still. "She liked the sound of your laugh. That's actually how she recognized you at pottery, in case you were wondering."

I had not been wondering, but okay, that was cool. What was the harm in letting this woman think I would go out with

Shiloh? I didn't have to commit to anything here. And if I did decide to at least call this Shiloh, well wouldn't that be inviting my edges back? Perhaps an opportunity to get caught by life was presenting itself here. Dr. Browning would be pleased.

"So, yes, I would like to go do something with her and yes, I'd like her number," I said, some of the panic subsiding with the sound of Collette's laughter. I was funny. Good, that was a good thing and it made me feel like I had gained control over my cardiac flutterings. "It'll sort of be a blind date, I guess," I said.

Collette pursed her lips, appearing startled. She looked like she wanted to laugh, but wasn't sure she should. I smiled, so she smiled, and then she broke out in laughter again. She said, "You *are* funny!"

She gave me Shiloh's number, which I entered directly into my phone. I thanked her for passing on the questions, and I asked her to let Shiloh know I'd be calling her tomorrow. I figured that was enough time to not seem impatient and not so much time that I'd chicken out. After an awkward moment of do-we-shake-hands-or-what, we nodded at each other, smiled and each turned away. Collette went back toward her locker while I floated out of the Y's front doors. Dating, hmmm.

CHAPTER FOURTEEN

Double the Dating Pleasure

Because the tiny lights were so tangled, I took off my mittens to separate the multicolored bulbs from one another and the twisted green wires. After a few muttered cuss words, I eventually found one loose end, placed it in between my teeth and began working to free the rest of the lights. Nothing was loosening up, but I continued to work at it anyway. Finally I let the ball of lights and wires fall to the ground in an unholy mess. The cold sunlight caught in the miniature glass bulbs and lit them as if they were plugged in.

"Come on," I said to the string of lights. My phone rang, muffled by my down jacket. I reached in to see who it was. Apparently, I wasn't fast enough. I had missed the call. I looked at the screen and the word that ran through my head was less than festive. Mickey had called. My mouth, which had been sort of drooly from holding the winter lights, went dry. I was glad I hadn't just answered the call without checking who was on the other end. I hadn't talked to Mickey for a month or more and I wasn't sure I really wanted to now. Why was she calling?

When I heard Mickey's recorded voice, my insides tightened. I didn't realize I had a death grip on my phone until I loosened my fingers to replay the message, "Uh, hi Al, this is Mickey," her voice began again, "I was calling you…uhm, of course I was calling you. Guess I didn't need to say 'you.' Anyway, I'm calling to see if you'd like to…uhm, maybe get together this coming weekend or sometime. You know, with the holidays…maybe we could go get dinner or…or something. Uhm. Okay, call me and let me know what you think. Okay. I was thinking of you…bye."

"Fuckity fuck fuck mcfuckerson," I said as I deleted the message. No. I didn't want to go get dinner or something. I didn't want to do anything with Mickey. Although I was tempted to call her back immediately and tell her no, I thought I should at least consider it because this apprehension that filled me must be indicative of an unresolved issue. The reminder of failed love, the dread of having to consider rekindling that love, and an unfathomable uncertainty had all been perched, with nervous legs crossed and palms sweating, on uncomfortable chairs in the back of my mind. I'd call Mickey back later. Maybe tomorrow. I'd see how I felt tomorrow and then go with that.

I considered the tangled winter lights at my feet. I wanted to kick them but their messy state was not their fault, so I brought them into the house to continue unraveling them in the warmth of the indoors.

"Hi Dwight!" I hollered up the stairs as I entered the house.

"Hi lilfella!" he hollered back to me.

I peeled off my winter coat and scarf, removed my boots and looked at the postcard from Mom that I had read earlier. Gladys had escorted her Pips to Mississippi and was taking them next to Arizona, even though they were scheduled to meet friends in Florida in a week. Why were they crisscrossing the states like that? Florida to Arizona and then back to Florida? They were like teenagers with their first set of wheels. I shook my head and padded up the stairs with the snarl of lights in my hand. Maybe Dwight would enjoy some company. I would certainly enjoy his company as I tried to unravel this travesty. I was unnerved by Mickey's call. Dwight had already proven himself a good listener, so I planned on working out how I felt about her offer with my cockatoo as my counsel.

Dwight's crest feathers rose toward the ceiling as I entered the office. Sunlight streamed in the window, creating blue glints in his black feathers and intensifying the red bands in his tail. The sun also made visible the veins in his bare belly. Dwight cooed to me, and I did my best to coo back at him. Patrick had taught Dwight this cooing business a couple of days ago when he came to meet Dwight for the first time. According to the Humane Society, Dwight would need to be socialized with a few new people every month or so, to avoid becoming territorial or possessive of me. But they warned I was not to overdo it lest he become even more stressed than he already was. So far, only Patrick had met my new companion. He claimed not to be into big birds, but I could tell from Patrick's face as Dwight had yelled, "Hi lilfella," down the stairs to me, that he might soften. And then the minute Patrick laid eyes on Dwight, a big "Oooooooh" escaped his lips and he couldn't take his eyes off the half-naked bird.

After I introduced them, I busied myself downstairs in the kitchen making a snack. I let Patrick and Dwight get on with their socializing and through the vents I had heard Patrick's voice and some nonsensical responses from Dwight. When I entered the office they were taking turns cooing back and forth to each other.

Now Dwight was cooing at me. So I cooed back, hoping he took it for a happy noise because my coo sounded rather like a growl. I tried again, smiling this time and immediately pictured dogs facing off over the carcass of something tasty. Would Dwight now see my bared teeth and hear me growling and think I was being a menace? No, Dwight thought I was wonderful, and to show me so, he bobbed his head with his feathers raised high like a showgirl in Vegas and cooed back.

I pushed my desk chair aside and sat down on the area rug, with the ball of horror in front of my crossed legs. I told Dwight about the call from Mickey while I worked on the lights. He clucked and whistled at various stages of my story.

"I just don't want to go there again with her," I said.

Dwight bobbed his head and chortled.

"I'd rather call anybody else in the world except Mickey," I concluded, which made me think that I should call this Shiloh woman. Even a cold call was more enticing than speaking to Mickey. So I grabbed my cell and looked at the contact list in my phone. I paged over to the S's and found Shiloh's number. I looked at it for a minute before making the call.

As it was ringing, I panicked. I didn't even have a plan! What was I going to say? Could I still hang up? No, she'd see my number on her caller ID and would know I chickened out. I could call later and say that I had lost...

"Hello?" a woman's voice answered.

"Hi. This is Shiloh—I mean, is this Shiloh?" I stumbled, oh Goddess, lend me a hand here!

"Yes, this is Shiloh," the woman's voice had laughter in it. "Who is this?"

"This is Allura. Collette gave me your number..." I let the sentence end without actually ending it.

"Allura!" she said, "Hi! I'm glad you called."

"Oh." Come on Goddess, some help, please?

"I, uhm, I didn't know how to get a hold of you," Shiloh said, "so I asked Collette to help me out if she ever saw you at the club again."

"She did...help you out..." I said. I bit my bottom lip hard enough to consider a piercing. I think my heart stopped beating.

"She must have because here you are." Shiloh's voice was bright. She laughed a little and said, "So do you want to go out sometime? Maybe we could do dinner, drinks, or maybe, I don't know," Shiloh paused and said, "yoga?"

Okay, there it was. I had already had the worst embarrassments that I could probably ever have in her presence, twice, so I took a deep breath. "Well, how about dinner and a movie?"

"A movie?" Shiloh asked.

"Yes and dinner. Maybe dinner first and then the movie," I said, feeling bolder now.

Shiloh started laughing. "You really are funny! Okay dinner and...a movie." From the way she said the word, I wondered if "a movie" had become a code word for something else since I'd been out of the dating scene. Shiloh was still laughing. I'd have to check with Falina. She'd know what the movie deal was. But Shiloh's voice was warm. And she had a nice, light laugh, almost like little bells tinkling against each other, so I joined her even though my palms were sweating so badly that my phone was about to slip from my hand.

"Would you like to go out this Friday?" I asked. "You can pick the restaurant and I'll pick the movie. How does that sound?"

"Mmm," Shiloh mused. I could still hear the smile on her face as she spoke, "Well, I guess that sounds like a plan."

I was going to ask her if she wanted to drive when she suggested I pick her up at seven. I told her that was perfect, so she gave me her address. My heart was still not beating properly, so I figured it would be graceful to end the call before I went into cardiac arrest.

"Okay, I'll see you at seven on Friday, then," I said.

"Sounds good! Bye, Allura."

"Bye, Shiloh."

"Shiloh," Dwight said as I ended the call.

"Dwight!" I yelled. I jumped up to look at him, happy to hear his new word, "You said Shiloh!"

Dwight said nothing, but he bobbed his head and eyed me like we shared a secret.

"Shiloh, Shiloh, Shiloh," I repeated loudly to Dwight. Then I panicked and looked at my phone to make sure I hadn't accidentally stayed on the line just to be overheard by Shiloh. What would she think of me calling out her name like that? She'd think I was some obsessed stalker. The call had definitely ended.

"Shiloh! Shiloh Shiloh! Say Shiloh, Dwight!" I called, but Dwight just looked at me.

The phone, still in my hand, rang. I was so startled that I answered it without even reading the caller ID. Now Dwight repeated his new word, "Shiloh!"

"Hello?" I said, thinking it might be Shiloh calling to say she'd changed her mind.

"Hi, Al." Mickey.

"Hi, Mickey," I said, my already panicky heart giving a little lurch in my chest.

"Hey, how are you?"

I took a deep breath, trying to loosen my ribcage. "I'm okay, how are you?"

"Not too bad," she said, "not too bad at all." I tried to lower the protective barrier I felt go up as I listened to Mickey's voice on the phone. I'd definitely need to deal with the frayed end of our relationship. Before I did, I'd need to deal with my frayed nerves and get rid of this emotional blockage. Throughout our conversation, Dwight practiced his new word. Shiloh, Shiloh, Shiloh.

Book of Shadows
Spell to Break Through Blockage

Cast the circle around the bathtub.
Burn myrrh.
"Blessed be Creatures of Light."
Light tiny white candles on tin plate to bring luck.
Greet and honor the four directions and the universal
elements.
"Thank you, essential oils of anise, frankincense, rose
and vetiver
for allowing me to recharge and re-energize my life and
to break through
the blockage that has enveloped me.
I will take the best you have to offer,
and in return, allow my blocked energies to wash down
the drain
when we are done."
Three drops of each oil go into the tub of water.
A small handful of salt follows the oils.
A good soaking ensues.
"As the water is drained, so is my blocked energy.
Replacing it is a wealth of decisiveness and creativity."
Pull the plug.
Thank the four directions and the universal elements.
"Blessed be Creatures of Light."
Extinguish candles.
Open the circle.

CHAPTER FIFTEEN

Reunion

Blair's blond hair, whipping around her face as she turned to bitch at Tootie in Mrs. Garrett's kitchen, made me realize how happy I was to not have fallen into that beauty trap as a teenager. Blair was all about being gorgeous, Tootie was all about being mischievous and cute and so far this whole *Facts of Life* episode was based on these two rubbing each other the wrong way. I watched the rerun waiting for something to click inside my head or heart. Why had Dr. Browning suggested I watch TV shows that I had seen as a teenager? I was supposed to be reflecting on things that I had perceived as crises during my teen years, but honestly, what good was that going to do? Had I ever really had any crises when I was a teen?

Ah, now that's more like it. Jo Polniaczek had entered Mrs. Garrett's kitchen and was successfully changing the subject thereby ending the commotion Blair and Tootie were creating. A huge, juvenile grin plastered itself across my face as I noted Jo's softball jersey and hair feathered back into a ponytail. Back in the day, Jo had been my sole reason for watching this show.

There weren't that many TV characters that I had lusted over as a teenager, but Jo was certainly the cream of a very small crop. She was tops, always showing up in scenes with motor oil smeared seductively across one cheek, holding a wrench, talking about getting new parts for her motorcycle. No one had ever alluded to her sexual orientation on the show, but really with the softball jersey and motor oil—who needed to question it? She was hot. And she was as gay as I was.

I was disappointed when the phone rang because Jo was still in the scene. I considered not answering it but then a commercial started, so I grabbed the phone before the voice mail kicked in. It was Trisha, heading out to happy hour after work and inviting me to join her and a few friends.

"Sure, thanks for thinking of me," I told her.

"We're heading over to The Chatterbox," she said, "I should be there by five thirty, but Elizabeth and Heather are there already. They've been there a few hours, so this could be interesting," Trisha laughed. "Oh, and Elizabeth and Daniel just broke up again. So, well…it could be very interesting."

"Okay," I said, panicking slightly, "okay." I silently took a deep breath. Elizabeth and Heather were friends of Mickey's and mine. It had been a long time since I'd seen them. Heather was an easygoing soul, but Elizabeth was one to watch out for— she always made me uneasy. She had a habit of going for my jugular. Mickey used to say it was jealousy on Elizabeth's part, but I never figured out what made her jealous, so I wasn't sure Mickey was right about that. I didn't want Trisha to know that I had any reservations about seeing friends that I hadn't seen since I was with Mickey, so I steeled myself up and said, "Right. I'll be there and thanks for the heads-up about Daniel. Will you let them know I'm coming?"

"No problem and yes, I will," Trisha said.

I tried to think of a plausible excuse for not showing up at The Chatterbox. I was not ready to see Elizabeth and Heather. They were, I was sure, still in close contact with Mickey, which shouldn't matter, but for some reason it did. It made me feel at a disadvantage, as if I had been second choice as a friend for them.

Ahhh-ha. Now here was one of my teenaged crises that still came up as often as did weeds in my garden. Being excluded by friends had always constituted a crisis for me. As a kid I enjoyed being alone only if by choice. When I wanted someone around, I really wanted someone around. Alaina and Falina had usually been good in a pinch but nothing was worse than when a friend chose someone else for sleepovers or hanging out. Ooh, yes, those were crisis times.

How was it that this still constituted a crisis? Heather and Elizabeth had been friends with me long before they were friends with Mickey, but I knew from Trisha that they still saw Mickey occasionally and they had not once called me. Was the point of Dr. Browning's vintage TV program viewing and crisis analysis to show me that I'd lived through what I'd considered to be catastrophes? Would I fail her therapy if I instead learned that I still suffered the same youthful angst? Or had I failed at life—at being an adult? Well, Goddess, there was a grim thought. Wait; maybe Elizabeth and Heather's temporary exclusion wasn't really a crisis now. Was it? My feelings were hurt, but was that a crisis? No, not really. Probably not, anyway. Okay, Dr. Browning, this assignment may have worked. I guessed I'd find out once I saw them.

I checked the time, trying to leave so that I wouldn't get there before Trisha arrived. Hmmm. Did needing a buffer-friend put this at crisis-level? No, I didn't think so. I inspected what I was wearing: a black pencil skirt, my black cowboy boots, turquoise beads and a pale blue shirt. The pale blue would never do—it made me feel too vulnerable, so I changed it and the beads for a deep red cable-knit sweater and an onyx choker. Red enhanced personal strength and onyx would absorb any negativity so that I wouldn't have to absorb it myself, just in case there was any. Fingers crossed there wouldn't be, but why take any chances? I checked the time again. Four forty-five. Okay. It wouldn't take more than ten minutes to drive over to The Chatterbox, so I could at least finish *The Facts of Life* episode before leaving.

Jo was nowhere to be seen in the second half of the episode, so I killed time by making small talk with Dwight upstairs in the office. I tried anyway. Dwight was more interested in listening to me fret over seeing Elizabeth and Heather than he was in talking back to me. He did bob his head encouragingly though and he raised his scaly foot a few times as if to say, "Easy there; it'll all be okay." I hoped he was right about that.

I said goodbye to Dwight and carried two empty coffee cups to the kitchen sink downstairs. I thought a coffee might be nice and then reconsidered. I was jumpy enough. Tea perhaps? Pagans in need of assistance sometimes used specific teas, and with my apprehension, I thought I might benefit from a protection tea. The magic didn't really come from the tea, but rather it came from the ritual that accompanied making and drinking the tea. Most cultures have good luck and protection practices such as the smashing of plates at weddings to protect the bride and groom, or the wearing of a crucifix to ward off demons or even carrying a rabbit's foot or some other trinket to protect one's luck. After checking off the list of flowers and herbs I'd need, I discarded the idea. The co-op shopping list I had made that morning had valerian and elderflower at the top. A protection tea without those two ingredients would just be, well, just tea.

Since the magic came mainly from the intention and the requests behind the actions, I decided instead to imbue a few household tasks with requests for protection. I wasn't taking any chances and had a feeling I'd be greeted with at the very least, a low level of animosity. I wasn't as worried about Heather who had always been cheerful and nonjudgmental, but I was expecting some backlash from Elizabeth who usually seemed to be in a huff over something. I asked the powers that be for some protection from negativity as I looked after a few mundane chores. I straightened up the kitchen even though it didn't need it, checked the mail, watered the windowsill herb garden, threw on my pea coat and a white woolen scarf, and then finally admitted it was time to leave.

On the short drive to The Chatterbox, I convinced myself that it would be just like old times, only without Mickey. Elizabeth and Heather would be glad to see me, I'd be happy to see them, and it would all feel normal. When I entered I saw them both tucked into a corner booth so I had time to secure a smile to my face before approaching them. Elizabeth was overdressed, as was usually the case, in a burgundy silk pantsuit. Her deeply parted dark blond hair was swept back on one side with an oversized sapphire-encrusted barrette. Heather was dressed more appropriately for a neighborhood restaurant. She wore a pine green cardigan with a teal camisole beneath it. Her style ran to delicate, yet simple lines, and she wore a choker of yellow glass beads interspersed with small metal squares. Her dark, chin-length curls were pulled back from her pale forehead with a thin green headband. When she spotted me, Heather jumped up with a genuine smile. She hugged me tight.

"Oooooh," she exclaimed, "good to see you! Good to see you!" Her voice muffled itself in my scarf. Elizabeth, on the other hand, waved without smiling and said, "Allura."

She didn't stand up, so I skipped the hug. I slid into the booth next to her so I'd be across from a friendly face instead of Elizabeth's scowl. I smiled to myself as I realized how much Elizabeth resembled bitchy Blair from *The Facts of Life*. She sighed as she scooted to make room for me. I had beaten Trisha there. Damn. Why hadn't I looked for her car outside before coming in?

Heather and I got caught up on news, as Elizabeth kept silent. Heather told me things were better than great between her and her partner Julia. A brief flicker of guilt and apology crossed her face when she said this. I wasn't sure if it was for me and the loss of Mickey or for Elizabeth and the loss of Daniel, but I didn't care—it was so good to see her. She said her job was going well. I lied and told her mine was too. No sense in my bringing us all down since Elizabeth decided to do that for us as she complained about her new position at a private school. She hated the principal and according to her the teachers were all incompetent morons.

I eyed Heather as Elizabeth droned on. Heather had put on a little weight, which she had needed, and she looked bright-eyed and happy. Her cheeks had a glow and her curly hair looked more buoyant than ever. She looked…I checked my breath, no…she couldn't be. I snuck a peek at her beverage. It appeared to be cranberry juice. It could have gin or vodka in it, I reasoned. When I glanced back up into her eyes and saw her looking like she was dying to say something, but at the same time, didn't want to say anything, I knew—she was pregnant! I raised my eyebrows, not knowing if I should ask out loud. I didn't have time to further debate whether or not to ask.

She squealed, "Yes, I am! I am!"

We both shot up out of our seats and hugged each other, jumping up and down beside the booth like we should be carted off to a sanitarium. I started to cry a little out of happiness for her and Julia. I held her at arm's length to get a good look at her, and she had started to tear up as well.

Elizabeth, her voice a paper cut, asked, "What are you two talking about?" Her face was impassive and her eyelids low, apparently bored with our excitement.

I looked at Heather and she nodded.

"Heather is going to have a baby!" I exclaimed, hugging Heather one more time before sliding back in to the booth beside Ms. Crabbypants.

"I am! I'm due in June!" Heather was all smiles as she, too, slid back into the booth. She changed her mind, scooted back out of the booth, yanked open her sweater and pulled her camisole up to her ribcage. She turned so we could admire her nonexistent baby bump.

"Hello, little one," I said, leaning out of the booth to rub her still flat abdomen.

"Huh, really," Elizabeth said. "I would have thought," she leveled a gaze at Heather, "that you would have shared this news with people you actually see long before you shared it with those people you don't see."

Heather beamed and said, "I haven't shared it with anyone but Julia and my doctor yet—you two are the first to know!"

"Don't you mean Allura was the first to know? You must have told her at *some* point." Elizabeth's face was now angry and red.

"She didn't," I said. "I just guessed now."

"Whatever." Elizabeth sighed and tossed down the remainder of what I knew to be her favorite drink, a Captain Diet. As the ice cubes cascaded toward her upper lip, I hoped they wouldn't come flying out all over the place. We didn't need any more fuel for her bad mood.

"Honestly, Elizabeth, I didn't tell anyone yet. Allura guessed, that's all," Heather said.

"Maybe it's easier to notice the differences when you don't see someone for a while," I said. Why was I trying to console her? She was going to choose her own reaction, wasn't she?

"I'm just very happy that you are the first two to know... well, Trisha, too." Heather was still trying to make amends.

"Trisha already knows?" Elizabeth looked askance.

"No, but I'm going to tell her as soon as she gets here."

Heather looked at her tiny art deco watch then up at the door. I could tell, as the furrow between Heather's eyebrows dissolved, that Trisha had just come in the door. Trisha slid in next to Heather after quick hellos. She shrugged off her lightweight tan down jacket, shivered in the cream-colored Henley she wore and then pulled the jacket back on. She readjusted her messy topknot that had come undone and was cascading halfway down her shoulders. With her pale hair and this outfit, she made me think of a field of wheat, graceful in a gentle fall breeze.

That pleasant image was shoved aside as Elizabeth drilled Trisha regarding any prior knowledge of Heather's pregnancy. Elizabeth was so ferocious that the good news was almost hard to recognize as good news. She seemed to want to turn it into a point of contention, to make it about her being the last to know rather than an event to be celebrated. I realized I did not miss Elizabeth's company at all, and that some losses, as Dr. Browning might refer to my having fallen out of touch with Elizabeth as, were gains in disguise.

Trisha, Heather and I all lost interest in trying to appease Elizabeth. The conversation turned to brighter topics such as the quirky décor, the old-school board game selection and the variety of patrons. Our voices dwindled to silence as the appetizers were ceremoniously set on the table between us. The ensuing munching turned to squeals, guffaws and yelps as Heather and I played *Atari Frogger* on one of The Chatterbox's big-screen TVs. I couldn't get my frog through the river of rushing logs, but Heather was a natural. Her frog was successfully crossing his third level of the game. Elizabeth was pointedly silent as Trisha cheered Heather and me on. But then, during a lull between players as I once again sacrificed my frog's life to the almighty upstream logging company, Elizabeth decided to share.

"You know, you really disappointed us when you left Mickey just when she needed you most," Elizabeth said.

Before this statement fully registered with me, I was thinking it sounded like a sad old country-western song. Then it hit me that she was talking to *me*. Heather looked surprised. Trisha's face pulled into a grimace as if smelling something foul. I gathered that when Elizabeth said "we" it was really only "she" who was disappointed. Trisha began to speak, but Elizabeth cut her off.

"Addictions are medical conditions, Allura," Elizabeth chastised. "Would you have left her if she had just been diagnosed with cancer? That's basically what you did."

Oh my Goddess, did she really just say that? It was rare that I wanted to punch someone or to run away from a scene; I usually fell somewhere in the middle of the flight or fight spectrum, but in this case, I wanted to throw a left hook right up under Elizabeth's jaw and then run, thereby satisfying both fight and flight urges. I was at a bad angle since I was seated next to her, so instead I took a deep breath.

"Elizabeth," I said, exhaling, "Mickey left *me*."

"Whatever," she countered, "you deserted her emotionally before she left you." She angled her eyes at the approaching waiter and spat out, "I'll have another." The waiter blanched but quickly recovered. He asked the rest of us if we wanted more drinks or appetizers. We said no through apologetic smiles.

"Elizabeth," Heather and Trisha said in unison. Trisha went on, "it isn't fair to–"

"It isn't fair to leave someone when they have an addiction!" Elizabeth announced to us and to the rest of The Chatterbox's patrons.

What a hypocrite. Wasn't this something like the eighth time she and Daniel had broken up? And wasn't each breakup due to Daniel having an affair with some co-worker or bar friend? If that didn't sound like an addiction, I don't know what did.

"Why'd you leave Daniel?" I asked, not interested in playing fair anymore.

"What?" Elizabeth shook her head as if to better understand my question.

"Why did you leave Daniel?" I wished I weren't sitting so close to her. Her anger was tangible, and I hoped she wouldn't hit me.

"I *had* to leave him because he had an affair!" she screeched. "How dare you compare me to you!"

"So, was his affair with a woman or with a bottle? Because you know what? There's not a whole hell of a lot of difference," I said, my voice so calm that it actually scared me. Inside, though, I was pissed because she made me swear in anger, which to me always seemed like giving away a shred of power to the person who made you do it. And so much for the "do what ye will and harm none" adage I tried to live by.

"Excuse me," I said before getting out of the booth.

My legs were shaking, but they carried me to the restroom, where my plan was to collect myself. I locked the door behind me, turned around and gripped the edges of the sink with both hands. I closed my eyes and took a deep breath. Through my eyelids, the overhead bulb cast dark red and bright blue patches separated by zips of yellow. I took another deep breath and considered practicing some laugh yoga. The thought made me smile, so I opened my eyes. The mirror reflected a cool, calm version of me and made me wonder how many people had an exterior that belied the boiling blood in their veins and raging acid in their bellies.

I turned on the tap and let the icy stream glide through my cupped fingers. Then I figured as long as I was in the restroom, I might as well pee. Not only would I feel better, it would give

Trisha and Heather time to slap a muzzle on Elizabeth. This confrontation wasn't exactly the hostility I'd prepared for—it was worse—but I'd lived through it. I made sure my skirt wasn't tucked into my underwear and flushed with the toe of my cowboy boot. Perhaps that's what Dr. Browning wanted me to understand about crises. They weren't always the ones you armed yourself with worry lines for, but usually you came through unscathed. Did she want me to see that worry was futile? If so, kudos to Dr. Browning.

When I rejoined them, Trisha and Heather were there in the booth, looking both spooked and relieved. Elizabeth was gone.

Book of Shadows
Spell for Good Luck on a First Date

Cast the circle.
Burn cinnamon incense.
"Blessed be Creatures of Light."
Light pink candles in glass holders to bring romance.
Place the big rose quartz between the candles.
Greet and honor the four directions and the universal elements.
"Eight of Wands, I invoke the love at first sight which your arrows represent."
Place the Eight of Wands Tarot card against the rose quartz.
"Eight of Wands, please let hot romance in my sullen heart make a dent."
Thank the four directions and the universal elements.
Panic, reconsider, feel the fear...
Want desperately to take the words back—I'm not ready for this!
Deep Pranic breath. Deep Pranic breath. Deep Pranic breath.
Focus on the dancing flames of the candles
knowing that Mother Earth, the Goddess and the Universe will do what they will.
Deep Pranic breath.
"Blessed be Creatures of Light."
Use that deep Pranic breath to extinguish candles.
Open the circle.
Walk away wondering what damage may be about to occur.

CHAPTER SIXTEEN

First Impressions

Shiloh stood in her doorway, framed by dark red brick, bright white wood and clear glass. Behind her the house glowed, warmly lit and smelling of cinnamon. Shiloh was beautiful. And she didn't stare at my crooked bangs.

"Hi Allura," she said, with a hint of question in her soft voice.

The tentativeness with which Shiloh extended her hand made my heart ache. I took her hand, but didn't shake it the way I usually would. Instead, I held it for a few seconds and then released it.

"Yes, hi, Shiloh," I replied. I smiled at her, and she smiled back but seemed to be looking a few meters beyond me. I turned to inspect my parking job, thinking she might have an issue with it, but it looked okay to me. Maybe she was into cars. I hoped my little green Honda measured up. I turned back and saw that she was looking down now. My pre-date anxiety quickly evolved into early-date anxiety. I hoped it would somehow be dispelled before it became a full-blown case of mid-date anxiety.

"Do you want to come into the house for a few moments?" she asked. "I just need to grab my coat and some cash."

"Sure, of course," I said, and as she turned and walked back into the house, I followed her.

Shiloh wore a slightly oversized cream fisherman's sweater and gray flannel trousers. They fit her perfectly. I tore my eyes away from Shiloh's backside and took a look around me. The foyer's floor was tiled in textured terra-cotta. The walls were painted a warm shade of golden yellow. The house's interior woodwork was dark, and it appeared to be original.

She ran her hand lightly along the wall as she walked toward what I expected to be the kitchen, so I did the same. The walls had a gritty sand-like texture in the paint. I wondered if she did this every time she came through the foyer. I would, as it felt good.

Her kitchen struck me as the most inviting I'd ever been in. The ceiling was beaten copper and two of the walls were red and dark orange brick. Her countertop was poured cement with some sort of iridescence in it that made me think of sunfish I had caught when I was a kid. Her pots and pans hung from a rack suspended over the range, and the floor in here was the same style of tiles from the foyer, in the same hues, but they were twice as big. The scent of cinnamon, stronger here than at the front door, made me feel like I had just stumbled into an Indian spice market. I watched Shiloh moving her hands across the countertop.

"Whew, I would not mind coming home if I lived here!" I exhaled. She laughed. Then, realizing the double entendre, I said, "I mean, that sounded forward, didn't it—that's not what I meant."

Shiloh looked in my direction and laughed. "No, I get it. It's okay."

"I just mean I like your house. You have a nice style here," I said. And I was relieved to see that there were no signs of a cat anywhere. No hairballs coughed up on rugs, no litter pans tucked into corners, no shredded scratching posts.

"That's what I thought you meant, thank you," she said. She was still running her hand along the counter as if she was seeking the purse that sat not ten inches from her hand. Then it hit me.

"Shiloh!" I said, "You're blind!"

She stopped and pulled both of her hands back toward her abdomen. "You didn't know that?"

"No, I didn't know." Wow, how had I not known? "You didn't mention it."

"But you had seen me at yoga and at pottery," she said, "Collette said you knew who I was when she talked to you. I didn't think I'd have to mention it."

Her voice was a combination of sadness and accusation. Did she think I was going to change my mind about our date?

"You probably thought I was kidding about the movie then, hey?" I asked. I twisted the beads at my neck.

"I did," she said. "I mean, I do listen to movies, but usually at home so someone can tell me what's going on. Scene-by-scene narration doesn't really go over too well at the theater. And I did think you were being funny when you brought it up, you know, because I had just made that yoga comment. I thought you were teasing me in retaliation."

"Oh wow, that would have been a great comeback on my part, but I…" I said, "I just really didn't know you were blind."

"The yoga comment was funny though, wasn't it?" she asked, smiling again.

I nodded, putting on a rueful expression. Then I stopped as soon as I realized what I was doing. Words. I had to use words. "Yes," I said, "it was funny. Funny like coming out of an important job interview and looking down to find your panties peeking out of your open zipper funny." Shiloh laughed and I continued, "But you know, about that yoga, I really need to explain…"

"I think I know what happened," she said.

"Uhm, no, I don't think you *could* know," I said, trying to figure out how to tell her the whole story without sounding like a twit. Or more like a twit than I had already sounded that day. She probably thought I forgot to take my meds before yoga class or was having a nervous breakdown highlighted with hysteria. "I read this article in the *Star Tribune* about laugh yoga. I thought I was in the laugh yoga class, but I was at the wrong

YMCA," I said all in one breath. "I think I ruined what could have been a very nice yoga class."

"Well, you made my day—I wrote that article," Shiloh said. You could have knocked me over with a Pranic breath, on both accounts. "That's exactly what I thought happened, too, by the way. I laughed once with you so you didn't feel bad, but after someone shushed us, I got self-conscious and couldn't do it, even though I knew whoever was laughing needed someone to join in. I'm sorry I didn't laugh with you, Allura," she said.

"That's okay," I said. "You wrote that article?" I tried to picture the byline on the article…Shiloh Liebermann, I thought it said. Yes, it had said Shiloh Liebermann.

"Yes, so I guess I'm partially to blame for your misadventure." She laughed and then said, "Sorry."

"Hmm, well, if you'd like your share of the embarrassment, I guess I could give up, oh, maybe a quarter of it?" I teased.

"No, no, give me my full half, I can take it," she laughed.

"Okay, but no fair trying to give it back, okay?" I asked.

"Okay," she answered.

"Hey, you're a writer. I am, too."

"You are?" Now she sounded surprised.

"Yeah, I am. Are you freelance?" I asked.

"Yes, mostly. I try to concentrate on fitness magazines, but occasionally I get picked up by the *Star Tribune*," she said. She explained that she also taught a fitness class at Davidoff Academy for the Blind three times a week, which she loved as it worked in perfectly with her writing. She said a structured class schedule made her write more. Without it, she said she wasted time with not writing until the deadline's very last minute. "Right now I'm trying my hand at a novel, my first," she added, somewhat sheepishly.

"What's it about?"

"A retirement ranch for lesbians is the site for a murder." When she said "murder" she stood up straight, jutted out her left hip and did the "jazz hands" thing. Then she laughed at herself and leaned back against the counter. Goddess, she was about the cutest person I had ever been in the same room with.

"Murder?" I asked, "Do you get scared writing it? Hey," I got excited and wondered why I didn't think to ask immediately, "are you using an OutWrite?"

"No, I don't get scared—maybe that means my novel isn't very effective," she mused. "And about the OutWrite, I wish," she said. "I'm using Soundbyte software. It's sort of outdated now, but I'm used to it. The OutWrite would be a dream. How do you know about it?"

"I'm doing an article on it," I said. "It's the first article I've liked writing for quite a while—seems like a quality piece of technology." I regretted saying that it was the first article I liked in a while. I hoped she didn't ask about that. It would be a downer. There were eight hundred things I'd rather be than a downer on a first date.

"It is. I have a friend who uses it, in case you want a resource for your article," she offered.

I told her I would appreciate that. She didn't jump to get the friend's number which made me happy because I took that to mean that we'd do that later, and that meant that there would be a later. It got quiet in her kitchen then, so I brought the conversation back around to her joking yoga comment. "So as long as you are willing to share the embarrassment, I guess I forgive you for bringing up the non-laugh yoga experience," I said.

Shiloh laughed. "Yeah, I guess I should have been called for unnecessary roughness on that one. You just sounded so nervous on the phone when you called—you sounded like you had misdialed and were surprised to suddenly find me on the other end of the line, so I figured I'd lighten up the situation for you."

"Well, that you did," I said, "and truth be told, I *was* surprised to hear you on the other end of the line. I wasn't ready to call, but I dialed before I had time to, uhm, well, chicken out. I was nervous."

"You still are," Shiloh said.

"Aren't you?" I asked.

I opened the front of my coat and threw it off my shoulders a bit, suddenly warm. Maybe it was the conversation. My carefully chosen paprika silk shirt matched the floor tiles. Shiloh wouldn't be able to notice. I thought of Dr. Browning again and about how we prepare for the wrong crises.

"I am," she said.

She was still leaning against the counter and facing me. If she really was nervous, she hid it well. I glanced behind her at the small purse on the counter near the wall. That was what she had been feeling for earlier. I looked at her beautiful face, at her blue eyes framed with dark lashes, her pointed chin and her smooth lips. She didn't look nervous at all and that was incredible because here I was, essentially a stranger in her house, and she trusted me not to hurt her or rob her or do any of the horrible things people did to each other. How could she trust like this?

"Shiloh?" I asked. I toyed with my tiger's eye beads.

"Mm-hm?" she said.

"Do you still want to go out to eat?" I asked.

"So, no movie then?" she asked, the corners of her mouth turning upward.

"Yeah, no, I think we should save the movie for another time." I smiled too, not for her, but for me and because I couldn't help it.

"So you still want to do something with me, then?" she asked.

"Yes, I do," I said. I did. I wanted to do many things with her. I wanted—the thought jolted my core—to do everything with her.

"Okay, good. Let's go." She turned around and quickly found her purse.

"Okay," I said, holding still so that she might walk through the kitchen before me. I followed her as she took a rich red woolen pea coat from behind the dark wood door of the foyer closet. I let her put it on by herself, wondering the few seconds it took her to do so if I should be offering to help her. I followed her out the door. She stopped on the front step, and I remembered now the way she had stood in the yoga studio with her arm crooked in front of her. How had I not noticed she was blind?

"I'm here," I said, taking her arm in mine, our inner elbows pressing our coats together. I wanted to tell her I was also wearing a pea coat and wanted to ask her if she thought that was funny, that we both had on pea coats. We might look like a set of salt and pepper shakers to anyone who set eyes on us, only we were more like two pepper shakers. She was cayenne pepper, and I was gray pepper.

"Thanks," she said as she gripped my arm.

She stepped very lightly. I wondered if she needed my arm at all. I walked her to the car door and took her hand in mine. I pressed her hand to the top of the back of the passenger seat. "It's a Honda Civic, so go low," I said, wondering if I should put my hand on top of her head so that she didn't bang into the roof of the car. I didn't think I should because I didn't want her to feel like a little kid. She did just fine, sliding in with grace. I closed the door and ran around to my side, jumped in and asked where to.

She wanted to go to Sea Lavender's in St. Paul. She told me they had the best salmon lasagna she had ever eaten and a whole wall of the restaurant was an aquarium.

"The salmon lasagna is for me. The aquarium is for you," she explained, facing straight ahead until I spoke. Then she tipped her head toward mine.

"That sounds good," I said. "Is it off Dale Street? Near Lexington?"

"Yeah," she answered, "I think so anyway." She smiled, so I smiled, too. She was exquisite.

"Okay, if it's not, we can GPS it from my phone," I offered.

"Sounds like a plan," she said.

I rolled away from the curb and took us off on our first date. We drove less than a mile in silence, and I was just about to say anything to break the quiet when Shiloh broke it for me.

"Allura, do you know anyone else who is blind?"

"No," I answered.

"Okay," she said, "then I am going to ask a very big favor of you."

"Okay," I replied, not knowing what to expect at all.

"All right, I…I think you might be thinking a lot, then, not knowing anyone else who is blind…" She faltered, not seeming to know how to say what she was kicking around in her mind. "I mean, you're probably wondering what to do with me, like what you can ask and what you can't ask and when you can help and wondering what I need and all of that…right?"

"So far, you are exactly right." I hadn't noticed how tense I had been until she said all of this. I couldn't remember the last time I was this keyed up. "What do I need to…to know, or do, or…what is the favor?" I asked.

"Okay, well, I want you to ask whatever comes to your mind. I promise I won't be offended and will answer if I can." She laughed. "Or if I want to. And if you think that you can do something physically that will help, like when you took my arm on my front steps, well, I appreciated that."

"You did?" I hadn't wanted to seem patronizing and didn't want to take advantage of a situation where I could touch her for a good reason, when I found myself wanting to touch her for no reason at all. I stopped for a yellow light so I could look at her. She had tucked her hair back behind her left ear. And with the way the streetlights glimmered on her lips, I thought she must have just licked them. I had to swallow hard. Was this taking advantage of the situation, to stare without her knowing? I felt rich.

"Yes, I did and stop staring at me," Shiloh said. My eyes got big. Thank Goddess she was still smiling. I snapped my glance back to the road, the light turning green. I drove and felt busted.

"Sorry, it's just…how did you know I was staring?" I asked.

"Mmm, it's hard to explain. I just know," she said, "I'll try to think of how to explain that, but later, okay?"

"You're just really…beautiful," I said, deciding to be honest. What did I have to lose? Shiloh didn't say anything in response, so I asked the favor that had popped into my head a minute earlier when she had asked me her favor.

"Shiloh," I began, "will you return the favor and ask me what you want and tell me what you're thinking, especially if there's something I'm not doing right?"

"Wait," she said and put her hand lightly on my thigh.

How did she know where my thigh was? Was she really blind or was she pulling my leg, no pun intended. Her eyes were clear, not the eyes I expected a blind person to have. I didn't recall seeing a cane or a Seeing Eye dog at her house. Maybe this was some ruse...some reality TV stunt. "You never said whether or not you'd do the favor I asked for," she reminded me.

"Oh," I said, "yes, I will. I promise. Will you?"

Her hand still rested lightly on my thigh. I felt even richer than before.

"Yes, I promise I will. So we have a deal then," she said, patting my thigh for emphasis. Too soon, her hand was back in her own lap. I knew she'd say yes, but even so, when she did, my ribs felt two sizes too small. I realized I had just wrapped my necklace so tightly around my fingers and neck that I was threatening to cut off my oxygen supply. I unwound my fingers and grabbed the steering wheel with both hands.

Before long though, we walked arm in arm into Sea Lavender's and were seated. We ordered a bottle of Chianti and I told her we'd be here a long time if she expected me to drink my share of the bottle and still be sober to drive her home. She laughed and said that they closed at one and we should try to outlast anyone else who was here. Sometimes it seemed she could see me. She looked right at my eyes, I swear, every time I said something. It made me want to keep talking because I *wanted* her to see me. I wanted to feel her looking at me. But instead of asking her about that—I didn't know how to phrase it anyway—I asked another question that had kept cropping up entire drive over here.

"Okay, so, without hesitation, Shiloh, I'm going to make good on my promise right now."

"Good, shoot."

"So you let me into your house and you know nothing about me. How can you let yourself do that? I mean, what if I robbed you or hurt you?"

"Well, I guess that would have sucked, but what if you didn't and we hit it off?" she asked me in return.

"Hmm, good point. So have you always been this trusting?"

"No, when I could see I didn't trust anyone, really."

"You could see?" I was surprised. She seemed so happy and well adjusted. Why wasn't she bitter about losing something she had once possessed?

"Yes, until I was thirty-three, but even then my vision had started to deteriorate. I feel more trusting now of others and can't really explain why. Maybe it's because I have no choice but to trust, you know?"

"I guess...kind of," I said.

She told me about how she was diagnosed with retinitis-pigmentosa and about how her vision went crazy. As she put it, it was like living life in front of a fun house mirror. Then she said it just started disappearing slowly, bit by bit. It made me sad to think that she had once seen and now had nothing but darkness. I didn't tell her this, but I felt it all the same. I didn't pity her exactly. I didn't get protective of her either, which surprised me, but I did feel bad that she couldn't see the aquarium and the filled wineglasses. I was saddened that she couldn't see the pristine paper tablecloth that was expecting fresh artwork to be created upon it with the four crayons—red, blue, green and yellow—that rested near the little spice set in the middle of the table. I wished she could see me and then felt selfish for that.

When dinner came, she told me all about her novel. I spent more time laughing about the antics on the lesbian retirement ranch she had created than I spent eating or drinking.

"How did you know I was a lesbian?" I asked Shiloh after our dessert plates were taken away. I was leaning forward with my elbows on the table even though I was so full I might burst.

"You're a lesbian?" Shiloh's upper lip curled into a grimace as she said the word.

Oh my Goddess, what was this? How could she not like lesbians? She was writing about them! Wasn't *she* one? Wasn't this a date? Shit. Hadn't Collette asked if I were single? Yes, she had. Was this a trick Collette was playing on Shiloh? That nasty piece of work, Collette, if it was a joke.

"I...I thought you knew," I said, pulling my elbows off the table and distancing myself from Shiloh.

"I'm sorry," Shiloh burst out laughing. "That wasn't nice of me. I'm so sorry!" She held her hand out and laid it on the table with her open palm up. She said, "Come here." I put my hand in hers, and she squeezed it. She did not let go even after the squeeze ended. "I am so sorry, Allura, I was just kidding around. Are you okay?"

"Almost," I said, even though the blood that had drained to my feet still hadn't risen to anywhere near my brain. I didn't want to have Shiloh thinking I was okay enough for her to let go of my hand, which she didn't.

"I'm sorry," she said again. "I didn't know if you were when I first heard you laughing, but I hoped you were. I wanted you to be. And then after the pottery thing, where I recognized your laughter after all that clatter and the voices of the people who helped you, well, by then I really hoped you were a lesbian. Weird, hey? I had to ask Collette what she thought and she has no gaydar whatsoever, but she said you had potential." Here she laughed a little and squeezed my hand once more. "Collette told me your hair might be too long for you to be a real lesbian, but she said she thought you might fall into the 'lipstick lesbian' category."

"Oh nooo," I groaned. "I'm not wearing lipstick, just to let you know." I felt I should confess about the crookedness of my bangs as well, but didn't.

Shiloh laughed and continued, "Well, so that's when I asked her to at least ask you if she ever saw you again. And I figured if I hoped hard enough, you wouldn't stand a chance, that even if you were straight, you'd succumb to my sparkling charm and wit and you'd convert just for me."

I almost choked on the last sip of my wine. "And you'd win the toaster oven," I teased.

"Yes," she laughed with me, "and I feel it's only fair to warn you that I am hoping hard for a few more things now."

"So I *don't* really stand a chance, do I?" I asked, pretending innocence and compliance.

"No, I'm afraid you don't!" she said.

And that was when I knew Shiloh Liebermann liked me.

CHAPTER SEVENTEEN

An Unprotected Patron

I replayed that first date in my head so many times over the next few days that I fully expected to wear a groove in my gray matter and get stuck with the memory of the night playing over and over like an old-fashioned record with a scratch on it. I was walking to a coffee shop a few blocks from home armed with my work. I needed a change of scenery to cajole my creative juices from the bottom of the jar they were residing in lately. I was enjoying the unseasonably mild weather and knew it wasn't the smart thing to do, but I couldn't help comparing the night to my first date with Mickey. The memories were so far at the opposite ends of the spectrum that they were hardly comparable, but I did it anyway. With Mickey there had been very little conversation on our first date. There was no laughter that I remember and bantering like old friends never entered the picture.

Conversation was scarily easy with Shiloh. So was the laughter. I didn't expect this amount of emotion, of nervous joy and expectation, with Shiloh. I always have this idea in the back of my head when I have a first date that this could go really well, it could be great, even, but I never allow that idea to crawl to the front of my head. I certainly don't give voice to that hope. I turned left one block short of Minnehaha Avenue to avoid the rush of traffic. A tall wall that had been erected the year the light-rail was put in buffered the noise and cast a shadow across the street. I looked into the front windows of the houses wondering how the inhabitants felt about looking out onto a wall of wood. A glossy black cat with hair that was neither short nor long wound itself around a porch column at the house I was about to pass, so I slowed and considered turning back. The cat hadn't noticed me, so I figured I was safe to pass. He'd probably leave me alone, but I kept my eyes on him just in case.

I walked on as quietly as I could, hoping the cat would continue to rub his head on the post and keep his eyes downward. Just when I thought I was safe, his golden eyes locked onto mine. It was *the* cat. I was sure of it even before I spied his little black hind toes surrounding one white toe on each paw. The cat was giving me the bird. There'd be humor in this if it weren't so creepy. He was definitely stalking me.

I broke my gaze from his and forced myself to continue walking. I didn't look back even though I wanted to in case his stalking became a full-blown attack. I let myself carry on with comparing Mickey to Shiloh. Mickey's friends had been the instigators of our relationship. All of them had thought I would be good for Mickey. My friends encouraged me to get on with the relationship because, as they put it, how could she not be the right one after so many wrong ones?

With Mickey, our first few encounters found us surrounded by her friends in one campus bar or another, shooting pool and eating burgers. What I realized after Mickey and I were already seriously involved was that what her friends had meant was I'd be a better partner for Mickey than the bottle of Jack Daniels was proving to be. For the first year of our relationship, Mickey was kind and attentive, and even though I had the feeling she never really let herself be *herself* with me, I enjoyed the time we shared together. Initially I'd thought her drinking to be a cute quirk. She was a self-admitted germaphobe and would joke about the alcohol washing away any rogue bacteria.

But after the first year, Mickey started hanging out with her old friends at the campus bars again, minus Trisha who had pretty much started to devote all her time to Patrick. After a few months of accompanying Mickey, it got old for me. I was not cut out to sit around hammering back beers and drinks, chasing balls around a table with a wooden stick and forcing smiles over the same tired old stories that were smiled over last night and the night before.

I threw myself into my writing career. Mickey threw herself further into the bottle. Pretty soon I stopped going out with her, and she took it personally, like I was rejecting her and not the idea of sitting in a dank bar doing nothing productive or meaningful for yet another night. Mickey claimed I had changed. When I thought about it, I couldn't be sure that I hadn't.

I hadn't done bars much before meeting Mickey. I kept waiting for our relationship to get back to the place it had been during that first year. Ugh. As I thought about Shiloh, I asked myself why was I even opening myself to the possibility of that loss again. The possibility that I might be delusional, thinking that I found that forever person, going with the flow, giving all of myself to someone else, only to be left in the end and to be told that it "just wasn't working anymore." I would have hung in there with Mickey out of principle, but she didn't give me the choice to do that.

Eventually, after living alone but together, Mickey told me that she no longer felt the same way for me and that we'd be better off apart. After she moved into the guest bedroom, I suggested she get help for her drinking problem. It was as if I suggested she slice off an arm. She called me temperamental and judgmental, and maybe I was. But I couldn't understand going to the bar five nights a week, getting so wasted you could barely tell the cab driver your address and then sleeping it off until noon the following day.

Shiloh might not turn to the bottle to eclipse me out of her life, but my failed attempts at relationships before Mickey reminded me that most good things do come to an end. And was there really any point when something as equally heartbreaking would eventually happen, like it had with all my other relationships? Even for all of my ease with Shiloh a few nights ago, I still wondered if the intensity and hard work of getting to know someone new was worth it. I was still coming down from my high anxiety buzz from our first date. The phone conversations we had shared since had quelled my nerves, but the endings of those nerves still went haywire when I thought of her or heard her voice. This with Shiloh, whatever *this* might be, felt important and real. If it were real, then it would hurt that much more when it ended.

Additionally, I was becoming increasingly anxious about having agreed to see Mickey on the third of January. She was going to Vegas for Christmas and New Year's but thought it would be a good idea if we could see each other when she returned to, as she put it, "figure things out." I had told her that things were pretty well figured out, but she had pleaded, not in a desperate way, but in a way that made my heart break a little more for us, and so I had said yes.

The robust, skunky scent of coffee assailed me as I entered the welcoming independently owned coffee shop. The aroma dragged me over to the stainless steel counter and forced me to order the darkest roast they had. The young man who rang me up sported a bushy beard, chin length hair and a flannel shirt. Immediately I wanted to test him with a few snippets from a Kings of Leon song to see if his look was in tribute, but the only lines that came to me were from "Sex on Fire." As I had never met this young man, I kept my wonderings to myself.

I babied my overfull coffee cup to a tall, scratched wooden table by the window. I unpacked my writing bag and got to work. It was a full twenty minutes before I even looked up from my notebook. I needed a better word for "sought." I looked around as I considered my options. The coffee shop was littered with people who all looked busy. The girl closest to me was squinting at a Kindle and smiling to herself. Two women to my left were leaning over another woman's laptop and all three were snickering over what they could see on the screen. There were a couple of younger women in worn leather armchairs, each engaged with her own cell phone. A man in basketball shorts pecked away at his laptop in the corner and another man used his phone to take a picture of his still-life kids at the mini caffeine-addict-in-training table. Once he had an acceptable photo, he sent it on, and the kids came back to life. The Kings of Leon guy behind the counter watched soccer on the muted TV suspended over the serving area.

I realized not one of us had a real book or even a newspaper. I sipped away at my coffee, appreciating the dark flavors. What did people do before they had their own technological devices? Talk to each other? I hadn't frequented coffee shops as a kid so I didn't know, but I'm guessing it used to be a very different scene. I looked down at my notebook and felt out of date. I liked the lines and the smudges of pencil, but there might come a day when I skipped this step and went straight to the computer for my drafts. Not today though, I thought as I hunted for a replacement for "sought."

I had to smile to myself because I was feeling happy and that was a welcome change. If I admitted it, I almost felt content, like I was myself again. I swung my legs under the stool and grinned into the faces of strangers. Most of them smiled back at me. Could The Funk really be gone?

Then my own little piece of technology alerted me to a call. I scooped my cell phone off the table. It was Elizabeth. I hesitated before answering.

"Hello?"

"Hi Allura, it's Elizabeth."

"Hi," I said.

"Is this a good time to talk?"

"Yes, of course," I replied. I wouldn't have answered my phone if it hadn't been a good time to talk. Why was she calling? Did she want to apologize? Funny, I thought, how when a few things start going right, everything follows. I gladdened over the prospect of us mending what we had damaged the other day at The Chatterbox. I would apologize to her too, I decided.

"Good," she said. I waited for her to say more, but she was silent.

"How are you, Elizabeth?"

"Fine." She sounded curt. Maybe she wasn't calling to make up with me. I felt my smile disintegrate into a straight line. I reached up to my throat to twist my beads and discovered there were none. What the hell? Hadn't I put any on this morning? That was so unlike me. Or had they fallen off? Elizabeth finally spoke again.

"You know, I've been thinking a lot about what you said," she began.

My gaze swept the floor as I listened to her. I grasped the table's edge so I wouldn't topple off the stool. The only thing down there was a wadded up straw wrapper. No beads. I tried to remember what beads I had selected that morning. Nothing came to me. I probably hadn't chosen any. Very unusual.

"Yes?" I prompted the silence. No inkling of an apology lingered.

"Well, you were way out of line, Allura, way out of line. You have no idea what happened between me and Daniel and you were—"

"Way out of line, I get it." I tried to control my rising pisstivity. I took a deep breath. "Elizabeth, I think I got defensive with the way you came at me about Mickey. You're right, I don't know anything about wha—"

"You're right, you don't. And I should be coming at you hard about the way you treated Mickey!" She aimed her words like spears and chucked them at me through the phone. "We should all be coming at you hard for that. I don't know how Trisha and Heather can forgive you. You really screwed up."

"Elizabeth," I said.

"No! You were wrong on both accounts," she spat, "and you wait, you'll be wronged by someone soon. You just wait!"

"Elizabeth," I tried again as she took a breath, but she cut me off once more.

"You think you're untouchable? You think no one will ever cheat on you? You think that?" she ranted.

I pulled the phone away from my ear and looked at the screen, seeking reason or sensibility in the mundane icons. I could hear her tinny screeching even though my ear was more than a foot away from the phone. I caught my reflection in the surface of the phone's screen. My brow was knit and I was biting my lower lip. I raised my eyebrows at myself in the reflection. Smiling cow pose. I smiled at myself, but I was full of anxiety over Elizabeth's outburst.

Her rage was still audible, and I heard no signs of it ending any time soon. Something was seriously wrong with her. What did she mean when she said I thought I was untouchable? And I'd be wronged by someone soon? Would I? I knew it was the last thing I should do, but I disconnected anyway. My hand shook. Tears pressed dangerously close. I didn't want to cry, not over her and not in this coffee shop. I took another deep breath.

I tossed my phone into my writing bag, closed my notebook, packed up and then just sat there with my chin in my hand. No beads to twist. I looked out of the window, not seeing much. I had felt so good a few minutes ago. Had I been wrong to compare Daniel's sex addiction to Mickey's alcohol addiction? I hadn't said it to be malicious; I had said it to help Elizabeth understand where I'd been coming from with Mickey. I had thought it might even bring us closer since we both had partners with addictions in common. Or exes with addictions, I should say. The acrid bite of my cooled coffee attacked my taste buds as I emptied my cup. The skies had grown bruised, and it looked like a cold rain, or maybe snow, was on its way. I slithered off the stool, grabbed my bag and let The Funk escort me out of the coffee shop.

Book of Shadows
Spell for Requesting Guidance

Cast the circle with burning sage.
"Blessed be Creatures of Light."
Light one red candle to take away the indecision.
Light one white candle to infuse self with confidence in decision-making.
Inscribe glyphs for the Sun, Mercury and Jupiter on a cut open paper bag.
Place the paper on the floor between the candles.
Stand with bare feet firmly rooted to the paper.
Greet and honor the four directions and the universal elements.
"Sun, I invoke the glow, warmth and steady energy you provide.
I'll let your brilliance guide me in all decisions.
Jupiter and Mercury, I request your powers of change and speed as I make decisions. I thank you for your presence. I trust that your combined guidance and powers will lead me along the correct paths in my life. Thank you."
Stay rooted to the paper and allow the energies of the Sun, Mercury and Jupiter
to travel upward through feet, legs, hips, belly, heart, chest, shoulders, neck and head.
Open self to the guidance that is present.
Thank the four directions and the universal elements.
"Blessed be Creatures of Light."
Extinguish both candles and open the circle.
Fold the paper glyph-side out and place it under the mattress so that the guidance
might be revisited each night.

CHAPTER EIGHTEEN

Solschristice

The acorn hit me square between the eyes.

"Hey!" I yelped, rubbing the spot where the pointy little cap or bottom made contact with my head. "What was that for?" I asked Veronica. We were sitting on opposite sides of Trisha and Patrick's low oak coffee table in their living room, gluing miniscule red ribbons to acorns so that we could dangle them from our Solschristice tree.

"Where are you?" Veronica asked me as Patrick plunked himself down on the floor next to her, holding his wineglass so high that if he did spill it, it would hit his dark green fleece shirt rather than just splashing the floor.

"Patrick, why'd you hold your glass high as you sat down?" I asked him.

"What do you mean," he asked.

"Hey!" Another acorn bounced off my head, this time hitting me above the ear because my face was turned toward Patrick.

"Quit changing the subject," Veronica demanded. "What's on your mind—you have been somewhere else for the last twenty minutes. What gives? Where were you?"

I had been somewhere else. I had been making out with Shiloh, letting her run her hands from my head to my naked toes, pressing her body into a huge four-poster bed with fat down-filled comforters tangled between our bare legs, pressing her bikinied body into the sand on a beach as the tide splashed us and added to the urgency of our passion, being kissed by her sweet mouth as December finally acted like December and the long-awaited snow drifted from the bitterly cold sky and covered our naked bodies that were pressed tightly together for heat—that's right, we were naked outside in December. It didn't make sense, but that's where I had been for the past few moments.

"Nowhere, I'm right here," I said. I tried to control the blush rising from the collar of my already red cardigan, but I was unsuccessful. My face was hotter than the fire roaring beside us.

"Yeah, whatever," Veronica said, winking at me.

She backed off when she saw my blush. She probably felt sorry for me if wherever my mind had wandered brought out this type of reaction. I made a mental note to make her an extra Yule gift this year for dropping the subject. Patrick sipped his wine with a bemused expression. Trisha was due home at any moment, so we were killing time before we ate dinner and began celebrating our hybrid Solschristice holiday together.

I was looking at Patrick's hand on the stem of his wineglass so that I wouldn't start daydreaming about Shiloh again, when I heard a frenetic popping behind me.

"Jesus!" Patrick yelled just as Veronica screamed, "Oh my Goddess!" We all jumped up, and they both lunged behind me toward the fireplace. Patrick dashed the wine from his glass onto our Solschristice tree, which was a good idea. Veronica flapped her full black taffeta skirt at it, which was a bad idea. The pine started to smolder—the long needles on its backside where it had been leaning against the brick hearth became wicks with little reddish orange sparks that were quickly traveling up each needle toward the trunk where they turned into bigger reddish orange sparks. The popping noise grew louder as more of the needles became fuses that were bursting into flames.

"Open the door, open the door!" Veronica cried out as Patrick tried to figure out a safe place to grab the tree. I scrambled toward the front door, shoving the big armchair out of the way and threw open the door. There stood Trisha with her gloved hand outstretched toward the doorknob.

"Move!" I hollered into her startled face, and she jumped aside as Veronica holding the tip and Patrick holding the trunk ran through the open front door like they were storming a castle with a glowing, smoking battering ram. Trisha and I stomped the little sparks on the floor as Veronica and Patrick beat the tree on the snow-less earth in the front yard. Tiny embers jumped away from the tree as they pounded it on the ground. I searched around for any renegade glimmers on the front porch. Trisha ran inside to do the same. When I looked back at Patrick and Veronica, they were staring down at the tree like they were paying respects at a funeral.

"I guess we won't need to make as many acorns as we thought," Patrick said, his voice sounding bright in the darkness.

"That could've been really bad," Veronica said, shaking her head.

"But it's all right," Patrick said. He leaned over, reached into an especially bare spot midway down the tree, grabbed the trunk, pulled it upright and said, "There's a lot of tree left."

I chewed the inside of my cheek and tugged my amethyst beads. The tree was more gone than here, but I could tell from the way Patrick was beaming at it that it was coming back in the house to be decorated with acorns, cranberries, popcorn and an angel in white. Patrick hoisted the half-singed pine over his shoulder and lugged it back in through the front door. I could hear Trisha inside asking Patrick if we were all okay and if the tree fire was completely out.

Veronica and I looked at each other. Her face went from frozen shock to devoid of emotion to bursting with humor all in a matter of seconds. We laughed like delirious hyenas right there in the front yard.

"Oh, my Goddess!" she hooted, pulling her cheeks down or warming them up with a hand on each side of her face. She laughed more quietly and said, "You know this is all your fault; your daydreaming took you away. We could have all perished in there!" She was still laughing and her brown eyes sparkled.

I delivered a playful shove to her shoulder and said, "My back was to the fire—you're to blame for this—you should've had my back!"

She grabbed my sweater front with both hands, pulled me so close that our foreheads were touching and said, "Happy Solstice, Allura!"

I hugged her and laughed a happy solstice into her shoulder. We walked back toward the house, leaving the tension of an almost-calamity out in the front yard. She kept one arm draped over my shoulder until we got to the front door.

"You know," she said, "whatever you were thinking about, you had a huge smile on your face the entire time you were gone."

"I'm sure I did." I let the mystery hang in the air. I was not going to jinx this Shiloh thing by talking about it just yet. It was like an unopened gift sitting under the Christmas tree. I wanted to savor the packaging, the bow and the hope.

Our Solschristice tree greeted us. It was now upright, half-burned and bedraggled, braced up in the tree stand opposite the fireplace.

"Good job, Patrick," Veronica said. Trisha, still in her down jacket and gloves, looked askance at her.

"Do you really think we should still have it in the house?" Trisha's eyebrows arched in question over her bright blue eyes. She had her gloved hands on her hips and was tipping her head from side to side, looking at the poor pine. No one answered her, so she backed up, looked at the tree again, dropped her hands from her hips and said, "Well, I guess it would be really disrespectful to put the tree through all that pain and anguish and then just toss it out in the alley. We better keep it." She pulled off her gloves and jacket and draped them over the banister.

"I knew you were a Pagan at heart, Trisha," Veronica said, beaming.

Trisha dropped herself into the big armchair, which still sat in the place I had shoved it when the tree was on fire and said, "Yeah, I probably am." She grinned.

We carried on with our dinner and our Solschristice celebration with more gusto than we usually had on our hybrid holidays, partly I think because we wanted to show the tree a better time than we already had. In between laughing and talking and listening and allowing myself impossibly short daydreams about Shiloh, I sent out silent thanks to God, Goddess and Mother Earth for giving me such exquisite friends.

CHAPTER NINETEEN

Pollination

I watched Shiloh's penny slice into the koi pond and hoped her wish would come true. I didn't tell her that my own penny missed the pond by six inches thanks to my phenomenal lack of athletic ability. This would be a great place to be if a person had a really bad cold or the flu. The moisture made the air palpable— how good it would feel as it filled sick lungs and clogged sinuses. I wondered how many people had the same thought. I looked around for phlegmatic children and hacking senior citizens. This conservatory could be a petri dish full of bacteria. Well, at least we wouldn't run into germaphobic Mickey.

We stood surrounded by orchids that would make Georgia O'Keeffe teary-eyed and most lesbians distracted. Shiloh had agreed on a second date. I had thought at length about where to go. I wanted her to experience the setting for our date as much or nearly as much as I would, so I had thought in terms of scents, sounds and textures. The big Minnesota Zoo was the first place to come to mind, but as some of the scents would be less than fragrant, I thought of the conservatory connected to Como Zoo in St. Paul. Shiloh thought it was a solid suggestion, so we moseyed through the light-dappled fern room. I held her arm even though the flagstones were even and smooth.

The conservatory was warm, and I felt even warmer in Shiloh's presence. Her laughter over my descriptions of the plants and blooms made me feel like a child seeking to impress her favorite teacher. We took turns breathing in the scent of every flower we could reach. By the time we'd sniffed our way through one of the conservatory wings, Shiloh decided it was time to sit and talk. A few birds resident in the great domed, glass building joined our conversation. We sat almost facing each other on a semi-circular stone bench surrounded by orchids.

"You have pollen on your nose!" I said laughing, and Shiloh brushed it off with the sleeve of her cayenne pepper coat.

"How rude!" she exclaimed, smiling. "You do too, but at least I was polite enough not to mention it!"

I laughed with her, leaned over and touched the tip of her nose before wiping the tip of *my* nose, just in case.

I pulled my phone from my pocket with the intention of taking Shiloh's picture, then hesitated. I would be able to look at the picture, but we'd never be able to reminisce over the picture *together*, would we? Isn't that what most pictures are for? They're to serve as reminders for a couple to say, "Oh look—our first date! Look at how short your hair was! I was so nervous—Look at how I've twisted my coat ties into a massive knot!" Then the couple laughs together on the way to the bedroom for some "remember when" lovemaking.

"Shiloh?"

"Yes?"

"Would you mind if I took your picture?" I decided I wanted to have a visual reminder even if we couldn't look at it together. I could always describe the picture to her when we were ninety years old, sharing a room in an assisted living apartment for lesbians. There probably wouldn't be any "remember when" sex at that age, or would there? At any rate, Shiloh's beauty was so enhanced by the surroundings that I had to capture it. She pressed her lips together, which brought lively color to them and said yes.

On the phone's screen, Shiloh looked small against the giant palm leaves. As I backed up to get her whole body in the frame, she grew even smaller. She didn't face the camera square on, so I captured an angled shot of her face with her black hair a strong contrast to her delicate features.

Later, when I downloaded the picture to my computer, my heart ached over her indisputable beauty. With the picture large on my screen, I noticed that perhaps accidentally and perhaps not, her thumbs and fingertips met and formed a definite heart in front of her abdomen. I sucked in my breath and held it behind a huge smile. The smile faded as fear poked at me like a garden hoe investigating weeds. I had gotten this involved with other women just to have the tender young relationships yanked from the soil, hadn't I? Yes. But if I were honest with myself, I hadn't felt this strongly for any of those other women. I looked at Shiloh's picture again and smiled despite my worries. I hoped her heart was on purpose.

CHAPTER TWENTY

The Four Senses

My desk chair spun emptily as I dashed from the office and raced down the stairs. Dwight's squawk reverberated after me, but I didn't answer. I knew what I was going to have to do. I had fought with myself all day, trying to write an article on a home security package that the owner could check using an Internet link from any computer at any time. It was an interesting product, but even more interesting were all the things Shiloh must be able to do without having vision. The first thing that had crossed my mind earlier as I made lunch was that Shiloh would have to be able to fix herself meals without seeing what she was doing. Did she use the stovetop? Was her microwave equipped with Braille? How did she know when there was mold on the bread or when the pot of pasta boiled over? As I prepared a salad and a bagel I marveled at what she must be able to do. How did she stay in the lines of a bagel when she put cream cheese on it? Did she make her meals or was there a service like Meals on Wheels that provided for her? Was there a special easy-to-make menu for people who were blind?

Later, after I was attempting to go back to work, I thought about how Shiloh got from place to place. She would always have to rely on others to drive her. She had told me on our first date that her mom teasingly called her the Jewish princess because she had to be chauffeured everywhere. Just moving, say through her house or the Y, would be a giant hassle for Shiloh. How did she do everything she did in a normal day? I tried to pull myself away from these musings and write my article, but every few minutes, I found myself wondering how Shiloh picked out her clothes or how she paid her bills or how she did her hair.

Eventually as a diversion from work I pulled out a blank piece of paper and wrote down every question I could think of for Shiloh for five minutes. Then I made myself work on the article for another fifteen minutes before I allowed myself more questions for Shiloh for another five. Working back and forth this way let me finish up the article. Then I had only one more question—in direct relation to the article I had just finished—about how a blind person viewed home security. I thought about it as I traipsed downstairs, ran cold water over my fingertips in the kitchen sink and then lit the burner under the kettle.

So here I was, rummaging through my foyer closet for a scarf to tie around my head so that I might be "blind" for the remainder of the evening. I was going to see what Shiloh went through every day. No, "see" wasn't the right word. I wanted to feel and hear what Shiloh went through every day. I found a white woolen scarf that wouldn't let me cheat, wrapped it twice around my head, blinding myself. For how long should I wear this blindfold to get an accurate feel for the way Shiloh experienced things?

Without mishap, I made my way, hunched and cautious, over to the red fainting couch. Should I really call it red now? Did the color matter as much to me with this blindfold on? In my head, I could still see that it was red, so what was the harm in calling it the red fainting couch? Did Shiloh still think in colors? Damn. My list of questions was upstairs on my desk. I had written, or scribbled somewhat legibly, in the dark before, so I knew I could handle adding a question about colors to the list, but I wasn't ready to tackle the stairs yet, so I sat and mentally added the color question. Surely I'd remember to ask.

A scream erupted from somewhere—it seemed to be all around me—Dwight? I ripped the scarf from my head, affronted by the cold and light that struck my eyes. I was halfway up the staircase when I realized it was my teapot whistling in the kitchen. I jogged back down the stairs and into the kitchen. I turned off the burner. Okay, I was going to do this thing. How easy it had been for me to un-blind myself the second I needed to. Shiloh didn't have that luxury. She couldn't say, "Let there be light," at the first hint of emergency and suddenly have her vision back to deal with whatever was screaming at the moment.

I wound the scarf around my head again, covering my eyes and told myself that it was for real this time. How long should I wear it? Why didn't I at least make the tea before I put it back on? I stood there. Had I turned the burner off, or had I just lowered the flame? Would my sleeve catch fire if I overshot the stove knob as I checked? I allowed my fingertips to seek out the knob. I found a knob—was it the right one? I'd check them all. I gave each of the five stove knobs, two of them rather greasy feeling, decisive clockwise twists. I leaned low and sniffed around at a safe distance from the stovetop. I smelled no gas. I stood up, feeling protected and victorious at having assured myself of this safety. There was a long, muffled creak somewhere above me. I stopped breathing. What was that? Dwight? My ears ached as I scoured the air with them. I heard nothing else. I let my held breath out in a quiet rush.

I'd make tea and then listen to Minnesota Public Radio as I sipped it. It would be peaceful and enjoyable. I turned to the cupboard in which my tea dwelt. Thank the Goddess my kitchen was tiny. I groped out the packages of herbal. It was too late for caffeine. It was also too late to mess with packaging loose tea into an infuser—I'd go with the pre-bagged. I located a box of tea that was still in its cellophane wrapper. Which tea had I not yet opened? What was the last type of tea I'd purchased? I held the box aloft, not wanting to lose my general sense of the cupboard's location. I'd risk it. I pulled out a pouch, tore it open and dislodged the tea bag. I hoped it was one of the peach herbals I knew was lurking somewhere in the cupboard. I raised the bag to my nose and inhaled. Peaches. Peaches like a sultry summer day. Yes. I had found it. Dumb luck and pride fought a short-lived battle within me. Pride won; I was a genius.

I felt around in the dish-drying rack for a mug. No luck. All I could feel were two plates and a big glass mixing bowl. Thank Goddess there were no knives. Okay, no problem. I shuffled my feet over to the cupboard that held the mugs, opened the door and grabbed the first one my hand recognized. I set it on the counter. I tried to drop the tea bag into it, but was alarmed to have my fingertips meet the unyielding bottom of the mug, which was in the wrong place. I laughed out loud and flipped the mug right side up. That would have been a disaster. I dropped the tea bag in this time, proud to have discovered the error before pouring the water. A low snapping sound shot out of the living room. My ears focused on the space where the noise had emanated from. What was that? I gripped the mug. I wished I had gotten down a heavier one if I was going to need a weapon. I listened.

All I could hear was the staticky nothingness that filled my house. No, wait…that was not true. I could hear the staccato clicking of the second hand on my kitchen clock. I could hear a faint whirring of something outside of my house and the miniscule pinging of a radiator. Most loudly of all, I could hear my thoughts, fragmented and somewhat panicked. And oddly enough, my thoughts were in my own voice. Why bother with attaching a voice to my thoughts…they were already my own, right? Why would my brain go through the extra trouble of "hearing" my thoughts in a voice at all? It's not like they needed a voice. Did the thoughts even need to be formally put into words? Why didn't they just come packaged as impressions or visions? I tried to stop thinking in words. I realized that wasn't going to work as I heard my own voice in my own head saying, "Stop thinking in words." Enough. I'd think, or not think, about this later. It was time for tea.

I reached out for the teapot before I took any steps. I wanted to find the handle before I found the hot pot. I already knew being blind would be dangerous; I didn't need any painful burns to impress that upon myself. I moved my hands through the air with excruciating slowness. I brushed the teapot handle, poked it with a finger to be certain I had found what I wanted to find and then grabbed it. I ran my fingers over the handle until I was sure of which end had the spout, shuffled the couple of steps I need to take in order to get back to my awaiting mug and stopped. How would I align the spout without touching it? I thought about this for a few seconds. I pictured several ways to do it and decided to go with touching the spout down onto the rim of my mug. That way no hands would be in direct contact with the boiling water or the hot metal. Great.

I found the mug's edge, held the teapot over the mug, lowered it until I heard the clink of stainless steel on pottery and poured. I heard the water filling the cup. I heard the small sigh of the teabag as its contents accepted the watery intrusion. I felt really good about this. I could be blind. No, wait. That wasn't fair. I had been blind for, what? Five minutes? Six? Ten? It was hard to say. Okay, maybe I had been blind for six minutes. That sounded about right. So being blind for six minutes while I made myself tea was not the same as, say, Shiloh being blind. No. She was really blind. Blind with a capital B. I-can't-take-this-white-scarf-off-my-head blind. I-don't-even-know-this-scarf-is-white blind.

What was I doing? I wanted to rip the scarf from my eyes, but I was immobilized by the overwhelming feeling that I was making light of something so monumental. My heart, stomach, everything rose into my throat. I held back tears. I shouldn't be doing this, should I? But I wasn't doing it flippantly. I wasn't doing it mockingly. And I certainly wasn't doing it perversely, was I? I was doing it to better understand Shiloh. I held the countertop's edge with both hands and took a deep breath. I would keep the scarf on. I would keep it on until the day was over. I wasn't sure how I would figure out when the day actually was over, but I would, somehow.

Okay, tea now. I wrapped my hands around the mug and raised it to my lips. I realized, in the absence of warmth in my palms, that I expected the mug to be hot. I also expected my scarf-covered face to be caught by the steam rising from the mug. Neither happened. I stuck a finger in the tea. It was barely lukewarm. How long had it taken me to make it? Shame over my gloating at being able to successfully and easily be blind brought heat to my face. I placed the mug on the counter. Millions of people lived without vision. Was I going to give up now or was I going to experience something that might allow me a more empathetic understanding?

I took the mug, with the tea bag still in it, since there'd be no way it would over-steep in the cooling water. I'd be lucky if the water leeched any flavor out of the leaves at all. I very slowly and cautiously made my way to the living room and set the mug on the fainting couch. It would be safe there. I inched over to the stereo. After what seemed like a long time, I found the power button and pushed it on. I then began searching for the function button. I wanted public radio, not the CDs. The CD would not help me discover the time, and I wanted some chatting to fill my mind. Music wouldn't fill the void right now. I knew my tea was already cold, so I took my time, trying to picture the buttons on the stereo. I was doused by splashes of country, rhythm and blues, pop, more country and finally talking. I listened to the voices until I recognized that they were indeed Minnesota Public Radio voices I was hearing. It was as if I had been reunited with old, lost friends. I sighed and stood up slowly. I made my way back over to the couch, looking for my tea mug with my hands before sitting down. Finally. I stretched out my legs, feeling every fiber of muscle ease itself into relaxing, from my hips all the way down into my toes. Finally.

I sipped my cold, barely peachy tea. It was tolerable. I should have grabbed a travel mug though. That way I couldn't spill it and no spiders or dirt could get into it. How would I even know if there was a spider in my tea? How would someone who was really blind ever know if her food was clean and safe to eat? There was another mental addition to my list of questions for Shiloh. I went to take a gulp of my tea—no sense sipping something that wasn't hot. My plan was to drain the contents of the mug before any foreign objects, or beings, could find their way into the beverage. I was overzealous about my gulp. The majority of the tea landed on my shirt. When I jumped at the shock, more tea sloshed out of the other side of the mug. I heard the tea land on fabric with a soft, wet ploff.

Great. I had a cold, wet spot on my shirt and another possibly on my skirt or on the couch. I wanted to lift the scarf enough to peek at the couch. It wouldn't really be cheating, would it?

I held my mug with both hands and guided it to my mouth to finish any dregs before they could do further damage. I heard the plop of the teabag as it dislodged itself from one side of mug's interior and fell to the other. Well, that was that; the mug was empty. I placed the mug on the floor. I let my hands look for a wet spot on the couch and then on my skirt. I found nothing. Mystery not solved.

The rest of the evening's experiment was no more gratifying. I hated being blind. My stomach growled. Dwight called from upstairs. Through the voices on the radio, I heard other, suspect noises from various parts of the house. The aura of needing to protect myself hung in the air about me, a residue leftover from working on my home security package article. My pulse pounded as I thought of horror movies. My phone rang three separate times. I thought about the article I needed to finish. My stomach growled more loudly, but not loudly enough to drown out my thoughts and questions. I sat still until it was time to sleep. It took me a long time to pee, brush my teeth and go to bed—hungry and naked save the scarf. I slept poorly knowing that behind every noise I heard, there was a homicidal madman, just waiting to get me.

CHAPTER TWENTY-ONE

Girlie Points

"Clitoris!" I shrieked.

"Yes, clitoris." Shiloh leaned back, crossed her arms over her chest and smiled. "And I'll take an extra twenty points for that."

"This isn't fair," I groaned. I recorded her points on the paper where she already had twice as many points as I did. We were playing Scrabble at her house on her Braille Scrabble board. She was beating the skirt off me.

"You were willing to play with girlie points, so it is fair."

"Yeah, but how was I to know you were going to have a triple word score with 'vulva'?"

"That was a good one, wasn't it?" she gloated.

"Yeah, forty-five points good!" Even though my pride was buried somewhere under her letter tiles, just looking at her made me feel like I had won. The many-paned windows rattled around us as the wind blew. The weather presented a stark contrast to the warmth of Shiloh's kitchen with its wonderful copper ceiling and red and orange brick walls. The wind was battling everything in its path, and it had started to sleet sometime during our game. I sat across the table from Shiloh.

She was here laughing with me, scoring extra points for every strictly feminine word, and it was amazing just to be in her presence. It was a busy way to play Scrabble—there was much more touching of the letters on the board than usual. I was in awe of her ability to memorize the board after feeling it. She was at no disadvantage, which was fortunate because she was quite competitive. I didn't mind losing once in a while, and if I had to lose to anyone, I'd certainly choose to lose to Shiloh.

"Quit staring and make your word," she said, smiling.

"Right." I rearranged my letters on the table. I wasn't confined to working in the tray since Shiloh wasn't going to see my letters. G, H, O, I, R, A and Y. Not much to work with, and I was distracted to boot. "Okay, let's see…" I said to let Shiloh know I'd stopped staring and was looking for a word. "Ohhh-kaaay." I drew out the word and re-rearranged the tiles. Y, H, O, R, I, G and A. I looked at the board to see what letters were open. The tiny bumps on the tiles caught the light from the hanging Tiffany lamp above us.

"Shiloh, how long did it take you to learn to read Braille?"

"A couple of months I think."

"That's fast, isn't it?" I asked. "I mean it's like learning to read all over again. Doesn't it take little kids longer than a couple of months to learn to read?"

"I don't think it takes that long for little kids, and anyway, I was really desperate to do it. I started practicing before my vision was completely gone. I think that may have helped."

"Why?"

"Why did it help?"

"Yeah."

"I still have pictures in my head of the letter and how the dots look from when I first started learning. So I had the added benefit of seeing and feeling them before I had to rely on feeling alone."

"I suppose that would help."

"You know, that being said, the kids at Davidoff Academy learn Braille really quickly, and many of them have never been able to see. I don't think it takes most of them even as long as it took me."

"Kids are better at learning, no offense."

"True," she agreed. "Plus, it's really lonely." She paused. "No, not lonely. It makes you feel really vulnerable, I guess, not to be able to read, to have to rely on others for everything. It makes you feel vulnerable and lonely." Even though it was still my turn, she began reading the words that had already been played on the Scrabble board. She picked off a few tiles and laid them down in front of her. She turned them toward me. They spelled my name.

"Here," she said and reached until she found my hand. She put my fingertips on the little lettered squares. "You're lucky, you only have to learn four letters for starters."

I closed my eyes and felt my name. One high dot for the A's. A line of dots for the L's. A funny fat T of dots for the R and a trio of spread-out dots for the U. I tried to memorize each letter.

A heated jolt rushed through my hands when Shiloh placed her hands over mine again, but I didn't open my eyes. I held still and reveled in her touch.

"Now close your eyes," she said.

"They already are."

She then held both my hands in one of hers and picked them up off the tiles. She held my hands for a moment longer before lowering them to the tiles, which were now in disarray. Was there a way to tell the tops of letters? I put them back in order, hoping I had the As and Ls in the right places, thinking I did.

"Okay, I did it. And if I'm wrong, well, I'll just have to let my parents know I've changed my name." I felt Shiloh's hands against mine and took mine away so she could read.

"You did it!"

"Did I?" I opened my eyes. I did! Just as I was going to ask for twenty extra girlie points since my name was strictly feminine, the doorbell rang. The pizza Shiloh had ordered and paid for over the phone was here. That had been the bribe she had used earlier that evening to get me to drive over—she'd provide a pizza and wine. As if I needed to be bribed.

"I got it," I said and touched her arm to let her know to stay seated.

"You can't. I have to sign for the credit card," she said, getting up and following me.

I let Shiloh pass me in the foyer and watched as her hair was blown about her face as she opened the door. She laughed as she pulled the delivery girl into the foyer. The girl set the pizza on the small table beside her and guided Shiloh's hand so she could sign in the right place on the receipt. Outside the sleet raced sideways on the wind. The trees were frosted, and my car was unrecognizable, covered in icy white in Shiloh's driveway. As the pizza girl left, a blanket of bad weather blew in the front door and melted into tiny diamonds on the terra-cotta floor.

"It's lousy out, hey?" Shiloh asked me after she closed the door.

"Yup, perfect night to get beaten at Scrabble."

Shiloh laughed like bells, music to my ears.

"You might have to stay the night," she said over her shoulder, one hand trailing along the wall, the other balancing the pizza.

I didn't know what to say to that. I wanted to make a joke, but I was so wrought up over the prospect of being near her all night that I couldn't. Of course, I'd probably be on the couch if I did spend the night. We hadn't really known each other long enough for anything else, had we? I felt like we had, but what was proper? And did I really care?

Around midnight I discovered I really did care what was proper. I didn't want to screw this up by jumping in too quickly. I wasn't sure it was right to start in the first place.

* * *

On the drive back home I pulled over to where I supposed the curb might be to tug at one of my frozen wiper blades, willing it to come loose from its icy mooring. I thought of the disappointment on Shiloh's face when I told her I couldn't spend the night with her. The truth was that I was really apprehensive, perhaps even terrified about getting too attached to her, yet I desired nothing more than to melt into her every fiber. I wanted to lose myself in her. But if I did, I ran the risk of literally losing myself again like I had with Mickey. And with Dr. Browning's help I was just beginning to recover, to pull myself out of The Funk. I most definitely did not want to go back there when it all fell apart with Shiloh.

The wiper blade finally gave way with a tearing noise that was muffled by my ski hat. I thumped it back down on the windshield a few times in hopes of being able to see clearly for the rest of the ride home. If only I could clear the view from my heart as easily. Then I could figure out what I wanted—a relationship with an intelligent, sexy, hot woman or a safe existence untroubled by the dangers of love.

I groaned out loud and threw myself over the hood of my Honda. It felt good to just lie there pressing my cheek against the frozen crust of sleet that still clung to my car. Eventually, I figured anyone looking out his or her window or driving by might worry, so I stood up and brushed off the front of my coat. Goddess help me. This love thing was making me get all dramatic. I looked back at the few feet of visible tire tracks. I could turn around and go back to Shiloh's. I could, I thought. But I didn't.

CHAPTER TWENTY-TWO

Seeing

Shiloh's voice was like a balm. On the phone she told me about her family's plans for a few upcoming get-togethers. The first of which was her youngest nephew's bar mitzvah at the end of this week. My mind spun with all of the arranging she had to do in order to be at each of the events. She had several nieces and nephews, and she laughed over how much she wished at least one of them were old enough to drive so she didn't need either of her parents, both of whom were beginning to experience EDS, or Elderly Driving Syndrome. Even though she couldn't see, she sensed that her mom's and her dad's driving skills were seriously impaired.

"How do you know then?" I asked.

"Okay, so last year, I started to pay attention to how many blaring car horns I could hear close by every time my dad drove me someplace. I tested my theory and counted fourteen honks in one trip from my parents' home to my house when my dad drove me and zero honks when my sister drove me the same route a few nights later. So I know, you know?"

I laughed in response.

"And then!" she continued. "And then when my mom drives it feels like I'm in the middle of a badly behaved ocean on a small boat. She slows down and speeds up and slows down and speeds up and slows down and speeds up constantly." I began to feel seasick myself. "I don't think it's just because I can't see that I am more aware of this—I think it's just really shoddy driving. Oh! And both of them have bad eyesight and refuse to spend any extra money on new glasses for themselves. They complain about it all the time, but aren't willing to do anything. Speaking of complaining, listen to me! I'm sorry, Allura, I think it's sort of funny—here I am complaining about all of their complaining!"

"It's okay," I assured her. And it was; I would have gladly listened to her talk about anything.

"I just miss being able to drive myself sometimes," she said.

"I bet you do," I commiserated. "But at the same time, you probably save a bundle in car insurance!" That was a stupid joke, but she laughed at it anyway.

"Thank you for pointing that out," she mused.

I spun in my desk chair and stopped when it made an almighty squeak that Dwight copied. I smiled at him and looked past his perch into the dull day beyond the window. The sleet and snow from the night before was short-lived. We were back to somber grays and browns. I spun my chair away from the window and let the colors of my books and office artwork warm me.

"Hey Shiloh?" I wanted to ask something I'd wondered a lot about ever since our first date. "What do you miss the most about being able to see?"

"Hmm, good question." She was quiet for a moment and then said, "Well, of course, I wish I could see people's faces, like yours. I wonder what you look like. But that's not what I miss the most because you can tell me and I can feel your face, if you let me, and I can still remember what my family and friends look like." She was quiet again, and I didn't say anything to fill the silence. "I think," she began, "that I miss taking really big steps the most."

"Big steps?" I echoed.

"Yes, I miss being able to really walk, or no, to run! I miss being able to take big steps without worrying about running into something." We were both quiet again, and then she asked me, "What do you think you'd miss if you couldn't see anything anymore?"

"Whoa, I don't know," I said, "let me think...wow, I just don't know! I'd miss everything, I think. But for what I'd miss the most, I can't say for sure. I think I'd miss seeing people smile—especially people I care about. I think, but I don't know for sure."

"You get used to it, eventually," she said. "You get used to listening for how people are feeling."

"Really?" I asked. I was amazed and perplexed.

"Yeah, you get to a place where you can tell what a person's face is doing just by how they sound," she explained. "I think I'm luckier than some of the kids I work with who have been blind since birth. They have to sort out other people's emotions in a totally different way, but I can still picture what people's faces do depending on how they are feeling."

"Wow," was all I could think to say. Wow.

"Like you," Shiloh said, "you are almost always smiling when we talk." She sounded shy.

"I am, it's true," I said, getting shy myself. What was this, junior high? What the hell was she doing to me?

"It's funny," she said.

"What is?"

"Well, no one has ever asked me what I miss most before. Everyone I know is either not thinking about my blindness, or in denial about it, or not caring." She said this in a matter-of-fact tone.

"Sorry," I said, "I know you are a million other things in addition to being blind, but...I do think about it." Goddess, did I offend her?

"No, I honestly like that you think about it, it makes me feel, I don't know, like you...like you are taking every aspect into consideration, like you care what I feel and...all that." She trailed off and became silent.

I had never heard her so much at a loss for words. My heart went soft.

"No one has asked?"

"Well, an occupational therapist asked me a thousand questions when I first knew that this was permanent. But none of my friends or family asked me anything at all. My family makes sure I have what I need like rides and groceries and help around the house, but my last serious ex…well, she was with me while I was losing my sight, and I think she chose to just pretend it wasn't happening, you know? She never asked me anything about what I missed or what I wanted…or anything, really. Can you imagine losing your vision and your partner pretending like it wasn't happening?"

It just about killed me to hear Shiloh ask this. "No, I can't imagine."

"Yeah, she just never brought it up. She left me to sort it out for myself. It was weird, too, because she was a good person, but only after we broke up did she start realizing, I think, that it was real. That I really would never get my sight back. She calls or comes over a few times a year, and she's more helpful now than she was when I was first fully blind and we were still together."

"I don't know what that would be like," I said, "to watch your partner lose her vision, but it must have been really hard for you to feel like she wasn't there for you one hundred percent." I hoped I didn't sound like I was taking her ex's side. That must have been really difficult for both of them, but especially for Shiloh.

"Everyone I've dated since then has tiptoed around the issue. No one has asked how to help or anything. It's like not mentioning it will make it go away. As if." Her laugh sounded genuine and warm, not derisive in that way most people sounded when they laughed after saying "as if."

"You've dated a lot since losing your sight?" I had to ask despite not wanting to hear the answer. Shiloh's romantic history had nothing to do with me, but I knew I'd be even more hesitant to fall further for her if she replied that she had dated many women.

"I guess about five or six, no...seven women. That's it. And no one asked about being blind. They couldn't joke about it, we didn't talk about it, nothing."

"Whoa," I managed to utter. Seven women. None worked out. Why did I think I might be the one? My odds were not looking good here.

"Yeah, but hey, that was then, right? And here we are now and all I know is that you are asking me, so thank you for that," she said.

CHAPTER TWENTY-THREE

Jest Between Friends

The cloak that Veronica gave me on the night of All Samhain's Silent Supper hung heavy over my naked shoulders, and I laughed at my reflection in the full-length bedroom mirror. I looked like a dominatrix ready to overtake some unsuspecting victim. I pulled the cloak closed over my nakedness and held it tightly to myself as I twirled in front of the mirror. Where had Veronica found such perfection? It was as if it were made for me. I opened it up again and searched inside for a tag in the deep green satin lining. Nothing. The outside was a paler green crushed velvet with gauzy glitter looped here and there in swirls and crescents. The cloak had no buttons or hooks. It would catch the wind, giving it even more life than it already seemed to possess.

Earlier between writing my article and answering the phone, which seemed unusually overworked today, I read *Drawing Down the Moon*, the book Veronica had given me. I had been looking for some new ideas on how and when to do a ritual of gratitude. I had several motivations behind this ritual, the two at the top of the list being Dwight and Shiloh. But the book was more about the history of Paganism. So much oppression and fear down through the ages was dismal although I still appreciated Veronica's gift. The book was fascinating, if not inspiring. But I'd look elsewhere as it needed to be much shorter than the Drawing Down the Moon ritual. Tonight, after seeing Patrick and Trisha, I'd come home, cast a circle outdoors, light a couple of candles and again give thanks for these new developments.

But at the moment, I had to get ready. I let the cloak slide down my arms, feeling the slippery lining whisk across my skin. I laid the cloak over the back of the chair and turned to look in the mirror. My body looked more angular than I had realized. I knew my clothes weren't fitting well anymore; my skirts needed belts, and the belts needed tightening. I turned my back to the mirror and twisted to look back over my shoulder. My butt looked small and insignificant. I didn't want an insignificant butt; I wanted some real significance back there.

Maybe I could lift more at the gym, or start eating more, or both. I had eaten my fill on my last date with Shiloh because, even though we laughed most of the evening away, spelling out naughty words and flirting, we sat and drank and nibbled until the pizza box and wine bottle were both empty. It had been the first time in a long, long time that I had helped anyone to empty a pizza box. But even so I was torn between fear of my being just another woman Shiloh had dated and the fear of being more than that to her. I knew how relationships went. They were satisfying at the beginning, comfortable during the middle and hellish at the end. Did I really want that again? My heart hollered yes, but my mind trembled no. Shiloh had dated seven women since her last serious relationship. That seemed like a lot. Perhaps she was a serial dater, and I'd just wind up being number eight on a long list of adoring fans. Of course, I'd dated more than seven women on my way to my big relationship with Mickey. And I wasn't a serial dater, so maybe I shouldn't be so apprehensive about Shiloh's track record.

I sighed and left the mirror to its own reflection. I consulted the witches' calendar on the wall beside the closet door and discovered that today's color was blue. Right then, blue it was. I went over to my chest of drawers and from the top one pulled out a pair of blue panties and a white bra with blue edging. I checked my reflection again. Geez, I looked even scrawnier in underwear. I would have a double helping of bread tonight, I decided. And in a couple of days, my bangs should be long enough to even them out. Or perhaps I should let a professional deal with it.

From atop my chest of drawers, I pulled a strand of lapis lazuli beads and wound them around my neck into a choker-length necklace. The dab of rosemary oil between my breasts was meant to bring me into the present moment, but instead I found myself thinking of Shiloh again. My plan was to say nothing about her tonight while I was with Trisha and Patrick, just as I hadn't mentioned her as we celebrated Solschristice. I didn't want to jinx anything by being overly excited about the whole affair. Even if I might find myself too afraid to unwrap it, she was still that unopened gift under the tree.

Three hours later Patrick was slapping the table demanding to know why I hadn't yet kissed Shiloh. My plan to savor the wrapped gift had been a good one in theory, but in reality when faced with two sets of really good ears I blew it, spilled my guts and jinxed everything. I was sure of it.

"Really Allura, how could you not end that stormy night with a kiss? It would have been the textbook date," Patrick said and sighed with mock disgust. He threw his hands up. "You may have botched it up beyond repair."

"Hmm, I don't think so, she said she'd enjoyed my company and wanted to know if we could do it again sometime," I told him, even though I was wondering the same thing. Three dates, three perfect chances and not one kiss.

"Sometime?" he repeated. "Did she really say 'sometime'?"

"I think so," I said.

"Well, that's it then! What does 'sometime' mean to *you*, Trisha?" Patrick asked.

"I know you want me to say it means 'never,'" Trisha began, "but honestly Patrick, look at Allura, what's not to want to date?"

I hadn't told them yet that Shiloh was blind because I was still reeling from my not having picked up on it in the first place. But I decided now was the time since Trisha had just alluded to my appearance and with much too much flattery, at that.

"Trisha, you are too kind—thank you for the compliment," I said, "but I don't think my looks are what will keep Shiloh coming back for more."

"Oh, reeeeeallly," said Patrick, raising his eyebrows and looking more like a leprechaun than the devil I think he was going for. "So you didn't kiss her after Scrabble, but you did manage to wow her with some other extraordinary skills? Maybe you cast a love spell on her," Patrick said, wriggling his fingertips at me as if he were bewitching me, "and made her blind to all your evil ways?"

"Uh, no Patrick, she is blind," I said. "She is blind to all my evil ways and blind to all my not-so-evil ways. She's blind. Period."

Both Patrick and Trisha looked at me with their faces wide open and surprised, like I had blindsided them. Figuratively. When I think about it now, I don't know why they should have been so surprised. There are blind people, after all, and they have to date other people. Now I was just one of those people. And I don't know why I was surprised that they were surprised, but I was. Truth be told, I was also a little offended, for some reason.

"You're kidding!" Patrick said in disbelief.

"No," I said, "I'm not kidding. She can't see."

"Wow," exhaled Trisha, her face returning to its normal glowing Scandinavian-ness.

"Wait, how'd you play Scrabble?" Patrick asked.

"Braille. I feel kind of stupid, because I had seen her or had sort of seen her, noticed her, I guess, is a better way to put it. I noticed her twice before, once at the Y during the non-laugh laugh yoga," I began explaining, but was cut short.

"Shut up! She was at that infamous yoga class?" Patrick hooted.

"Yes," I continued, trying to look indignant, "she was. Hey, speaking of the yoga class, Shiloh is the author of that article you gave me on laugh yoga. Pretty bizarre, hey?" I asked.

"Is she really? That is bizarre." He tugged at his chin.

"Yes and she was also at the pottery studio one night when I was there. So I had noticed her twice, but never did I get the impression that she couldn't see."

"Too many coincidences. Maybe she really can see, and this is one of those TV shows where they prank some poor person," Trisha offered.

"I know, I thought that too, for a few minutes," I confessed, "but I'm pretty sure she really is blind. I only figured it out when I was picking her up to go out on our first date."

"What happened? Did you try to shake her hand, and you guys missed? Or what?" Patrick asked, cracking himself up with his imagined mishap.

"Patrick." Trisha's tone held a warning. I think she thought he was going to take joking too far.

"No, nothing like that. She went into her house to get something, I followed and from the way she ran her hand along the counter to find her purse, I could tell. I felt absolutely stupid for not knowing. I think she thought I was going to call off the date."

"Did you want to, at all?" Patrick asked. The joking was set aside for the time being.

"Not once," I answered. "And it could have been a really awkward evening except she made me promise to ask whatever I needed to and to do whatever I thought would help her, you know? So it's going well and…and I really like her."

"Cool," Trisha said.

"Yeah, that is cool," Patrick said, looking really thoughtful. "You know what's even cooler?"

"What?" I asked in response.

"The fact that she couldn't see your bangs."

Book of Shadows
Offering of Gratitude

Cast the circle using Magnolia Incense.
"Blessed be Creatures of Light."
Light a wine-colored votive candle. Place it in a glass jar
at the center of the yard.
Greet and honor the four directions and the universal
elements.
Focus on the flame of the votive remembering that
"votive" means "offering."
Consider the feelings of the first person to discover fire
and the first person to use fire
as an intensifier for her desires and needs.
Recall the mysteries around fire and its light.
Pour gratitude into the flame
Thanking it for its light,
its guidance,
and its comfort.
Pour gratitude into the flame for the Goddess,
God, Mother Earth and the Universe.
Request that the flame bring the gratitude to these
profound entities.
Thank the four directions and the universal elements.
"Blessed be Creatures of Light."
Do not extinguish the candle but let it burn
until it extinguishes itself.
Open the circle.

CHAPTER TWENTY-FOUR

Big Steps

The smell of coffee woke me. As I padded down to get a cup from the coffeemaker, which was on a timer, something felt different. There was a hush around me, like someone had turned down the world's volume, but I couldn't put my finger on what was different. I pulled a handmade-by-yours-truly mug from the cupboard and admired the iridescent brown glaze job on the clunky thing. At thirty dollars a visit, I'm sure this was the priciest, ugliest coffee mug ever, but I liked it. I had built it with coils of clay and had only smoothed out the inside for easy cleaning, but the outside was left ribbed. When I ran my hand up and down its side, my knuckles clacked together in a way that sounded strange but felt good.

I poured a cup and watched the steam rise lazy as a kid with a remote control. I held the cup to my lips but didn't sip it yet. Instead I breathed in the steam and turned, with the cup still to my mouth, and looked out the kitchen window.

"Hot damn!" I hollered and put down the cup.

"Hot damn!" Dwight echoed from upstairs.

Through the windowsill herb garden I could see a brilliant white landscape in the park across the street. I was surprised that there wasn't one kid in the park, but it was pretty early and a school day. The vast expanse of unbroken snow was almost blinding. Shiloh. I was going to call Shiloh to see if she knew that it had snowed. She was an early riser. She had told me this over the Scrabble board. Any excuse to call her seemed like a good one, but the first big snowfall was an exceptionally good excuse. She picked up on the third ring.

"Hello," she said not even sounding sleepy.

"Hi Shiloh—it's Allura," I said. I didn't allow myself time to get shy with her even though I felt it coming. "It snowed last night! Did you know?" I asked right away.

"No," she laughed, "I didn't. What kind?"

"Uhm," I said bending over to peer through the window, "it's the kind that sticks to tree branches. Everything is outlined in white, you know? And it stayed on the ground. There's actually quite a lot of it out there." I leaned closer to the window. I could see my neighbor shoveling a path down the sidewalk. I gasped. It looked like it was over a foot deep. From my kitchen it seemed like the kind of snow that a person could fall down into without getting hurt. I looked harder at the burgeoning path down the sidewalk. No, a person would definitely not get hurt if she fell in this stuff.

"I knew it felt different this morning when I got up!" Shiloh said, sounding happy about the snow.

"Hey Shiloh," I asked, "do you have an hour or so free today?" If she had time, I had a plan.

"Yeah, I don't have to be at Davidoff to teach class until noon," she said.

"Do you want to come and play in the snow?" I asked.

"Oh, I'd love to!" she cried. "Come get me!"

And so I did. I picked her up at her house and then drove her back to mine. We didn't go inside, however. Instead I held her mittened hand in mine. I walked with her to the middle of the park. We were the only people there, and there was not one thing around for at least 150 feet on all sides of us. It was perfect. I described what was and what wasn't around us, so she could picture it.

"Shiloh, remember when you told me the thing you missed most was taking really big steps?" I asked her, still holding her hand, but not walking any longer.

"Yes?" she answered.

"I think this is your chance," I said. "There's nothing around, and if you do fall, you won't get hurt. The snow will protect you."

"No way!" she laughed, clasping my hand more tightly in hers.

"Yes, come on, we'll take really big steps together to start out. Then you can do it on your own," I said. "I'll watch to make sure you don't get in trouble, and I'll holler if you need to stop."

I looked at her face. I could see she was trying to decide. She was breathtaking. She had an enormous blue knit hat pulled down over her head. It pushed the wisps of her black bangs toward her light blue eyes. Her cheeks were red. I didn't know if it was the cold or the idea of big steps that reddened them. Either way, she was the prettiest person I'd ever seen. I hoped this was a good idea. I hoped she would enjoy it.

"Wait," I said, "let me see something." I let go of her hand and fell backward into the snow before I could think about it and chicken out. It was perfect. It didn't hurt a bit. "You'll be safe and pretty comfortable if you fall. I just tested it," I said, standing up and brushing snow off my butt. I took her hand in mine again.

"Okay," she said and bit at her bottom lip, "but I'll tell you when to let go of my hand."

"All right," I said. "Let's take big steps in this direction first," I said as I guided her forward. She took big steps, and I trotted alongside her. It was hard at first to stride out because the snow was on the heavy side, but once we got going we could almost run. Shiloh started laughing, her breath coming out in a wonderful puff of fog that we both blasted right through with more big steps.

"I love it!" she yelled. "Let's turn around. You can let go of my hand, but stay next to me!" She sounded exhilarated but a bit scared.

"I'll stay right by you." I turned her around while still holding her hand. We started taking really big steps back. Then we got our speed up. "Okay?" I hollered.

"Okay," she hollered back and let go of my hand. She didn't slow down at all but kept running. She was taking huge steps and shrieking the entire time. I had to race hard to keep up with her, she was going so fast. We ran all the way across the park, leaving a path of churned up snow behind us. Shiloh started to slow down right when I started thinking about warning her to do so. She was still laughing as she held out her hand in my direction, but she didn't stop altogether.

I grabbed her hand and swung her into my arms, and before I knew it, she brought her face close to mine, close enough for me to see that there were tears on her lashes and cheeks. Then she was kissing me. Our mouths were warm even though our noses and chins were cold. We were both out of breath, so it was a gaspy kiss, but it lasted and lasted until Shiloh pulled me down on top of her in the snow. I tried not to squish her as I landed. I rolled to my side while keeping my arms around her. She was laughing and I think crying. She pushed her face near mine again and murmured, "Thank you, Allura." So I kissed her again.

CHAPTER TWENTY-FIVE

Soundtracks

I stretched my legs up the wall and blushed even though no one could see my bare thighs when my bathrobe fell back and pooled around my waist on the bed.

"So, then I decided that we needed to have a soundtrack for the wedding," Shiloh was explaining why she spent her thirteenth summer grounded to the house, "because everyone had the traditional songs, and my brother and I thought my sister deserved something extra special since she and her soon-to-be husband could only afford a backyard wedding at my parents' house."

"This isn't going to end well, is it?" I asked.

"Not as bad as you might think, but if I had to do the whole thing over, I think we could have chosen less provocative songs," Shiloh continued.

"'Walk Like an Egyptian?'" I tried to think of the worst 80's songs possible.

Shiloh laughed. "No, that would have been benign compared to what we chose. The worst part about it was that we thought it would be especially magical if it were a total surprise. If suddenly the music were to emanate from hidden speakers. We waited for days, listening to the radio, for the disc jockey to play the songs we wanted. When the songs came on, we hit record on our boom box, and we felt like we won the lottery or something. Lucas and I spent all night prior to the wedding rigging up the wires and the speakers to blast out over the backyard from his bedroom windows."

"'Hungry Like the Wolf'?" I tried again.

"No," Shiloh laughed. "We got all the way through 'I Might Like You Better If We Slept Together' by Romeo Void and half way through Madonna's 'Like a Virgin' before my dad found where the music was coming from and ripped the wires from the speakers." I was laughing too hard to comment, so Shiloh went on, "These were the most romantic, wedding-appropriate songs two thirteen-year-olds could come up with. We did it with respect and love in mind, truly, but my parents saw it differently. We got grounded. My sister has since told me that her friends still talk about it now and then, so she at least saw the humor in it."

"I love it," I said. I did love it. I loved having my ear pressed to my cell phone listening to Shiloh's laugh. I loved that she had called me once a day since our snow date, just to chat as she put it. With my free hand, I bunched up a pillow under my head and then switched hands on my phone because my right elbow was starting to ache from being bent for so long. I should have found my Bluetooth earpiece. Tomorrow, I'd have it ready for Shiloh's call. Or maybe I'd actually call her first.

"Okay," she continued, "so you asked me about my first love, and I got sidetracked."

"I don't mind at all," I reassured her.

"Well, the whole grounding thing was partly responsible. My cousin Althea's parents, my mom's sister and my uncle, were having some trouble with their relationship. Apparently they needed some space and time to discover whether or not they should stay together or if they should split up, so Althea came to live with us for the summer. And Althea's best friend, Mary

Claire, visited a few times in late May, when Althea first came. I'm going to tell you it was love at first sight, but Mary Claire would tell you otherwise because I was sort of horrible to her at first."

"Why?" I asked.

"I think it was because I liked her, *like that*, and I didn't know what to do with that, you know?" Shiloh almost sounded thirteen again as she told me this. "So I had this crush thing happening. It caught me off guard because I had expected it to happen, of course, but not, definitely not, with a girl. So I picked on her, called her names, ruined her time with Althea. I still can't figure out why they spent so much time around the house when they knew I'd be there because I was grounded. Althea and Mary Claire were lucky enough have a break from me in June when they went to summer camp together. When they came back in July, I had sort of come to terms with what I was feeling, so I was a lot nicer to her."

"And were your feelings reciprocated?" I asked, hoping for Shiloh that they were.

"Yes, but not acted on, you know?" she said. "It was fabulous and terrible all at once. I knew she knew I liked her, I knew she liked me back, but we were never alone. Althea was always around and…well, I'm glad today that the tension didn't kill us both. July was a long, hot month that year. And I never got grounded again."

"Ughhh! I feel for you!" I sighed. "Do you still see her?" Dumb word choice, I realized half a second later.

"Not really, not on purpose anyway." Shiloh didn't seem to notice or care about my faux pas. "We were both at Pride a few years ago though, and she recognized me. She came and said hi. Funny, hey? How we know before we even really know?" she asked.

"Yeah, it is funny," I agreed, thinking about the first girl I fell in love with. She had been gay, and the thought had never crossed my mind that she might not be, or that I might not be. We never even checked with each other, we just knew or assumed. In my experience now, we always check with people before we let ourselves assume anything. Hadn't Shiloh checked with me first? Well, hadn't she had Collette check for her? Why was that? Why couldn't we just trust ourselves to be good judges of who might be right for us?

"Hey, did you say 'two thirteen-year-olds' when you were talking about your brother?" I asked, my mind wandering back to her soundtrack story. "Are you twins?"

"Yeah, we are. Don't look a thing like each other—he's blond with brown eyes—but we're twins," Shiloh said.

"Does he live here in Minneapolis?"

"Yeah, he's married to a woman, and they have three adorable kids. He's a good guy."

"Is he...can he still see?" I hoped that question wasn't callous or hurtful, but how strange would it be if he also lost his vision—then again, how strange if he hadn't lost his vision.

"Yes, he can see." The tone of Shiloh's voice let me know that my question was not hurtful. "As far as we know, he doesn't have any sign of retinitis-pigmentosa. Thank goodness."

"That's good," I said, without thinking. Then I thought, oops. "I mean..." I didn't know what I meant except that I had just implied that being blind was bad. Well, it was, wasn't it? Or it was at least harder than having sight.

"It's all right, I know what you mean. It is good that he can see," Shiloh responded.

"Shiloh, if someone created a soundtrack for your life," I started to ask, needing to change the subject so I could not worry about stepping on my tongue as I spoke, "what songs would you want on it?"

"Hmm, good question...I'm hoping this is not going to be played at my wedding," we both laughed at her comment, "but is it a funeral-type soundtrack? Do you mean when all is said and done, what do I want played, or do you want to know what songs would sum it up today?"

"Uhm..." I didn't really know, so I went with the present. "How about if we went up to today?" I said but wondered why she wouldn't want it played at her wedding. Were the songs that embarrassing? Was she referring to the surprise soundtrack at her sister's ceremony? Or was she so anti-commitment that she knew she'd never want a wedding of her own?

"Okay," she said and then was quiet for a moment. When she spoke again, she sounded absolutely certain that she had her answers right. "I'd want 'Shiloh' by Neil Diamond, for obvious reasons, even though it's sort of a sad, ironic song. And I'd want the good old 'Barracuda' by Heart for its hard-driving beat and danger." She laughed at herself. I didn't join in this time because I was too enthralled with her. "How many do I get?" she asked.

"Oh, I don't know," I said, "I think you can have as many as you want." My gracious answer probably gave away the fact that I'd give her anything she wanted at this point, and that made me feel uncomfortable and vulnerable. What the heck was happening here?

"Sweet, so I'll choose one more, a really big headliner for my soundtrack, okay? And then I want to hear yours," she said, her voice gentle.

"Okay," I said.

"So for my one really important one, the one that would sit on top of the heap today, I'd want 'Home' even though it's kind of folksy and down-homeish," Shiloh said.

Her statement sounded more like a question with the way she expectantly raised the tone of her voice on the last words. It was as if she were looking for a reaction from me. I couldn't place the song right away, so I wracked my brains for lyrics with the phrase "home" in them. There were so many songs with that word, but the one I knew the lyrics to was by Edward Sharpe and the Magnetic Zeros with the lyrics that went something like, "…Home, yes I am home, home is wherever I'm with you." My heart gave an almighty lurch in my chest. It was a love song. I half hoped she meant a different song because this one made me think of how very entangled and dependent two people can become. And how very broken a home can feel when the relationship finally collapses. Maybe her song was a different "home." Maybe it wasn't dedicated to me, but I wasn't sure what to do with the simultaneous dread and hope that I experienced when I thought it might be for me.

"By Edward Sharpe and the Magnetic Zeros?" I asked.

"Yep, do you know it?" Shiloh asked back. She sounded cautious but like she was smiling.

"I do." Ugh! Did I really just say I do?

"Good, now let's hear your soundtrack!" Shiloh was impatient to move from her soundtrack to mine, I think, but I couldn't do it. My mind was throwing an unholy fit, and I suddenly needed to get off the phone before my head exploded into bits and pieces all over the place. I couldn't let this be a repeat of me and Mickey where I get attached to Shiloh, Shiloh changes for the worse and gets pissed at me when I want things the way they used to be when we first met, and eventually Shiloh dumps me. Then I'm left alone, with no edges to snag on to anything worthwhile in life.

"Uhm, Shiloh, I have to go." I knew I sounded somewhat desperate to hang up. For a second I worried that she might feel like she'd scared me away, but truth be told, she had. For now, just for right now, I was scared. Terrified. I panicked. Without waiting for her response, I hung up.

CHAPTER TWENTY-SIX

Learning

I pulled the now flannel-like sheet of paper from my coat pocket for the third time. I unfolded it and looked over the notes on writing I had made for Cami's English Eleven class. Whose idea was this anyway? The topics that might amuse the high school students now seemed overly idealistic. Why wasn't I going to really tell them how it was? Nowhere on the paper did I mention how nerve-wracking it was to wait for rejection notices, or how rattling it was to have a piece accepted only to have it be rendered pretty much unrecognizable by an editor. Maybe I should start with these humdrum details and save the good stuff for last. I could end with how it feels to have someone you run into comment on your article and tell you how it helped them figure out a bit of their life. Or how exquisite it is to play with words, arranging them into patterns like boxcars that no other train conductor has ever connected before. On second thought, that might be a good place to start, seeing as how this was an English class after all.

You know who would amaze the kids? Shiloh. Wouldn't it blow their minds to know that you don't even have to be able to *see* to write a publishable article or novel? Maybe it wouldn't, seeing as how this generation had grown up with technology that swiftly adapted itself to each individual's needs. The students might not be overly impressed that one could tell the computer what to write, or type it in if the person knew the keyboard already, have the words read back with punctuation read aloud and then tell the computer how to revise and edit, all without ever seeing the keyboard or the finished product.

I jumped as the bell sounded in the office where I was waiting for Cami to come pick me up and walk me to her classroom.

"Horrible sounding things, aren't they?" asked an auburn-haired woman typing away at a computer behind the front counter. She looked at me through big glasses, which she shoved back up the bridge of her nose with the back of one hand.

"Yeah," I agreed. "It must take a while to get used to them."

"I can't really remember getting used to them, that was a few years ago, but I'll tell you, sometimes I wish I had them at home," she said, shaking her head. "If I had them at home, I think I'd get more done. And I'd get more out of my kids, I bet."

"Really? Like how?" I asked.

"Well, here I work on attendance until the fourth bell, then I work on lunch accounts until one more bell rings, and then it's a hodgepodge of random computer things, you know, entering field trips, scheduling substitute teachers, stuff like that. So if I could do the same at home, I'd watch TV until the second bell, make dinner until the third bell, eat at the fourth, and the kids could do dishes at the fifth…see what I mean?" she asked.

I liked her idea. I was a writer who didn't have to follow an hour-by-hour schedule, so a bell system could probably help me out with time management. I was going to tell her so, but just then I saw Cami through the office's glass door. For school she'd done away with the clingy sweater and yoga pants. Today she was wrapped in an artsy beige velvet jacket with raglan sleeves and rose-colored jeans. Less revealing of her athletic form, but still flattering. She came in, hugged me, said hello, grabbed me by my elbow and whisked me away. All I had time for was to say thank you with a wave goodbye to the woman behind the desk.

Cami's classroom was bright with fluorescent lights blasting down from the ceiling and daylight streaming in through the windows. Student work covered the walls. A buzzing swarm of teenagers entered the room behind us. A few of them looked me up and down, probably assessing whether or not I had anything good to offer them. I hoped I did, as I hopped up on the stool in front of the room where Cami told me to make myself comfortable as she introduced me.

I shared my story of how I got into writing—I had a crush on my English 101 instructor and the only other courses offered by that instructor were a journalism course and a creative writing course, so before you could say "fraternization" I had signed up for both. At first the students weren't sure whether or not they should laugh at my story until Cami burst out in a guffaw. Then the students felt comfortable following suit. Once they laughed the first time, I felt encouraged, so I went on, keeping them laughing almost the entire hour.

Near the end of the class, I asked them if they had any questions and pretty girl with braids and an angular face raised her hand. She wanted to know if I had ever had any embarrassing typos make it into my published articles or column and who got in trouble for a mistake like that—me or my editor. I told her about the time my article's title ran as "Breast Features of The New Year's Technology" and the time when "Deathalyzers: Saving Lives" showed up in the magazine. The students laughed, and I felt like a rock star. Their energy was so clear and vital that it made me happy to be there with them. Another student raised his hand and asked who got in trouble for those typos. I had forgotten to answer the second half of the girl's question. This guy was gently reminding me so that the girl's inquiry didn't go unanswered. How nice was that? I told him that we both took the heat, to some degree, but that it was *my* name printed under the title, so I was the one who had the most to lose. The students nodded soberly, considering what I had told them. I felt I should drive home the point of doing your best work always, despite having an editor on most articles.

"You know," I began, "having an editor is like having a net under you as you perform on a tightrope. You know he or she is there, but you hope that you never have to rely on her to save you, you know?" They nodded. "Most editors are happy to help catch grammatical errors, and nobody dies if you misspell a word or if you miss a period, but—"

"Ha," I was interrupted by a student voice, "at my house somebody dies if I miss a period!" There was absolute silence in the room until I burst out laughing. That was really clever! I said so, and the rest of the class started laughing, too. Cami told the student that shouting out was rather disrespectful, but that she recognized it was almost too funny to not point out. Then the bell rang. The students applauded and thanked me, gathered up their backpacks and notebooks and poured out into the hallway.

I listened to my voice mails as I walked through the parking lot to my car.

"Hi Allura, it's Shiloh." When I heard Shiloh's voice I stopped walking. Passion and affection cemented me in place. How could I let myself get this emotionally connected to a woman I barely knew? And why did I find myself wanting to get even more emotionally, not to mention physically, connected to her despite knowing how badly it hurt to be dumped by a person you trusted and loved? This was crazy.

"Sorry if I scared you with that soundtrack thing." Shiloh's voice sounded canned as it emanated from the tiny speaker in my cell phone. She continued, "I didn't mean to put any pressure on you—I just like that song...anyway, give me a call when you have a minute. Bye!"

The song thing did have me questioning where I wanted this to go. I'd call her back later, after my heart had a day or two to rest.

Once at home, I busied myself with tidying up and going through the mail. I saved my mom's postcard for last—something to look forward to. This one had a huge orange sun sinking into the desert.

Dear Allura Tuki Satou,

My Dear—what the hell is this dried-up root thing in Gladys' wheel-well storage? It looks like one of your witchy doohickeys. Can I cook with it? Tired of takeout.

Love, Mom

She had found the comfrey from the Home Goodbye and Relocation Protection spells. I smiled and hoped she put it back into its place in their RV.

CHAPTER TWENTY-SEVEN

Resolutions

Mickey tapped her fingertips on the tabletop but I didn't recognize the beat. She arranged and then rearranged the salt and pepper shakers and the drink menu. Her small hands unfolded and then refolded her linen napkin. Her nerves must have been absolutely jangled because I had very rarely seen her fidget. That was usually my hobby, not hers. But today for some reason, my nerves were rock solid. I was not nervous about seeing Mickey.

Her short silver and black hair still had its tiny spiky bangs, she still dressed in tailored clothing that was more masculine than feminine and she still balanced the mannish style with her favorite pale pink shirt beneath her black sports coat. Her nose was pert as ever and her rosy apple cheeks buoyed her serious dark brown eyes. In fact, sitting across the table from Mickey was akin to putting on my favorite old sweatshirt. Recognized, comfortable. This surprised me because before seeing her I had felt so reluctant.

We met at the Loring Pasta Bar because it was midway between my house and her new apartment. But the real reason

I had agreed to the venue was because we had never been there together. Mickey had suggested several places where we had gone in the past, but I was not interested in revisiting history. Veronica had advised me to perform a protection ritual to ward off any negative energy I might be subjected to. I hadn't felt as if I'd need it, so I didn't. In hindsight, it may have been a good idea to do one.

"So," Mickey began, "how are you?"

"Fine," I answered. I was okay, so I wasn't technically lying. The holidays had been decent enough; I'd spent them with Alaina and Falina, and then Patrick, Trisha and Veronica. I was feeling subdued because of the way things had gone with Shiloh—we had spoken briefly on the phone a few times after the soundtrack conversation, but we never really picked up our original energy. I was sad about this when I let myself dwell on it, so I didn't let myself do that, or at least not often. Not more than once a day, anyway. But on a positive note, my writing assignments were more enjoyable, mostly because I just whipped through them. And Dwight Night, Jr....well, Dwight was dewightful. Yes, I was in love with that bird and not ashamed to admit it. He was the best addition to my life all year, which made me happy and sad all at once because I had honestly thought he'd be one of two wonderful additions, not the only one. But there it was.

"Fine," I repeated.

"That's good," Mickey said, tugging at the collar of her pink shirt.

And suddenly I was tired, like this was going to be more work than I could muster. Mickey must have picked up on that because she decided to turn on the charm.

"Did you make any New Year's resolutions?" she asked, smiling broadly with both her mouth and her dark eyes. The apples of her cheeks bobbed. It was good to see. There hadn't been much smiling from either of us in our last months together.

"No, not yet," I said, "did you?"

"Yes." Her eyes glinted in the warm, dim interior of the restaurant. "I did."

"Hmm," I said. I wasn't sure if I should ask what her resolutions were. I wasn't sure I wanted to know.

"Guess what they are," Mickey said, leaning forward so that her full chest was pressed tightly to the table's edge.

An attractive woman with jet-black hair, which of course made me think of Shiloh, delivered Mickey's Diet Coke and my wine to the table. "Thanks," we both said, looking up at the waitress who dashed off because the restaurant was getting crowded. She was going to have a busy night. I wanted to ask Mickey if she had resolved to stop drinking because I was thrown by her choice of beverage. I had never witnessed her passing up a chance to order a drink. This was something, and I wanted to mention it, but at the same time, I didn't think I should.

"Okay, so guess," she prompted.

"Well." I squinched my eyes at her, pretending to size her up, "Well, I think you resolved to stop sending hate mail to the Pentagon, to buy foreign and to…uhm…to shave your head." At this, Mickey ran her hand through her short salt-and-pepper hair, the salt strands becoming gossamer under the low lighting above us.

"Oh my God," she said with mock awe in her voice, "you are so good." This last part came out seductively. Parts of me that shouldn't have responded did. I tasted my wine, not making eye contact with Mickey.

I glanced around the dining area and my eyes rested on the back of a head that made me almost choke on the tart wine. The black bobbed hair swung, its owner laughing. The laughter, with its sound of little tinkling bells, reached my ears and hit me with the same force as a physical blow. I held my breath to encourage the wine to go down the right pipe. Shiloh was sitting with her back to me, and judging by her animation, she was facing a wonderfully engaging woman. The woman was pretty with eyes like Shiloh's and a bright, easy smile. As I watched, the woman talked, holding Shiloh rapt with her story. Then they were both laughing again. I realized as I sat there, that this was exactly what I had feared in the first place with Shiloh—that I would get attached and she'd move on. I took a deep controlled breath.

"Okay Al, so my first resolution," Mickey was saying. I brought my reluctant gaze to Mickey's smile. She started over now that I was looking at her. "My first resolution is to fix several things that I broke this past year."

She was looking hard at me, but I couldn't get on the same wavelength. "What did you break?" I asked.

She looked surprised that I had to ask.

"Well, our relationship, for starters," she said, watching for my reaction. I tried not to let my face betray my dismay at her having brought up something I wasn't sure I wanted to discuss. In fact, I was certain I did not want to discuss it, not now with Shiloh sitting a mere twenty or so feet away. Mickey was waiting for some sort of response, but I couldn't give her one.

"I know I was wrong to say that we had nothing in common anymore, Al." Mickey started toying with the saltshaker again. "And I was stupid to leave you," she said and looked up at me. "I'd like to start over with you," she said.

She was telling her truth. I could see it in her eyes. How easy it would be to pretend that nothing had ever gone wrong between us. We could go back to being Mickey and Al. She could stop renting her apartment, and we would just go back to the way we used to be with her living in my house, her cleaning fanatically, me trying to set boundaries within which I could have messes that would remain mine alone. We could watch TV and take turns making dinner. I heard Shiloh laughing again, and I had to look. The woman across from her touched Shiloh's mouth with the corner of her own linen napkin. My mood plummeted. I dragged my eyes back to Mickey's familiar face. I still didn't have anything to say.

"So, that's one resolution," she said. "My other one is to live greener."

That was it? To start over with me and to live greener? Not to give up drinking? Well, maybe that was one she was leaving unsaid, I thought as I looked at her Diet Coke. It felt odd to have my future lined up next to living greener in her short list of resolutions. I didn't like it.

"I guess those are decent resolutions, Mickey. And it's good that you can actually control one of them," I said, not caring if my words bit her. What the hell? Did she think she was the only one to have a decision in the restarting of our relationship? I was shocked, but not so shocked that half my brain wasn't trying to decide whether or not I should go say hi to Shiloh. I would be interrupting. But wouldn't it be wrong not to let her know I was there? It seemed unfair of me to not go announce myself or something.

But when I put it that way, announcing myself was the last thing I wanted to do with her over there yukking it up with that woman who was touching her mouth. Even if I had the upper hand that twenty-twenty vision gave me, I didn't feel like intruding. How could I possibly do it anyway? Stand there at the side of the table until the other woman ripped her eyes from Shiloh's beautiful face long enough to notice me? And then what? And then say, "Hi, I wish I were sitting where you are." Yeah, no, I didn't think so.

I had to offer Mickey my strictest attention so as to not burst into tears. I had huge emotional distress potential at that moment, and I wasn't even PMSing. So, I told myself that here—across from Mickey—was where I was, so I'd better make the most of it.

Mickey was sitting there in silence, watching me. "I'm sorry, Mickey, for saying that," I began, "but I don't think you can make a resolution when you are only one half of the deciding force behind following through on it." I said it kindly and was surprised to find that I was a little bit sad to be saying it. Again I thought of how nice it would be to be with a known entity and have all the uncertainty of just getting to know somebody obliterated from your life, just like that.

"I know," Mickey said. "I know that I'm not the only one deciding, that's why I wanted to see you, to tell you." She looked at me when she said this. "Or to ask you, I mean, what you think."

"I don't know what to think, Mick. This is pretty out of the blue, wouldn't you say?"

"Maybe for you," she said, "but I haven't stopped thinking about you since, well, since I moved out."

"What do you miss most?" I asked, feeling mean and not totally because of Mickey but also because of where I'd rather be sitting and the fact that someone else was there right now.

"The bickering about your drinking? The messes I leave behind me everywhere I go? Never being able to be home on your own because I am always there?" The last one had been a more recent complaint. It was a complaint that had sprung up only after we had decided not to pursue our relationship, but before she had moved out on her own—and it was a complaint, I was fairly certain, that had come about because she was ready to start a relationship with some new drinking buddy-slash-girlfriend. I reminded myself then that this bitterness would probably return to me threefold, if not more, so I stopped. But I was really rattled. She made me think about going down that road with her again, and I didn't want to consider it. Not really. Damn.

"Allura," she said, using my entire first name, which I can only remember her doing once or twice before. "Allura," she repeated, "I am sorry."

I looked at her. Her eyes were watering, her eyebrows were knit together and her lips were beginning to quiver in earnest. I didn't want her to cry. That would have killed me. Mickey was not a crier. If she started now because of what I had just said to her, well, that would have been terrible.

"Okay, okay," I crooned quietly to Mickey. I held out my open hand across the table and let her take it in her own. Her bottom lip stopped quivering. I breathed a sigh of relief. She squeezed my hand, and I let her hold it there on the table. I thought of the last time I had my hand held on top of a table. I looked over at Shiloh. I certainly wouldn't be going over there tonight. Not now.

The woman across from Shiloh caught me off guard. She was still talking to Shiloh with her voice low, yet she was staring straight at me.

I followed her gaze down to my hand in Mickey's, and then I looked back at the woman. She was glaring at me, I was sure of it. What the hell? Now she looked back at Shiloh, who was standing up, feeling for her coat on the back of her chair. She found it and put it on while the other woman took a few bills from her wallet, placed them on the table, put on her own coat and escorted Shiloh out of the restaurant. The other woman didn't look back at me and obviously neither did Shiloh.

The rest of the evening passed by me in a blur. I was left feeling sick in the pit of my stomach, like I'd ridden one too many rides at the amusement park. Even my head reeled as I explained to Mickey that now was not a good time to rekindle anything and that there might never be a good time to rekindle. I told her we couldn't go backward. She told me that deciding to move forward was not going backward, especially if we changed how we did things. I considered her words. Maybe she was right. After what I'd just felt as I watched Shiloh with another woman, part of me thought that life with Mickey looked awfully safe. Comfortable. We'd already been through what I considered the worst with each other, so how could there be any future hurt or letdown? I'd be going in with my eyes wide open. I'd know what to expect.

I felt The Funk wrap its arms around my shoulders. I felt it nuzzle my ear. I closed my eyes for a second.

"Al, are you okay?" Mickey asked.

"Yeah," I answered. I opened my eyes. "I just need to go home, I think." Home. That made me think of Shiloh's soundtrack. Was she that much of a player that she'd let me believe that song was for me and then show up with another woman so soon?

"You've barely touched your—"

"I know," I interrupted her. "I'm sorry, Mickey. I've got to go."

Mickey's heart was practically laying on the table between us. I felt like we'd attempted surgery and had just given up. And that's not the way I wanted to leave things.

"Mickey," I said. "We can't start over. I can't start over with you. No matter how right you suppose things could be for us, I'm not right for you anymore. It wouldn't be good for us, either one of us."

"You say that now, you think that now, but what if we checked in with each other? Say, in a month? Maybe you'll feel differently then."

I was desperate to go home and be miserable alone. Or with Dwight. So I took the chicken's way out and said, "Maybe. I don't know. Maybe."

As I drove home, I reminded myself of all the reasons a person should refrain from falling in love. Near the end of the list was that you never really stopped loving anyone. Not really.

CHAPTER TWENTY-EIGHT

Ab-BRA-cadabra

"Shiloh, Shiloh," Dwight called out for what must have been the thirtieth time in the past hour.

"Dwight, really," I said back to him, "can you say something else? How about lilfella? Huh? Lilfella, lilfella, lilfella." I tried to get him going on one of his other favorite phrases. I was in the middle of an intense solitaire game on my computer, the window with my half-written article for *The Indelible* minimized. Today it was an article on a bra available from China. It was ridiculous. What made it appropriate for my column, but just barely, was that the bra contained technology, if one could call it that, which allowed the wearer to increase or decrease the amount of breast that was pushed up and squeezed over the bra's edges. The cup size was controlled via a remote control. Part of my assignment was to address the impact of the text in the highly effective advertisements.

Wondering how I was to approach this article, I ate a slippery hunk of overripe avocado from the plate on my desk. It was a food that Patrick told me would help me put on healthy weight.

I was tired of my clothes hanging off my bones, looking like they felt sorry for themselves for not belonging to a curvaceous owner. I wanted to get a good start on the article because Veronica was due to come over in an hour.

"Shiloh!" Dwight called.

I sighed.

Usually, Dwight was happy to try new foods, and it was gratifying to watch his reactions as he rolled novel bits around on his tongue. So to replace Shiloh's name in his mouth, I held out some avocado to him as he leaned over to meet me.

"Here you go, Dwighty, my boy," I said as he inspected the green goo on my fingers. He leaned back without sampling the avocado.

"No, really, taste," I encouraged. He leaned forward and then changed his mind again.

"C'mon, Dwight, don't play hard to get; it's for you." I waved my fingers under his beak. He gingerly tasted the avocado. I took the opportunity to smear a bit more under his top beak. He played with it in his mouth and bobbed his head.

"Good, hey?" I asked. He didn't answer. Maybe he was trying to decide whether or not he liked it. I grabbed a tissue, wiped my fingers and started writing.

At first I fumed that I was writing over such a banal, mundane, frivolous piece of lingerie, but then as I wrote more I began to see the humor. This was one article where I might actually be able to get away with writing tongue-in-cheek. The heart of the article was meant to question whether such a piece of lingerie and its resulting bodily enhancements would be popular here in the United States and if the quality of the writing in the ads would promote its popularity. I was toying with writing from the angle of the correlation between the depth of our cleavage and the depth of our vanity. And I was sincerely impressed with the ads.

Since that angle wasn't working as well as I had hoped and Dwight was still practicing saying Shiloh's name, I considered calling her to share a laugh over the bra and maybe get her perspective on how I might write the article. I hesitated after what I had seen at the Loring the night before, but I figured that if there was another woman I should at least try to keep myself in the running. Then again, maybe I should call her and say goodbye once and for all—remove the temptation she presented and save myself from the impending heartache while forcing the inevitable parting of ways.

Would I be able to give her up, just like that? No, I was going to call and see what unfolded. Why couldn't I open myself to the possibility that things would go well? My hands were already sweating as I picked up the phone to call before I could change my mind.

Shiloh's phone rang seven times before I heard her voice on the other end. "Hi there, you've reached Shiloh. I can't answer or find my phone right now, so please leave a message. Thanks!" It was her outgoing voice message, which I had never heard before. I wondered for a split second until the tone went off for me to leave my message whether or not she was being funny about not being able to find her phone. I believed she was being funny on purpose and of course, that lodged her even further into my heart.

"Hi Shiloh," I said, "it's Allura. I was calling to tell you about this bra that I'm writing about—it's hysterical. And I'm struggling with the article, but I thought you'd appreciate the bra and…" Should I mention I saw her last night at the Loring? How would I explain not coming over to say hi? No, I decided not to say anything for now. "So anyway, just call me when you can, if you want. Okay. Talk to you soon, I hope. Bye!"

Oh Goddess, did I sound desperate? I hoped not. I didn't think I did, but you never knew how you sounded to the person on the other side of the message, did you? Oh well. I clutched the phone to my chest. If I was wearing the Chinese remote inflating bra, I'd be able to tuck my phone into my technologically enhanced cleavage and wait for Shiloh's call, but as it was my B-cup-wannabe's weren't going to hold up much. I set the phone on my desk beside my computer and empty plate.

"Shiloh, Shiloh," Dwight chanted, "Shiloh!"

"I know buddy, I'm right there with you," I commiserated. "Shiloh."

CHAPTER TWENTY-NINE

In the Cards

Dear Allura, Mom's postcard began.

We are up to our armpits in sand. Has it snowed there yet? I can't say I miss it right now. Your dad is asleep with his big sunglasses on his face—shall I wake him or enjoy the reverse raccoon mask that is, as I write, certainly being created by this wonderful Arizona sunshine? I'll let you know my decision in my next postcard, love Mom.

I looked again at the front of the postcard. They were in Scottsdale, Arizona. My guess was that she woke him, but I'd have to wait for the next installment to know for certain. There was a knock at my front door, and then a bolt of sunlight splashed the foyer as Veronica bustled through the door she opened for herself. Her swing coat was closed up to her neck. Must be cold out today despite the sunshine.

"Hi!" she beamed. "Are you ready to roll?" She thrust an upside-down bouquet of dried herbs at me, narrowed her eyes, and then turned and walked across the room to hang the bouquet from the back of a dining room chair. "Leave those there, in the middle of your house. They'll be helpful there," she explained.

"Will do. Thank you," I said. I set the postcard beside the others on the plate rail that circled the four walls of my old-fashioned dining room.

"Goodbye, Dwight!" I hollered up the stairs. He didn't answer. I figured he was eating or rough-mouthing his rope toy or rawhide.

Veronica and I were heading to a psychic Tarot card reading. We'd decided to take the light rail, so we walked to the station closest to my house. Veronica had heard psychic Madame DuVaulle speaking on Minnesota Public Radio and had been impressed. I happened to trust MPR to not give airtime to a fraud, so even though her name had me a little suspicious, we were on our way to see what each of our futures held in store.

Veronica had prepped me and told me I would need to have a question ready and that I would probably need to divulge it to Madame DuVaulle. Veronica had shared with me that her question was going to revolve around three aspects of her future: her career, her parents and her love life.

Veronica was a floor manager at a dialysis clinic, but what she had been talking about doing for years was opening a small Pagan garden shop in the Lyn-Lake area of Minneapolis. She knew just about all there was to know about gardening. She loved socializing while helping people develop their gardening passions. I witnessed it all summer long in her garden as people from her neighborhood would stop by to chat, learn and get herbs or veggies. And she had a great mind for business. So every time she spoke of the possibility of opening her own shop, I encouraged her because it would be the perfect fit. Her parents were aging, and not extremely gracefully, so I wasn't surprised to hear she wanted to know their future as well. And her love life had been set on the back burner for as long as I had known her. She had had many admirers who were attracted to her competent, independent demeanor, but she had let none of them in, save for a few lucky men and women with whom she spent no more than a few weeks of casual dating. So Veronica's plan for the psychic made sense.

But what the heck would I ask about? My thoughts over the past few days had been bouncing between my own career and whether or not it was still fulfilling, and new love versus old love. Those were not necessarily in order of importance. I didn't want to build a question around either of those. Wait. That wasn't the truth. It was just that I was woefully under-prepared to hear what the psychic might have to say on these matters. That was the truth. The way I looked at it, if I received a reading that hinted at a new career or a new love, I'd freak out about all the changes I'd have to go through. However if I heard I was going to have to stay with my old career or go back to my old relationship, I'd go mad with the stagnation.

Veronica said, "So, what's your question for the psychic?"

"Ah...I don't know for sure," I said.

"You must know." Her little boots made sharp taps on the cold pavement as we walked. "What are you going to ask? It's not like you've got nothing going on to ask about right now," she reminded me.

"Come on!" I pleaded, knowing she wouldn't let me off the hook.

She shook her head and said, "Okay, why don't you ask Madame DuVaulle what the outcome of your parents' travels will be? Oooh, or you could find out what will happen with Brian and Falina! Or perhaps you could ask when Trisha and Patrick will need a new roof." She looked at me with over-expressed mock enthusiasm in her face before she climbed onto the light rail that arrived at the station as we did. We found seats together at the front of the car. Veronica undid the neck of her swing coat as she sat down.

"I know what you are doing," I said. "And I don't approve."

She was cornering me into admitting that I actually had a question that mattered to me. How did she know me so well? And why hadn't I taken acting classes rather than pottery classes? That way I could have kept my business to myself and not be drinking out of handmade coffee cups. Had I taken both pottery and acting classes, I could have maybe fooled myself into believing that I wasn't torn up about Mickey's emotional plea to resurrect our still-dying relationship, that I wasn't sorely missing what Shiloh and I might have been able to have together and maybe even that I enjoyed having ugly, thick pieces of pottery littering my home.

I did make Dwight a bowl that he seemed to prefer over his smooth white perfect bowl and his gleaming stainless steel bowls. That was definitely not acting on his part; he was always the real deal. Dwight Night, Jr. coming at you live every day. What you saw with that bird was what you got. I was feeling like I was too much the same lately. For the past few months I felt like I had no choice except to be as transparent as a soap bubble and just as delicate. Yes, acting lessons were next. And if I could convince myself with high-quality acting that I was not stuck between going back to my past with Mickey and going into my future with Shiloh, ha, well, that would indeed be something. It would be worth a few lessons.

"So really Allura, tell me. What do you want to know from Madame DuVaulle?" Veronica prompted.

"Okay, yeah, because my wheels are spinning and I'm going to drive myself crazy if I just keep avoiding the subject in my head," I said. A sigh escaped me. It sounded like the sigh of somebody who held all the Y's weights across her shoulders. The exhalation made me laugh because here I was thinking about acting lessons and who needed more drama than was contained in that exhalation? Veronica laughed with me. Then she put her hand on my knee and played at roughly shaking me.

"Hey, Allura, it's going to work out exactly the way it should, you know that," she said. "Right?"

"Yeah, I know it will," I said. And I did know it. Everything always worked out the way it ought to, but the uncertainty was bugging me. And the idea of more change and maybe a little more loss was also bugging me. I looked at Veronica and knew she knew what my questions were. She had been here for all my lamenting about how the glamour of and passion for writing was beginning to fizzle. She had also been here for all the heartbreak with Mickey, and now she also knew of the brief up and sudden down with Shiloh.

When I had told Veronica about Shiloh and the other woman at the Loring, she winced but then she had come up with all these other possibilities—maybe this other woman was an aide? No, I had told her. Maybe she was just a good friend? No, I didn't think so. Maybe she was a stranger with whom Shiloh had accidentally sat? No, that was very, very unlikely. And ridiculous, but thanks for trying. The light rail car stopped and passengers were exchanged, but we stayed put.

"All right," I said as soon as Veronica took her hand from my knee. "First I'm going to ask Madame DuVaulle where I should look for an inspiring career change. Then I'm going to ask her where I should look for, uhm, well…love, I guess."

"Good girl," Veronica said. "But Allura, why are you asking the career question first? Is that the one that matters most to you?"

I tugged on my garnet beads. Why *did* I want to save the love question for second? It was the first thing in my mind every morning and the last thing I considered before falling asleep. Writing the column was tolerable, but this broken heart situation, well, that was not as tolerable.

"I don't know," I admitted. "Maybe I want her to have the chance to get warmed up, you know? If Madame DuVaulle screws up on my first question about my career because she's just getting to know my vibes or my energy or whatever, well, that would be acceptable. But if I asked my real question first—" Oops, there it was, my confessing what mattered most to me— out loud, no less—damn. "And she screws up on that one, the love one, well, I'd be pretty unhappy." The light rail car swayed as we took a corner. Veronica reached out to grab the metal bar in front of us.

"So, it sounds like you already know the answer you're looking for on that love question," Veronica observed.

"Does it?" I was surprised. When I thought about it though, I did know in some little chickenshit recess of my mind the answer I wanted to hear. Dealing with that answer was another matter.

When we got to our stop, Veronica and I left the warmth of the light rail car and walked, with the stinging wind in our faces, the three blocks between us and the knowledge of what the future had in store for us. As soon as we were inside Madame DuVaulle's aged, red brick building I realized it wasn't going to be an office, but rather a chamber or a lair. The air in the long hallway was heavy with sandalwood and frankincense. I filled my lungs with the perfume. It was the right scent for opening your mind, the wrong scent if you wanted to remain logical about and distant from what you were about to discover. Damn.

The corridor was walled with wooden paneling that had been painted various colors. Along the hallway were small, old-fashioned placards hanging above the doors. Our first option was the door in the green section of paneling, which was labeled "ReKnewAll." That was all. I had no idea what went on behind that door, but I had to admit I found myself intrigued. For some reason, I pictured a virginity restoration clinic. I had heard those places existed.

Veronica led me past a door whose placard read "Clean Scene" and another that had the name and words "Trixie Kaeteri Consignment–Yours For Now." I smiled, thinking that "Yours For Now" might be good words to hang above your door if you were involved in the oldest profession, which I wouldn't have been surprised to find here. Not that any of the doors or the hallway looked shady—it just wouldn't have surprised me.

What I believed to be frankincense grew a bit stronger as we moved toward the far end of the hall. We passed two more closed doors, "Trials Publishing" in the pale pink section of paneling and "Rapture" in the dark pink section before coming across the only open door in the baby blue section. It was labeled "Art's Art." I took a quick peek inside. Art, I presumed, was standing behind a counter talking on the phone and gesturing. His massive arms were a myriad of tattoos. A small orange tabby cat sat watching his arm as it waved in the air. Ugh. I hoped the cat stayed put. The last thing I needed was this cat wandering around plotting its hostile takeover under my feet as I tried to pay attention to my future. I took one final glance at the walls of Art's place, tattooed as heavily as Art. I trailed after Veronica through the last door, this one in the yellow-gold paneled section.

A woman, slightly stooped and draped in layered shawls, met us as we entered. The room was candlelit, overheated. A red couch that reminded me of my fainting couch at home took up one short wall. The backs of three mismatched, well-worn wingback chairs pressed the opposite wall. Everything in the room was richly and deeply saturated with color. There was barely room to move among the furniture. A large person might be uncomfortable here. And I realized the frankincense hadn't been wafting from here. Rather, cinnamon and orange were the scents du jour. The cinnamon gave me a Shiloh pang in the heart. Damn.

The woman showed Veronica where to lay down her coat, and I followed suit, draping mine over Veronica's on a dark blue wingback chair. The table in the middle of the tiny room was covered with shawls similar to those that covered the woman. Behind a dark green wingback was another smaller, but taller table with a tin lantern holding four short, fat white candles, the only light source in the room. This table had no shawl covering it. In the candlelight I could see that it was inlaid with an intricate pattern. There was another closed door, beside this smaller table.

The woman, diminutive under her shawls, stretched out a veined, scrawny forearm adorned with a multitude of gemstone-covered bracelets. She pointed to the couch and said, "Sit there," to me and indicating the other half of the couch, "Sit there," to Veronica. So we sat down, sinking in much further than either of us expected. We both said, "Oh!" at the same time. Madame DuVaulle chuckled and perched herself on a rose-colored wingback. She looked like a proper psychic, and that was reassuring. Good old Minnesota Public Radio. It had never let me down.

"You," she said pointing at me again, "are happy that I look like I know what I am doing."

Oh my Goddess. "Yes," I said. I hoped that that was okay with her.

"Yes," she said back, nodding her little pointed chin, "yes. We will read Tarot today?" she asked Veronica.

"Yes, please," Veronica said. "Your website said we should pay ahead of the reading?"

"That is a good idea; that way if you do not like what I have to say, I can still feed my dogs the fancy food." Madame DuVaulle cackled at her own joke. We each paid her and gave her a little extra to ensure a good reading. The money disappeared into a pocket under her shawls.

"Okay, we will read you first," she indicated Veronica with another nod of her chin, "and then we will read you." She looked at me, and I saw that her eyes were clouded with age and cataracts.

Madame DuVaulle asked Veronica what she wanted to know, so Veronica told her the three areas where she needed some perspective. Pulling a battered Tarot deck from beneath the table, the psychic slowly shuffled the deck, her knobby knuckles and crooked, wrinkly fingers reminding me of Dwight's feet.

"You tell me when the deck is ready," she said to Veronica.

Veronica nodded her understanding and watched as she shuffled. "It's ready now," Veronica said.

Madame DuVaulle stopped shuffling and placed the deck before Veronica.

"Now you make three cuts in the deck," she said. So Veronica cut the deck into three piles, two skinny and one healthy. "Very nice," Madame DuVaulle said and stacked up the three piles into one deck again and began dealing them out in a pattern on the table. Three cards were dealt into the middle of a circle, with eleven cards in all being laid out. Madame DuVaulle peered at the eleventh card she dealt. She didn't seem satisfied. She laid another card atop the last card. This one she scrutinized as well before laying one more card on top of it. She frowned at this one, but she didn't cover it with another card this time. Instead she held the remains of the deck in one hand and passed her other hand over the top of the leftover cards. Her lips moved, but no words were spoken aloud, and she turned to set the unused cards next to the lantern on the small, tall table.

"Okay, what is your name?" she asked Veronica.

"Veronica."

"Veronica, my dear, you will have some decisions to make on your own, according your cards here," she said, pointing to the stack of three cards in the eleventh position. "But overall, you have some answers, or shall we say guidance," she continued. She went through Veronica's cards, one by one. Veronica listened, her eyes growing small and squinty at times and getting big and round at other times. Some of what Madame DuVaulle said was completely cryptic to me, but it all seemed to make sense to Veronica.

I tried to figure out the exact wording of my questions. I was guessing it was as important as the wording in a spell, so I wanted to get it right. The heat in the room that had at first seemed oppressive and cloying was now soothing, encouraging me to get comfortable physically if not mentally. Okay, how to word the questions? Maybe I could ask whether I should go forward or backward, but no, that question carried its own answer, didn't it? A person couldn't really go backward, ever. So no, that wording wouldn't do. How about a question about whether or not I should pursue the unknown? Yes, that might work. And I could ask if I should pursue the unknown in my love life and in my career. That way both aspects would be taken care of. Solid. I felt good about my questions. I leaned back into the soft couch and listened again to Veronica's reading.

"And here, in your Near Future position you have the Ace of Cups. This is your card that forecasts unconditional love, so if you want to pursue a lover, chances are very strong that you will find the right one in the near future." Madame DuVaulle let a quiet, knowing laugh escape her wrinkled lips. Her smile was youthful and content. "You have someone in mind already, do you not?" Madame DuVaulle asked Veronica.

"Yes," Veronica answered and my head snapped around hard enough to make a vertebra in my neck pop with a loud thunk. Yes? She sounded certain about the fact that she had someone in mind, yet she hadn't mentioned one thing to me. Oh, how unfair!

Madame DuVaulle laughed again and said, "You will have some explaining to do, it seems."

"Yes, you will," I said, giving Veronica the how-dare-you-hold-out-on-me look out of the corner of my eye. She laughed with a hint of guilt and ducked her head slightly. I turned back to the Tarot cards. How dare Veronica not spill her guts the way I always did? Of course, I had never really asked her to spill them, had I? No, not that I could remember.

It was different asking Veronica to tell all. She had kept her own secrets close ever since we had first met. And I had never wanted to ask her about her love life and what she wanted for herself because I almost always had some sort of relationship going on and she only had infrequent, casual encounters. She had always seemed to want more, but hadn't ever actually said anything to that effect. So I hadn't brought it up. My fault then, that I didn't know about this person in the works—or this person Veronica wanted to be in the works. I'd ask on the ride home, that was for sure.

The last cards in Veronica's reading were all Minor Arcana, which was why Madame DuVaulle had been frowning at them. Apparently all it meant was that Veronica would have more influence over the matters she was asking about. I wasn't sure how Veronica would see this, but I guessed that she'd view it as a negative. Especially in regard to her parents where I think she wanted some definite solution so she didn't have to worry about how they'd age.

"Do you see any pattern, or anything that should encourage me to open my own business?" Veronica asked.

"Your Significator card is The World card, so yes, if you are contemplating opening your own business, you are in extremely good shape to do so," Madame DuVaulle answered. I exhaled in relief for Veronica.

"What other questions do you have?" Madame DuVaulle wanted to know.

"None, thank you," Veronica said, looking satisfied. She leaned back into the couch just as I was pushing my butt forward to get ready for my reading.

Madame DuVaulle was putting the Tarot deck back together. "What is your name?" she asked me. I always thought it funny that psychics would ask this question, but I answered her anyway.

"It's Allura Satou," I said, wondering why I gave her my last name too.

"Pretty name," she said.

"It has too many vowels," I said. Why? Because I was nervous. I could feel Veronica looking at me, and Madame DuVaulle laughed.

"It is still pretty," she said. She was shuffling the cards now, and my palms grew clammy. "What is your question?"

"I...I uh, I want to know," I stammered. Shit! What did I want to know again? I couldn't remember the perfect wording I had sorted out earlier.

"It is all right," the psychic said, "you take your time. Your question is in you, I know. You just let me know when it is ready to come out."

Suddenly she reminded me of Dr. Browning. I knew now was not the time to screw around, but all these really funny, at least to me, questions were floating around in my head. What if I asked her to tell me what the weather would be like on my seventieth birthday? Or what if I asked her what color underwear the cards recommended I wear next Saturday? How about if I asked which wall I should paint red as an accent in my living room? What if I asked her what I really wanted to know? And why did that seem as farfetched as the first three ridiculous questions? I took a deep breath and blurted out my question.

"Should I take my love life and my career into the unknown, or should I stick with the familiar?" I asked in one loud, fast exhalation.

"There it is!" Madame DuVaulle said as if she just took first place in the homegrown question contest at the Minnesota State Fair. She nodded and said, "I knew your question was in there. Now, you just tell me when to stop shuffling. You tell me when the cards are ready."

Then I realized she had been shuffling with those old, likely arthritic hands the whole time I had been stalling, so I told her to stop right away. The deck did seem ready to me, but I also didn't want to make her shuffle more than she already had. She stopped shuffling and set the deck in front of me. I divided the deck into three piles as she instructed. Then she picked them up and compiled them back into one deck, which she dealt out in front of me in the same pattern she dealt out Veronica's. My eleventh card was The Tower card, one of the Major Arcana, so Madame DuVaulle stopped there and dealt out no further cards.

I tried to remember what The Tower card represented, but I couldn't. I had some recollection from past readings that it was a card that shook some people up, but I was already shaken up, so I let it go for now. I looked at my Significator card, the card that represented me, my essence, and it was the Son of Wands. Madame DuVaulle saw me looking at it and asked if we should start. I told her yes, we should.

"Your Significator is the Son of Wands. He lets us know that you love making people laugh and that people appreciate the exuberant energy you bring to their worlds. That is who you are deep, deep inside. If it is also who you want to be, you are in luck," she said, looking at me to see if I understood.

I nodded, recognizing myself in the card. No question about that one—it was right on the money.

"The reason you are asking this question is represented by the Emperor card," Madame DuVaulle began. She shook her head, not liking the card apparently. "This card tells us that you have somehow been made to fit into a rigid, inflexible schedule or position. Either you or somebody else has brought you too far into the thinking realm of life and has made you leave the feeling realm for a time. Do you know who this card represents?"

I had to think about that. It could be Mickey. It could be my current editors or even my whole job. I had deadlines, formats and word counts to follow. With Mickey, I had to think hard all the time, leaving little room to feel. But I wasn't sure.

"I can't really say who it might be," I said.

"Well then. This is someone who has somehow sent you the message that you are not safe if you are feeling things, but that thinking through things constantly is just fine," Madame DuVaulle offered.

Oh. Now I knew. Damn.

"Did you say it could be me doing this to myself?" I asked.

"Yes," she answered.

"Okay, I know who it is then—it's me. What do I do?"

"You simply decide to start feeling things again," Madame DuVaulle said.

Oh. I had held back as much as I could from feeling the pain of the breakup with Mickey, and then I had held back from feeling everything I could while getting to know Shiloh. Damn. Not only had I bought tickets to *Depression: The Musical*, I had also reserved a seasonal front row seat for myself. Or was I deciding to cast myself as the star in the whole production?

"Now, your Cross Current card is here—Judgment. You have already made a healing decision for yourself, but the trouble is you are not willing to go with that decision just yet because you are being too judgmental of your decision," Madame DuVaulle said. "Do you know what I am talking about?"

"I think so," I said.

"You know what you need. Now you can be the one who runs blindly through the snow. If you fall, the universe will protect you, understand?" she said. I thought I felt the couch tilt beneath me.

Had she really just said that? I had been looking at the Judgment card, but when she said I could run blindly, I looked up at her face. She was peering intently at me with her eyes cloudy as can be, but I felt she could see into my soul. I didn't answer, because I knew she already knew what I would have said, which was simply, "Okay."

"Let us look at what is underneath all of this. Let us look at what keeps you going. Ah, we have the Magician holding you up. You, Allura, want to be the alchemist who changes the bitter acid of suffering and pain into the wine that allows everyone to dance and feel good. Did you know that?" Madame DuVaulle asked.

"No, I didn't," I answered. "In fact, I'd have said I have selfishness at my root rather than wanting others to feel good." I had to be honest because I had the feeling she'd see right through me if I lied and said that I always put others' interests above my own.

"This Magician sometimes benefits others in benefiting himself," she explained, "but that does not negate the good he does for others, does it?"

"No, I don't suppose it does."

"Well, my dear, the energy and consciousness that you have underneath all else is a positive force for yourself as well as for those around you. This card," she said as she picked up the Death card, "shows that you have recently let go of something. You have been given a chance to break out of a rut, a negative pattern, or maybe that unhealthy relationship. It is behind you now, so let us see if there will be a rebirth of sorts." She set the Death card back in its place and patted it as if it were a child that needed soothing.

I nodded.

"In your conscious mind we have The Ace of Wands! This means you recognize you are like a tiny new baby bird that has just burst from her egg. You know this is a time of rebirth, or new beginnings. Look at all the new beginning cards! So, Allura, once you let go of that old doubt and judgment—" she tapped the Judgment card and then the Emperor card, "—you will be a new woman."

Goddess willing.

"Here you have The Lovers sitting in the position that tells us that this is what you most desire and, at the same time, what you most fear. That makes sense, does it not?" She didn't wait for me to respond, but continued, "You know, someone recently tried to give you her song and you panicked, you ran away."

My mouth dropped open. Shiloh's soundtrack with "Home" pumped itself through my memory. I didn't have to answer Madame DuVaulle.

She said, "You just get over that fear now, because look at all these birth cards—they say it is not too late. And look at this." She picked up The Son of Cups and waved it in front of me. "You are going to fall in love, so you can stop fighting it now. There is nothing you can do about this."

She set the Son of Cups back on the table. "You know," she said looking hard at me, "falling in love can refer to people. It can also refer to what you do to earn a living. The universe does not see a difference or a boundary between the career Allura and the love Allura, so it would appear that you are going to have to go into that unknown you asked about in both your love life and your career life."

"Nothing I can do to decide differently?" I asked.

"No, because you have already made the decision. Now you just have to trust in it," Madame DuVaulle said.

"So can you tell what kind of career I should be looking for?" I asked.

"You do not know what you want to do?" Madame DuVaulle sounded surprised.

"Well, short of stand-up comedy, no," I said.

"That is the magician speaking there, stand-up comedy, hahaha," Madame DuVaulle chuckled. Veronica snorted softly next to me. I had almost forgotten she was there.

"She's not kidding about the stand-up comedy," Veronica said to Madame DuVaulle.

"Hmm, well, we all have to do what we think is best for ourselves, but did you not just have an experience with education that was similar to stand-up comedy? I see you doing well in a teaching role," Madame DuVaulle said.

How did she know this stuff? She was incredible.

"My thinking is that you will be teaching writing by this time next year, only your students will have exceptional needs," she predicted.

"Wow. Okay," I said. I didn't know what to think about that.

"So let us look at the energies that surround you," Madame DuVaulle went on, picking up the Strength card. "It would seem that you are surrounded by magical helpers," she said. "Do you feel that you are in contact with the natural world in some magical way, maybe with a pet or some earthy person? Or maybe with the earth itself?"

"I have a new bird named Dwight—well, he's not new, but he's new to me. He's been a helper of sorts," I offered.

"And you had news of his arrival before you met him, did you not?" Madame DuVaulle asked.

Did I? Dr. Browning had advised me to get a pet, a needy, homely pet, but I didn't think that was what she was…oh! The crow's feather! I hadn't thought about that since the day it fell at my feet on the sidewalk, and I put it in my woven shoulder bag as I walked home from Dr. Browning's.

"Yeah, I guess I did," I said. This woman was really incredible. How did she know about the feather? And what other things did she know? "Can you see the future or only the past?" I asked Madame DuVaulle.

"Well, I can see things that you have in your head but are not thinking of, but I cannot see the future," she explained.

"I was wondering the same thing," Veronica said. "You knew things I had kind of forgotten about."

"That is what I have been told by many people who have come to see me," Madame DuVaulle said as if it was no big deal, but I was blown away.

"We had better look at your outcome card, Allura," Madame DuVaulle said, bringing our attention back to the reading. "You should buckle up, my dear, because you are in for a big, big ride."

It was funny to hear her use this phrase, but it made me uneasy. "Oh-oh, what kind of ride?" I asked. I wasn't sure I wanted to hear what she had to say.

"According to the majority of your other cards the outcome will be better than you expect, but this Tower card predicts a major structural change in your life. But we saw that coming in all your birth cards, did we not?" Madame DuVaulle asked.

"I don't think I'm ready for a major structural change though," I said.

"The change is already underway. You are more than half-way through, I would say," she said.

"Really?" I asked, without having to ask because in that second I knew she was right and that I'd be okay. I'd start running blindly through the snow and let the universe catch me if I did happen to fall. I felt good about this reading. I equated the feeling with roughly six therapy sessions with Dr. Browning.

One the ride back home, I asked Veronica what she thought about her reading.

"I wanted her to read a card to me that said, 'Go for the Garden Shop,' just like that, you know? But she knew things, Allura, didn't she?" Veronica asked me with awe in her voice. "She is the real deal. She knew things that had happened to me that I hadn't thought were important at the time."

I had been so nervous trying to think of my question, not wanting the answer, but wanting the answer all at the same time that I hadn't listened as well as I would have liked to Veronica's reading. Some of the parts I did listen to had been a secret language spoken only by the psychic and Veronica. I assumed that parts of my reading were the same for Veronica—especially the parts where Madame DuVaulle had made reference to specific things like Shiloh offering me her song and the educational comedy bit.

I asked Veronica what things Madame DuVaulle had known about her, and she told me a few of them. I decided to wait to give Veronica grief about having a secret crush until later. I wanted to mull over what Madame DuVaulle had told me. I also felt it would be in bad form to sit through each other's readings, which kind of cut close to the bone for both of us, and then to tease Veronica about it. So we sat silent the rest of the way to our stop.

CHAPTER THIRTY

Lilfella

The black cat sat smack-dab in the middle of my front step. When he saw Veronica and me approaching, he stood up and began pacing back and forth in front of my door.

"Ooooh, pretty cat," Veronica murmured.

"Ughhhh," I groaned. "That thing has been following me."

"Really?" Veronica looked at me, surprised.

"Yes, look at his back toes, he's giving me the finger." I had stopped on the sidewalk in front of my house. I considered going around to the alley so I could enter through the back door. Veronica, however, walked right up to the cat and tousled him behind the ears, making the tufts of hair stick out even more wildly. The cat purred so loudly I could hear him where I stood, but despite the purr, I had the feeling the cat was rather panicked. He paced back and forth between Veronica's Victorian ankle boots. He seemed to like the petting, but kept glancing at the door. He didn't rub his head into Veronica's hand the way most cats would, trying to convince the petter that they are loving the attention when really they are just plotting the opening of the vein that has now come within reach.

"I think he wants in," Veronica said, looking at me from her bent over position.

"Uh-uh, not gonna happen," I said, trying to control my revulsion.

"He seems upset," she responded.

"Yeah, I see that, but he can't come in the house. Plus, Dwight would eat him...or he would eat Dwight. It just wouldn't be good."

"I don't know," Veronica mused, looking back at the cat.

"I do know. I know he's not coming in."

"He's here for a reason, though," she said. She stopped petting him and straightened up.

"Can you contain him long enough for me to get in the house?" I felt like a wimp asking that, but I visualized myself walking into the house and the cat snaking in behind me.

"Yeah, I'll hold him," she said.

"Thanks." I waited for her to scoop him up. He hung his head over her shoulder and stared at the front door. I rushed past her, unlocked the door and scooted in.

"Now you, without the cat," I said through the barely opened door.

"Thanks for stopping by, kitty." Veronica gently placed the cat on the porch floor and followed me in. The cat stared in after us, but he didn't try to follow.

"Allura, he might be homeless," she said after we were safely inside with the door closed. "He might be cold."

"Someone will take him in," I assured her. "Plus, I saw him on his own porch the other day." Without warning, I felt my already tense stomach tighten further as I remembered Elizabeth's threatening phone call. Madame DuVaulle had said nothing of that, I realized. I hadn't told Veronica about it because it seemed silly to be upset about it, but maybe talking about it would make me feel better. I'd put some tea on and ask Veronica what she thought. I got the kettle ready as Veronica made herself comfy in the living room.

Dwight hadn't said hello to me, and that was unusual. I ran cold water into the kettle. With the stalker cat on the porch, we didn't make the usual amount of noise as we came in, so that was likely why Dwight had remained silent. I set the kettle on the flame and headed out into the living room. Veronica was in the corner of the fainting couch and had her feet tucked up under her. She was leafing through a writer's magazine.

"I'm going to go say hi to Dwight," I told her as I took the stairs two at a time.

"Hi Dwight!" I hollered before I was even in the room.

I skidded *Risky Business* style across the open doorway to amuse him, and a cry caught in my throat at what I saw. Dwight was lying, beak down, on the floor of his cage.

"Dwight!" I cried. "Dwight!" He didn't get up. From downstairs I could hear Veronica's steps quickly crossing the floor and then coming up the stairs. I opened Dwight's cage, tears blurring my vision.

"What's happened?" Veronica's voice shook.

"I don't know." I touched Dwight's back, near his neck. He trembled. I jerked my hand back and then gently scooped him up with both hands. He was limp, but he wasn't dead, which was what I had feared.

"Dwight, lilfella, come on, wake up, buddy," I crooned with my face almost touching his feathers. I kissed the top of his head. "Come on, Dwight, wake up, you're okay, buddy."

"Allura, let's get him to the vet."

Veronica sped, driving my car to the vet clinic on Cedar Avenue while I cradled Dwight's body in my arms. We had wrapped him in a fleecy throw before leaving the house. For anyone who didn't know there was a bird in the blanket, it probably appeared we were rushing a human infant into the vet clinic. The veterinarians said they weren't experts on birds, but they took Dwight in the back room to see what they could do. The clinic that specialized in birds was all the way across the city. A few unbearably long minutes later, Dr. Dora came out to ask me questions. I realized through the haze of my panic that she looked like my father or how my father would look if he'd been born female. She had kind, crescent moon eyes and a wide, upturned nose like my dad. She was probably Japanese and probably in her sixties. Her trendy haircut, razor edged and streaked with auburn, made her look like an elf. I answered her questions through my tears and handfuls of tissue, no this had never happened before, no he didn't go through a trauma, no he hadn't sustained a blow, no he...yes, he *had* tried a new food, avocado.

"When did he eat the avocado?" Dr. Dora asked. She made a note on her clipboard.

"This morning, around eight or nine. Is it bad?"

"Well, avocado can be very toxic to some birds. We can treat Dwight symptomatically with supportive therapy, but there's no specific treatment," the vet said. She placed her hand on my forearm and said, "We'll do the best we can. I'll send a technician out to speak with you in a moment, and I'll go now to look after Dwight."

Veronica sat beside me with her arm wrapped tightly around my shoulders as we waited for the technician. We didn't speak.

I had poisoned Dwight, my lilfella.

I held Dwight's empty blanket to my abdomen. I felt like I was going to throw up. No wonder he hadn't just gobbled up the avocado when I offered it. He knew it wasn't good for him, and he'd eaten it simply to make me happy. What a damned fool I was! Poor little trusting guy, and I poisoned him. Goddess let him be okay. When the technician came out, both Veronica and I stood up.

"Are you here with Dwight?" she asked.

"Yes," Veronica answered. We were the only people in the waiting room.

"I'm Laura, the technician," she said. She appeared to be all of sixteen years old but with an edgy thin smile and sharp black eyebrows in her pale full moon face. Her black hair was pulled back into a tight, short ponytail.

"How is he?" I had no time for polite introductions.

"He has edema in his throat and fluid in his lungs and abdomen, but his heart seems to be fine, which is good news," she said. "We've already induced vomiting and cathartics to clear the avocado from his system. We might have to use oral-activated charcoal to absorb any remaining toxins." She looked at me to see if I understood her.

I nodded, so she continued, "If he doesn't respond to these treatments, Dr. Dora said we can try steroids, diuretics, oxygen and bronchodilators. He may not pull through this. But he's a big bird, so that helps." She grasped my forearm the same way Dr. Dora had. Her eyes looked sad, and her thin lips grew even thinner.

I nodded. It was hard to swallow in order to speak. "What do we do now?" I croaked.

"Let me go ask Dr. Dora," she replied.

Veronica and I sat back down. I smoothed the throw blanket out over my knees and then balled it up again against my stomach. I tried to take deep breaths to calm my heart and my stomach.

"It's going to be okay," Veronica said, putting her arm around me again. I leaned my head onto her shoulder. She squeezed me and kissed the top of my head.

"I know. It has to be. I'm so stupid." I started crying again.

"No, you didn't know."

"It's a jungle food, right? Avocado? And he's a jungle bird. I never thought…"

"It's okay. Hey, Madame DuVaulle never mentioned this, right? So there's that," Veronica said, jiggling me a little. I tried to smile.

"True," I sniffed. "But this could be my Tower card."

"No, I don't think so. Did you notice the cat was still there when we left?"

"No." I hadn't noticed *anything*, to tell the truth. Just Dwight, limp in my arms.

"He was," she said. "I think that's why he was there in the first place. Because Dwight was sick."

"I don't know. He's been around a lot."

"Maybe he's looking after you, like a familiar," she said.

I sat up and moved out from under her arm. "Oh no," I said. "Do you think he's here to replace Dwight?" If the Goddess took Dwight and sent me a damn cat, I would not be able to handle it.

Veronica grabbed me and tucked me back under her arm. "No," she said shaking me firmly, as if to get the thought out of my mind. "No, because Dwight is going to be just fine."

"Veronica, this is why," I said as she held me to her side, "it's never a good idea to fall in love with anyone." I sniffed loudly. "If Dwight doesn't get better, how will my life have been made any better by having loved him? I mean, the good times will make the bad, the missing him, even worse, right?" I don't know if it came out the way I meant it, but it was the best I could do to explain how I felt. It was the same way I felt about Shiloh, about love in general. It was dangerous. Yes, it was awesome, but it was so dangerous.

"That's stupidity and fear talking," Veronica replied. "And you're smarter than that, so as soon as the fear part is over—"

"No, it's reality!" I said, cutting her off. "Giving importance to someone, letting them into your heart, that's just ridiculous. It's how we entertain ourselves or something, so we don't get bored. We think we're supposed to fall in love because media and society tell us to, so we do, we let ourselves love, and then bam! It's over. The person dies, leaves you and then what do you have? Nothing but heartache."

"Are we talking about a person or about Dwight here?" Veronica asked.

"Well," I sniffled again. Who were we talking about? "We're talking about anyone—it's all the same."

I wasn't going to let myself love deeply. I could make myself believe that love was fabricated by corporations trying to sell things like greeting cards, diamond rings and boxes of chocolates. Veronica sighed and leaned her head against mine. She pulled me tightly to her side. I let her. I thought about all the reasons not to love as I sat cradled against her.

Dr. Dora came out of the back of the clinic. Veronica and I straightened up, but she didn't release me from her embrace. Dr. Dora's arms were folded across her white lab coat. Her stethoscope, looking much too big for a chest as tiny as Dwight's, hung around her neck. "Our patient," she said, "is calling very feebly for someone named 'lilfella.' I'd hate for him to have to call for long, so why don't you come back to see him. He's feeling pretty good right now, we think."

Forgetting all of my resolution and reasoning against falling in love, I jumped up. With a soft whoosh Dwight's blanket fell from my lap to the tile floor. I followed Dr. Dora to see my little man.

CHAPTER THIRTY-ONE

Shakespeare's Gay?

I was in Cami's class for what was my third visit in January. Being there was like a drug. I adored sharing what I knew about writing, the students seemed to appreciate what I was teaching them and I didn't have to watch my back in the classroom. Schools didn't allow cats inside. That crafty bugger had been showing up everywhere lately. To the credit of cats everywhere, they were intelligent and persistent, much to my personal dismay. I'd half expected to be greeted by his luminous golden eyes and unruly ear hair as I walked into the building, but I'd seen no signs of him here. On this visit I was teaching the students about concise writing, so they were rewriting long, overly wordy letters that had passed between William Shakespeare and his intimate companion, the Earl of Southampton.

The students were intrigued that William Shakespeare was married to Anne Hathaway while possibly having a male lover and surprised by the idea that more is not always better when it comes to writing. Their mission was to rewrite the letters using fewer words while still keeping each of the ideas and sentiments intact. Then in February, the students were going to have a lesson on language registers and have the chance to rewrite the letters one more time using today's slang. I could not wait to see how their writing unfolded. They were so absorbed in what they were doing that Cami and I had time to just stand back and observe.

"So, what's new on the home front?" Cami asked me.

"Nothing much," I replied. I didn't tell her that I was on pins and needles waiting for Shiloh to return any of the five or six voice messages I had left her over the past couple of weeks, I didn't tell her what had befallen Dwight and I didn't tell her that I felt like a fraud talking about the joys of writing as I stood here loathing my return home to continue a writing career that made me want to rip my face off.

"How's Falina? She still dating that Brian guy?" Cami asked. Her hazel eyes sparkled at me as she tugged at the front of her blouse, bunching it up in a way that let me know she had also been told the story of the mis-buttoned shirt. We laughed.

"Yeah, she is," I said, still laughing at her motions. "He has forgiven her for that, I think, because they are still hot and heavy." I lowered my voice as I said "hot and heavy," and she laughed at me for this.

"They're eleventh graders," she said, laughing and waving her hand like she was Glenda the Good Witch. "They only listen when adults whisper. Anyway, you could use a much more explicit phrase and they would still one-up you with something even more explicit."

"Oh!" I said.

"And after all, you're having them translate homosexual love letters here—you think there's anything more exciting than that for them? We could say whatever we wanted to each other and they wouldn't even hear us." She waggled her eyebrows at me in a suggestive manner. Heat rose from my chest to my cheeks.

"Yeah, but it's Shakespeare! And he was bisexual at best." I defended my choice of lessons and at the same time hoped to reroute the conversation from us potentially saying inappropriate things to each other.

"Hey, I know, I know. And I wanted to tell you," Cami said, lowering her voice now, "that you have an exceptional rapport with teenagers and you should consider teaching. And I'm not just saying that because you've been here helping me teach my classes and I feel like I owe you." She laughed. "I do appreciate that by the way, but I'm telling you this because good teachers matter. You know, there are some teachers out there who can't do what you do with these kids even though they've been teaching for years and years."

"Wow, thank you," I said. I was flattered by her sincere words. "Want to hear something crazy?"

"Sure," Cami said.

"I went to a psychic the other day for a Tarot reading, and she told me she saw me teaching kids in the future." I was watching as one of the boys in Cami's class got so excited with what he was writing that he was now standing up at his desk, bent over at the waist, scribbling furiously as he rewrote Shakespeare's words.

"See?" Cami asked.

"Only…" I looked around at these kids and knew they didn't quite match the kids Madame DuVaulle predicted I'd be teaching. "The psychic said I'd be teaching kids with exceptional needs."

Just then two girls and a boy began racing around the room, shrieking. One of the girls clutched her papers and was trying to stay ahead of the two chasing kids while trying to keep her writing out of their hands. A few other students looked up but then went back to their writing or collaborating. The girl in the front of the pack knocked over a chair before getting cornered and having her writing ripped out of her hands. All three of the kids were gasping for breath, laughing and hanging on each other. The rest of the class continued to work as if nothing unusual was going on.

"Allura, honey," Cami said, her voice calm and even and her eyelids at half-mast, "they *all* have exceptional needs."

Book of Shadows
Stagnant Negativity Cleanse

Cast circle around myself.
"Blessed be Creatures of Light."
Light pale green candle.
Burn cinnamon incense.
Pass egg over my entire body, head to toe,
while concentrating on surrendering negativity to the
egg.
Request protection and cleansing and renewal from the
Goddess.
"God, Goddess, Mother Earth,
Unmoor my ship from this stagnant berth.
Please weather my seas with passion and mirth.
Perfect egg, uncloud my skies,
complete egg, help me be wise."
Puff deep breath onto eggshell.
Thank the egg and break it in dish of water, examine for
impurity or blood.
(There was none, so no further actions are necessary.)
Flush the egg and water down the toilet.
"Thank you, Goddess, for the egg and for the cleansing."
"Blessed be Creatures of Light."
Snuff the candle.

CHAPTER THIRTY-TWO

Apply Myself Liberally

I guessed there weren't many teaching jobs for a person without a teaching degree, but I was scouring the Internet anyway. Dwight was walking around on my desk, moving pens and pencils from one side of the desk to the other. This was a new habit he had recently taken up. It was one that I would have to discourage because I was worried about him sampling dangerous edibles—his list of edible household items being much longer than my list, although I hadn't forgotten I was the one who forced the avocado on him. Also, he wasn't exactly litter trained yet. On the other hand, I should welcome the little gifts he left behind because at least he was here and alive to leave them...all over my books, papers, rocks, candles and chair.

I held out my arm to him and said, "Step up!" He stepped up, with heavy feet grasping my arm through my sleeve, and let me place him atop his cage where there was a play station with a cockatoo-sized jungle gym and food and water bowls.

"Good boy," I said, grabbing a peanut for him from the top drawer of my desk. I held the peanut out to him, and he grabbed it in his big, scaly foot. I loved watching him hold his food with his feet. Sometimes he just went straight to using his beak to break into whatever morsel he discovered, but when he used his foot, it just cracked me up. He still amazed me. Before the avocado incident, he had started to become more accustomed to his new place and was beginning to explore virgin territory every day. But since coming home from the clinic, he had become even bolder. It was as if after his near-death experience he resolved to live it up before I tried to poison him again. Dr. Dora had warned that he'd be subdued for a few days, but no such luck. I had to keep my eyes and ears open. I'd begun to appreciate the lock on his cage door which I had had no reason to use up until yesterday when I came home and heard his "lilfella" greeting coming at me from the kitchen.

He had wandered all the way downstairs. I saw that he had introduced himself to the herb garden in the kitchen window and had gnawed the basil into a stub of stalks. I was thankful he hadn't introduced himself to electricity by munching on an extension cord. I found little bird shits everywhere.

But now he was happy to busy himself with destroying the peanut. I knew he'd stay in the office as long as I was there, so I turned back to the computer to see if anyone wanted to hire me to teach writing. I typed, "Writing instructor Twin Cities not certified" into the search bar and got four hits. Two were at the university level, one was community education and one was at…wow. It was at the Davidoff Academy for the Blind where Shiloh taught her fitness class.

My stomach lurched, and I decided right then and there to apply online for the job, whether I was qualified or not. I also decided I was going to call Shiloh, tell her she scared the hell out of me and that I wanted to see her. I couldn't exactly spring myself on her or just show up on her doorstep, because that would be unfair. But what if I asked her to meet me at…I don't know…someplace at a certain time if she was willing to give this a go, or to at least see me? What the heck had happened anyway?

I was scared off by her soundtrack offering, hung up, didn't answer a couple of her calls, then I called her and she didn't answer my calls. And in between all that I saw her at the Loring with some woman who had touched her face, but she didn't see me, of course. Maybe she somehow knew I was there...and with Mickey.

Mickey. I needed to wrap things up with Mickey. We had talked a few times on the phone, nothing committal, just banter. Nothing seductive or exciting or heartwarming. There was just nothing there anymore. No matter how badly Mickey thought she wanted to start or restart a relationship with me, we just couldn't do that. There wasn't enough to keep us together the first time, so there was certainly not enough to bring us back together now. And I didn't want to go back.

I spent the next two hours perfecting my résumé and filling out the online application for Davidoff Academy. By the time I finished, the light of the full moon was bouncing from the eastern night sky onto the windows of the houses across the street and back into my office window. I pushed my chair away from the desk, feeling the relief of having done something monumental by sending the application. It felt good to take concrete steps.

Reflected in my neighbors' windows, there were no less than eleven moons staring at me as I gazed at them. I wished that Shiloh were here so that I could describe it to her. I decided to keep taking concrete steps tonight since that first one had felt so good.

I dialed Shiloh's number. She didn't answer in time to beat her voice mail, so I left a message, "Shiloh, it's Allura. Hi." I cleared my throat because my voice seemed to be stuck deep behind my pounding heart. "Hi," I began again, "I miss you and I'm scared to know you, but mostly I miss you and..." Hm, this message was not going the way I wanted it to go, but I tried to salvage it, "so, uhm, maybe you'll call me back and we can talk or go out, or something...okay, so call me back and...I love you." I love you? Where had that come from? I love you?

"*You have exceeded your time limit for this message. Please press one to send your message as it is or press three to revise your message,*" droned the computer voice on the other end of the line. Thank Goddess, a chance to revise my message, or just delete it altogether until I had a chance to collect myself. What number was for revising? I couldn't remember. One? Three? What were my choices again? Shit. I pressed one.

"Your message has been sent," the computer voice said.

"Noooooo!" No. Damn it. I pushed the three several times with all the desperation of someone who has just accidentally and badly sealed her fate while she was preoccupied with something else. It was no use, the message had been sent. I ended the call and tossed the phone onto my desk. I'd said, "I love you." What the hell? Maybe Shiloh would think it was meant to be one of those casual "love ya" comments we all made to each other. How pronounced was the "I" anyway? Pretty pronounced, I'd say, as the phrase echoed in my own damn voice through my own damn head. Fuck. Fuckity fuck, McFuckerson. I burrowed my head into my crossed arms on my desk and wondered what kind of crime it would be to break into a woman's house long enough to delete a stupid message that you had left. Would it really be a crime if you stole back your own message?

As if to prevent me from turning to a life of thievery, the doorbell rang. I looked at Dwight to make sure he'd be okay. He was wrestling the rope that hung from his jungle gym on top of his cage, so I padded down the stairs and looked out the wavy glass window on my front door. I almost fell over when I saw who was on the other side. It was Shiloh, and she was alone.

"Shiloh!" I said as I threw open the door. How in the world...? There was no car on the street behind her. How did she get here?

"Allura," she said, "is it okay that I'm here? I took a cab." She held her hand out somewhat tentatively, so I took it in my own and led her over the threshold. "Step up a bit," I said to her to make sure she didn't trip coming into the house.

"I am so glad you're here," I said. I didn't care if I was gushing and she heard it.

"You are?" she asked.

"Yes, I am!" Then I got worried—why was she here? "Are you okay? Did something happen?"

"No," she said, shaking her head. "I wanted to see you," she said. I saw her hesitant smile and knew she was wondering if I caught her joke.

I was still holding her hand. I pulled it toward me and placed it over my heart, which was testing the confines of my rib cage. "Can you see me now?" I asked, laughing at how cheesy my comeback was.

She pressed her hand hard to my chest. "Yes," she said, not smiling anymore.

I looked at her mouth, her eyes, and her hair peeking out from under her big blue winter hat. She was beautiful.

"What happened?" Shiloh whispered her question.

"I don't know. I got scared," I answered.

I looked at her clear, bright eyes again right before I took my hand off hers to tip her chin up. And then I kissed her. She left her hand over my heart even as she pulled me toward her with her other arm. She kissed me back, hard, and I thought I'd start crying, I was so relieved and so happy she was here. She didn't move other than to break her mouth away from mine.

"Allura, I miss you, and I'm sorry you're scared," she murmured. We kept our foreheads pressed together. I felt her words on my lips as much as I heard them.

"I'm not scared right now, and I miss you, too, Shiloh."

"Has anything changed?" she asked quietly, pushing her mouth alongside my cheek. "I mean, with the way you feel about me?"

Changed? "Yes," I said.

She began to pull away.

I held her to me. "No, I mean no. Wait, Shiloh, stay here."

She let me hold her to me, but I could feel through her pea coat that she wasn't soft in my arms anymore; she was tense.

"Shiloh, I miss you so much. I like you more than I ever have, so that has changed. It changes every day that I realize all the things I want to tell you and laugh about with you. And every day that has gone by without you has made me wonder what you are doing and want to hear your voice and want to know more about you. And I'm not afraid of being with you now. I was afraid of it because I couldn't bear to think of knowing you and then having things be over, you know?" This didn't come out the way I wanted it to, but I had to try to tell her what I was feeling. I wanted her to relax in my arms, to melt into me the way she had when she had first arrived.

"Really?" she asked.

Through her coat I felt her spine relax a bit and her hips pressed against mine again. "Really," I said.

"Have you moved on with someone else?" she asked.

"Moved on?" I asked. I didn't know what she meant.

"You were at the Loring with someone, and you held her hand. My sister told me. We were there at the same time you were. I recognized your voice." Shiloh sounded empty as she said this.

"So then you heard our whole conversation?" I asked, hoping that she had, yet I was slightly embarrassed at the prospect.

"No, I heard you ask someone what they missed most, and it made me think of how good I felt when you asked me that. Then the place got so busy and loud, I didn't hear you again."

Not to mention that I was sure I had lowered my voice, because I had wanted to maintain control over my emotions during that fraught conversation. Shiloh must have felt terrible when she heard me ask that question, the question that to my way of thinking was *Shiloh's* question. But it hadn't been the same question with Mickey. It had been the beginning of the end of the conversation. It had been when I hit the high point of my pisstivity.

Wait...Shiloh's words replayed themselves in my head—she had not been on a date!

"That was your sister?" I was overjoyed at this news.

"Yes," she said.

"I thought it was a...girlfriend or lover or someone," I said.

"You knew I was there?" She pulled away from me a bit.

"Yes," I said, not wanting to let go of her, but not wanting to force her to stay close to me if she didn't want to.

"Why didn't you come over to say hi?" she asked, her voice rising.

"I saw you were with someone. I was going to come over anyway, but then I saw her touch your face. That's when I realized I might be intruding on a date and…" I faltered.

No time like the present for honesty. What did I have to lose except the fear of moving forward with this intoxicating woman? I took a deep breath and said, "I didn't want to keep falling in love with you only to have you eventually gone from my life." Since she'd hear me pledging my love for her on her voice mail soon enough, what difference did it make if I told her the truth now? What difference did it make if I finally told myself the truth? "But I now understand that love and loss are entwined. They can't be separated. You can't protect yourself from the risk of losing love." I sensed, in the deepest recesses of my being, that she was right here with me, falling in love, so why not go with it?

"Allura," she whispered.

"You are here." I moved her hand from the center of my chest to the left side, over my heart.

"That's where I want to be." She began kissing me again and as her mouth grew more insistent, my knees grew less steady. I pulled her forward and took a few steps backward until I was able to lean against something solid. It wound up not being as solid as it felt. I had to catch both of us, still kissing, as the front door squeaked and slammed closed behind our combined weight. I hoped the stalker cat hadn't followed Shiloh in. Then I dismissed the ridiculous worry. I had more important thoughts to attend to at the moment.

"Hi lilfella!" Dwight cawed to us.

I broke our kiss to holler, "Hi Dwight!" up the stairs. Shiloh laughed like tinkling bells before resuming our kiss.

Shiloh's hand had slipped, purposefully I believe, from high on my chest to lower until she was cupping my breast. It was only a moment before my clothing frustrated her. She broke contact long enough to throw her pea coat and hat to the floor, reach for me and resume her exploration beneath my shirt. Without her coat, she was smaller in my arms. I pressed my hands up the back of her shirt against her bare skin. I could feel her muscles, taut and smooth. I tried to stop worrying about my knees giving out beneath us as I pressed her more closely to me.

Shiloh pushed me back enough to give herself some room as she traced her fingers lightly under my breasts and then across my nipples. I stopped breathing so I could better concentrate on my nerve endings meeting her fingertips.

"I need to Braille you." She laughed quietly, concentrating on me.

"Let's Braille each other upstairs, okay?" I didn't want to stop, but I knew I needed to stop worrying about staying upright.

I led her up the stairs and down the short hallway. My skin ached for her hands again. Goddess, thank you.

"Shiloh! Shiloh! Shiloh!" Dwight called out as we passed the door to my office. Funny guy. Shiloh stopped in her tracks, her face open with surprise.

"It's Dwight. Your name is one of his favorite words, sorry," I apologized as she laughed and held my hand, allowing me to lead her to my bedroom. I closed the door behind us. After a half-second's worth of consideration, I realized I didn't need any more shouted encouragement from Dwight, so I told Shiloh I'd be right back and went to put him to bed.

When I returned, Shiloh was sitting in the middle of my bed, cross-legged and smiling. I looked at her and was crushed by her perfection. I wanted to feel and taste and hear that perfection so badly that my entire body ached and purred. I knelt on the edge of the bed. Shiloh grabbed the first part of me her hands made contact with—my arms—and pulled me back onto her. Without asking, she turned me over onto my back and began undressing me, her hands light as she brushed each newly bared part of me with first her palms and fingertips and then with the backs of her hands, leaving trails of goose bumps. How odd to be able to watch her do this to me without worrying about what she thought of how I looked. How freeing it was.

"Shiloh?"

"Mmm."

"Can I leave the lights on? Are you okay with that?"

"Yes, you can leave the lights on, but that's all you can leave on," she said and laughed and yanked my last piece of clothing, my turquoise panties, from my hips to my toes. She tossed them, with quite a bit of flair, over her shoulder. I didn't see where they landed and then forgot to care as she continued to Braille me.

It was not long before Shiloh was as naked as I was, and she was letting me Braille her in return. I ran my hands over every part of her, first with my eyes open and appreciating and then with my eyes closed. I let my fingertips and palms trace her body, as she had mine. Then copying her out of curiosity, I trailed the backs of my hands across her skin as well. She was spread out, on her back, each part of her body slightly rising as I trailed my hands across it. I had to open my eyes again, marveling at how unselfconscious she was.

"You are beautiful," I told her.

"You are, too," she whispered, sitting up to find my shoulders, the back of my neck, my mouth against hers. She pulled me down into the pillows with her. She held the back of my head and kissed me gently, outlining my lips with her tongue, as she did the same with her fingers between my legs. She allowed the tension there to build and then backed off. I murmured my dissent at this. She shushed me.

She broke her mouth away from mine and began kissing a random line from my neck to my navel and finally, below. Her mouth teased between my legs, making little promises, but not sealing the deal. Too early, she was pulling away, crushing me. Soon her mouth was back up at my mouth. She left just enough space between our bodies for my hand to explore and arouse her. I could feel her smile against my lips. Shiloh swelled under my fingertips. She wiggled her hips between my open thighs until she was lined up where she wanted to be. There was no longer room for my hand so I wrapped my arms around her and held her to me. She kissed me with greater demand until her mouth abruptly left mine.

Shiloh arched her back and pressed the hardest part of her into the softest part of me. I had to tear my focus from between my legs, where she was wedged, in order to watch her exquisite face above mine. Her eyes were closed, her hair was destroyed with damp tendrils plastered to her forehead and her perfect lips were set in a determined pout—open just enough to give her the air she seemed to be short of. The heat continued to rise around my hips, and I couldn't stop myself from returning her unceasing grind. By my hips, she held me to her with a gentle ferocity that made my heart dance and ache. Her breath was sweet and heavy at my neck for a moment when she shuddered and moaned a dangerously sultry, "Oh God!" I held her as she arched. Shiloh was breathtaking.

I wanted so badly to continue watching her, but my eyes involuntarily closed with her second "Oh God!" She shuddered again, then held still, arched above me with her pubic bone pressed hard between my legs. Feeling her finish this way brought on my own climax and after a breathless volley of "Oh God," "Oh Goddess," "Oh God," "Oh Goddess," I arched up under Shiloh, searching for greater contact to bring closure to the last throbbing spasm.

Shiloh, now relaxed and panting in my arms, fell to the bed beside me, letting one arm and leg drape over me. Her grace and weight soothed my senses. I held Shiloh as tightly as she held me. She burrowed her face into my neck. I smoothed her damp hair away from her cheek. She moved her hand to my face to do the same. I turned my face to her palm and felt every part of me relax. Being a believer in Karma, I had to wonder what I had done right to deserve this.

CHAPTER THIRTY-THREE

Blindsided

The next morning, after refueling with bagels and coffee, Shiloh and I sped past the houses in my neighborhood in an attempt to get her home in time to make it to class at Davidoff. Shiloh's fingers toyed with the big, blue hat she held on her lap. I had warmed the car before we left, so her hat wasn't necessary. Goddess knows how but she had returned her hair to its usual glossy perfection. It was tucked behind her ear and the edges flipped coyly at her chin. How did I get so lucky? Shiloh had asked me that very question about herself right before falling asleep for a couple of hours earlier this morning. I hadn't had an answer, so all I had been able to do was kiss her gently until our breathing took on each other's sleepy rhythm.

"Allura?" Shiloh tipped her chin, the edges of her hair drawing my eyes from the road, "were you being funny last night in bed?"

"Uhhh…" was my response. Being funny *in bed*? This might be the all-time worst question after making love for the first time with someone you really wanted to make love with again. Quite possibly a world record, but I couldn't recall anything I'd said or done to be funny. What was she talking about? And did I really want to know?

I tried again, "Uhhh...what do you mean?"

"Well, I know how you think in humor, and you always try to make me laugh," she began.

Even if I didn't want to know what she was talking about, I had to ask, "And?"

"Well, when you were saying 'Oh Goddess,' were you being funny?" Her voice faltered at the end of her question.

Impenetrable walls shot up around me. She couldn't be asking me this, could she?

"I wasn't trying to be funny. Sorry if you thought I was." I was surprised by how mean I sounded as I said it. Feeling stupid was making me angry. My heart hurt. I frowned. "I was just being myself."

"I'm sorry." Shiloh's voice was quiet. "I thought you were playing around. The whole goddess thing has thrown me for a loop. Don't you believe in God, Allura?"

Whoa! What? Is that where she was taking this? Really? Who the hell had I slept with last night?

"Apparently not like you do," I bit out. Why was I getting so defensive? I tried to push down the walls, but I was too hurt to muster enough power to calm myself.

"So what, then? You believe in the goddess you were calling out to last night?"

"Yes. Is that a problem?" I had a feeling her answer would let me know that it was indeed a problem.

"It is a problem," she confirmed.

"I believe there are several powers, entities, that exist, but I don't believe there is just one, all by himself, who's in charge of us all. I most strongly believe in the Goddess and the Mother Earth. God is fine, but *he's* not so much my thing. I'm Pagan."

"Pagan?" Shiloh's voice was still quiet.

"Pagan."

"So you weren't just being...feminist?"

"Shiloh, don't do this, not now...not after..." I sounded kind of pathetic in my own ears.

"Don't do what?" Shiloh asked.

"I was being myself—Pagan." I had to take a deep breath. "Regrettably, I was not being funny, and I was not being feminist."

"When did you choose to be Pagan? And why would you choose a religion that is so obscure when there are real religions out there?"

Oh. My. Goddess. Hearing that, I decided I was done with relationships. We'd never discussed religion before. Why was it suddenly an issue? I couldn't take this. I quit. Well, I'd quit right after I set this woman straight. Ha. Straight. Ha ha…hmm. Fuck it. I couldn't even laugh with myself right now.

"Shiloh." I didn't care if I sounded condescending. "It was no decision. It was…well, it just was. It just is. What do you believe?" Why was I asking? I was through with this.

"I'm Jewish. I believe there's only one God, no goddess. Judaism includes Goddess references, so I understand the *notion* of the Divine Feminine, but it's just an idea. There's no literal goddess—but I can understand the concept, figuratively."

I doubted that. I felt crushed by the weight of the discovery that Shiloh was narrow-minded. I never saw that coming. Being blindsided like this made me cynical and that in turn made me mad at myself as well as at Shiloh.

"So that was your decision, then? To be Jewish?" This whole thing smacked of the hetero-slash-homo genetics-versus-decision argument. I couldn't believe we were having the bloody conversation. How could this go so wrong just after it had gone so, so right?

"No." Shiloh's one-word answer made me hope she also saw the futility of this discussion. "Allura, I get the whole Christian thing—been there, dated that. But Pagan?"

I had no luck; she was still talking.

"And to not believe in one God? Really, Allura? Isn't that kind of…I don't know…kind of prehistoric?"

I sighed in response.

"And," Shiloh continued, "nobody goes out and just chooses a religion. And if they did, who the hell would *choose* to be

Jewish? Who would choose to be oppressed like Jews were and still are?"

"That's the point I was trying to make, Shiloh. I didn't choose." That wasn't true. I did choose, but only because Paganism fit. My parents had raised me Christian, but it never really felt right, so after a lot of exploration, I discovered Paganism was a perfect spiritual match for me. I didn't need to explain myself though. I was right. "Who have Pagans ever oppressed anyway? It's not like we've ever gone out on our own version of a witch hunt to oppress anyone."

"That's not the issue," Shiloh said. "I wasn't saying Pagans were oppressive...I was saying my being Jewish was never a choice."

"Well, maybe it should have been," was my retort. I wasn't making sense; I wasn't able to put into words what I wanted Shiloh to know.

Trees, houses, traffic lights, pedestrians and of course a goddamn black cat all streaked together beyond my windshield. So that I didn't hyperventilate or cry in front of Shiloh, who might not even *deserve* my tears at this point, I started to focus on one thing at a time outside my car, rather than letting them wash into a big blur.

The trees in their late winter nakedness loomed cold and forbidding, arching over the street like claws. Under them an elderly man walking his ancient, gray-muzzled golden retriever, looked at me as we passed. His eyes bore into mine as if he knew all my secrets, of which there were not many. Time misaligned itself as my head swiveled to hold his deliberate, wrinkled gaze.

Looking at him made me recall Madame DuVaulle's words about falling in love. What, exactly, had she said would come of that love? I combed through the tangle of remembered phrases in my mind. She'd said that I was going to fall in love and that it might be with a career or with a person. Well. That wasn't helpful at this moment. Falling in love with a career was not much of a consolation prize for losing Shiloh. Damn it! Losing Shiloh was not exactly what this felt like. Rather it felt like having Shiloh replaced by some conservative, self-righteous person. It felt like we were breaking up, breaking apart from each other. God? Were we really breaking up over God? Kill me now.

Madame DuVaulle had also said that I could run blindly in the snow and I'd be safe, or something along those lines. I knew she had been speaking of Shiloh in the park, but maybe she had also been speaking of life in general. I could only hope so because all I felt right now was a monumental case of The Funk reappearing. I swerved to avoid a squirrel and Shiloh's right hand shot out for the door, but she didn't say anything. I looked back in my rearview mirror and the squirrel still sat, seemingly undecided on which way to go. Little fucker probably had his own big case of The Funk. If he didn't move his tiny gray butt, he'd have a case of death.

"Sorry. Squirrel," I offered Shiloh.

She didn't respond. What was she thinking? Without vision, without being able to let her gaze drift around, she did not have the luxury of giving her mind something else to chew on as she contemplated my crime of Paganism. Was she even thinking of that anymore? I peeked sideways at her face. She looked thoughtful, but beyond that, I couldn't tell what she was thinking. Her eyelashes were nearly resting on her cheekbones. Her eyes were downcast as if she were looking at something on the floor of my car. Her face was still emotionless, but her air was sad and vulnerable. Tears started to wreak havoc with my vision. There were only four more blocks to go before we'd be at her house. I couldn't bear to leave this unresolved.

"Shiloh, what are you thinking?"

"I'm thinking that we're really very different from each other."

She rolled and unrolled the belt of her pea coat around her hat in her lap. We were different from each other? Of course we were, but she was implying that her different was acceptable and mine was not. The judgment in that statement felt so heavy! Right. Now I was really done with this. If she thought we were so different, well, her loss. The tears that had started from sadness turned to angry tears. This relationship wasn't going to get a fair chance, was it? I felt robbed.

I pulled to the curb in front of Shiloh's house with a gentleness I didn't feel.

"Yes," I said, "we really are different from one another because while you are busy looking for deal-breaking differences, I'm looking for…" Where was I going with this? Indignation and hurt were pulling words from my lips faster than I could make sense of them. "…I'm looking for common ground in our differences," I finished. That was a definite lie on my part. I'd been the one looking for deal breakers. Would I have been more willing to listen to Shiloh's religious concerns had I not just spent over a month warning myself not to fall in love with her?

Before Shiloh could say anything, I unfastened my seat belt, exited the car as noisily as possible so she'd know what I was doing, went around to open her door, gently took her by the wrist and walked her to her front door. I expected her to start punching in her security code on the little numbered Braille pad, but she just stood there. In my head, I said goodbye to Shiloh. Maybe she wished me a silent goodbye as well. But as it was, I left her there without speaking.

I made it a few blocks before I had to pull over and succumb to the tears. With my forehead pressed to my steering wheel, I bawled. My tears fell into my lap like rain, but my sadness choked me, so I made no noise other than some tortured, tense rasps and gasps. What the hell had just happened? Were we so different from one another that we couldn't bridge the gap and be in love? What the hell was so bad about being Pagan? Did Shiloh have some misinformation from scary movies or children's fairy tales that she was confusing with Paganism? What the hell? Or maybe I could blame this all on Elizabeth. Maybe her revenge on me for comparing Daniel's addiction to Mickey's was to secretly make Shiloh's acquaintance and turn her against me.

I kept my head on the steering wheel even after my tears slowed and my throat loosened up enough to allow me to breathe again. I contemplated driving over to Madame DuVaulle to tell her to take her prediction of love and shove it up her psychic ass, but I figured she'd somehow hone in on that message as it floated about the cosmos. A snort of laughter, made sharp by a post-cry hiccup, forced me to pick my head up off the wheel and search for a tissue. I flipped open my glove box just as my cell phone rang.

My shoulders tensed, yet a jolt of hope coursed through me. Oh, thank you Goddess! I grabbed my cell, hoping to see Shiloh's name in the caller ID, but it wasn't Shiloh.

"Hi, Falina!" I forced lightheartedness into my voice so she wouldn't know I'd been crying.

"Allura…" Falina's voice cracked. Unlike me, she could not hide the tears or the fear in her voice. "Allura, Mom and Dad have been in an accident."

CHAPTER THIRTY-FOUR

Letting Go

Falina, Alaina and I, along with our mom's relatives were the first wave of a cheerless family reunion held in the waiting room of Flagler Hospital in Florida. Dad's only brother and his family were on their way from Seattle. They were expected to arrive in a few hours. Dad's sister would round out the reunion when she arrived the following day.

Mom was healing nicely. Her doctor and nurses were pleased with her recovery. Dad was still in an induced coma that, according to his doctors, would allow his brain and body to recover from his collision with the RV's steering wheel and doorframe. He was scheduled for surgery to relieve pressure on his brain. The seven of us in the waiting area had just finished filing through his room, one at a time, to see him. I was the last in the line.

When I exited Dad's room, I had to rest with my back against the corridor wall for support and tip my head back to keep the tears in check. Like this, they ran down the back of my throat instead. Behind my closed eyelids, I pictured Dad as I had just seen him, small and pale in his hospital bed, his chest rising and falling from the air being forced into his lungs. The blips of his heart monitor and the digital static reflecting his low blood pressure accompanied the mechanical sighs of the ventilator.

For a moment, when I had first entered his room, I doubted it was really my father. I knew the chart in his room would read "Benjirou Satou," so I didn't check it, but it was staggering to think that this was Dad beneath the tubes, the bandages and the unfamiliar, sterile sheet.

When I was able to open my eyes there in the corridor, I contemplated walking back into the waiting area and family reunion. But I found my body was uncooperative. Instead, I pushed open the door to Dad's room and reentered the dim chamber.

I didn't sit down on the bedside stool as I had the first time. This time I stood. I slid my hand under Dad's so that it felt as if he were holding my hand against the bed sheet. I tried to hear his voice in my head telling me he would be just fine, telling me he'd wake up soon. I tried to hear one of his jokes. Was he listening in his head for a reason to recover? How did comas work? Just in case he was listening, I whispered to him that I loved him and that we all needed him to wake up.

My resolution to stand only lasted until the tears got the best of me and forced me to sit. They seemed to come from an infinite well these past two days. What was the rush to get back to the waiting area? I cried into my bent arm, making sure not to lose contact with the palm of Dad's hand, until my head throbbed and my throat ached. Wake up, Dad. You're not done yet—wake up. We need you.

"Honey." The nurse's hushed voice broke into my silent pleading. I looked out from the crook of my elbow. I watched as the pale yellow slice of light from the corridor got wider.

"Honey, we need to prep your father for surgery," the nurse said.

I cleared my throat and looked back at my dad.

"Here, you need these." The nurse was at my side with a box of tissues.

I took them, looked back at my dad and sent one more silent plea for him to wake up. He didn't listen. I slid my hand out from under his and left his room.

Mom was allowed to have visitors in her room. She'd likely only be in overnight for observation, so we piled in like a reverse clown car. Once we'd all perched, leaned and sat ourselves around the tiny room, Mom told us of the accident. She and Dad had been pushing on toward an RV park later into the evening than they had planned. They were both tired. Dad was driving. A deer appeared in the arc of their headlights. Maybe Dad was so tired that he forgot he was driving Gladys rather than his old car and swerved to avoid hitting the deer. I didn't even know there were deer in Florida. Gladys careened off the road into a ditch where impact with a tree sent Dad's head into the steering wheel and then backward into the doorframe. Both he and Mom had their seat belts on, but only Mom's airbag deployed. Dad had been knocked out and had been out ever since. Mom had abrasions from her seat belt, a black eye from the airbag, and stiffness in her back, but she wasn't concerned about herself. She was too worried about Dad.

From the way she was telling the story, it was apparent her emotional injuries were worse than the physical ones. She said motorists were there to help almost immediately and an ambulance was on the scene faster than she expected. She began describing Dad after the wreck, but she broke down and couldn't go on. I started crying, and Alaina went to sit on Mom's bed and held her until she stopped sobbing.

I looked at Falina sitting on the windowsill next to me. I could tell she was holding her breath so as not to break down herself. Dad's brother's family looked dazed. They were all in various states of grief as well. Eventually we were able to look up and out of ourselves again. It seemed no one in the cramped room dared to breathe for fear of more crying and setting off my mom's tears again. Funny how we all tried to keep our emotions so self-contained for one another.

Over the next two days, the rest of the family arrived and we drifted between our rented hotel rooms and Dad's bedside.

He was still in a coma, but the surgery had gone well. I watched Mom troop through visits, phone calls and hospital decisions. I was saddened by her ethereal presence. She was fading. More than once, the idea occurred to me that I was lucky to have lost Shiloh early. I was lucky to be free of Mickey, too. Watching my life mate struggle for her life was not an experience I wanted to have, ever. It was hard enough to watch as a daughter, but when it was your *partner*, your future there in the hospital bed…no, thank you.

At the end of the fifth day, I wandered the hospital halls after buying a few trinkets at the hospital gift shop. I had cleaned them out of Almond Joy bars a day ago, but they still had a few items I needed. I headed out the front doors in hopes of some fresh air, a clearer perspective on things and the possibility of a plea fulfilled. In my pocket were my new purchases. I had three small crystal prisms, a miniature Raggedy Ann doll no taller than my pinky finger, a bag of dried apricots, a glittery bookmark and a tiny pewter acorn.

With these, I petitioned the fairies to assist Dad in healing. A petition is an earnest request for help, like a spell, but it's a spell over which one feels powerless to affect an outcome. I hadn't packed any salt, candles, or incense, so this was the best I could do here in the raised flowerbeds outside the hospital. I'd also left my Book of Shadows at home, so I'd have to record the petition later. I thanked the fairies in advance for any healing they could perform as I hid the gifts under the nodding blossoms of hydrangea and the broad leaves of the hosta plants. The small metal acorn was the last gift I offered. Its weight in my hand was satisfying. Such a small thing, yet it was so definite and dense. No wonder it represented life, strength and potential—exactly what Dad needed right now. I kissed the acorn and snuggled it into the earth under the big blue flowers.

I sat on the edge of the raised flowerbed and pulled my cell phone from my bag. The last time I'd used it had been in the Minneapolis Airport before flying down to Florida. I turned it on and listened numbly to the chimes announcing every voice mail and text I'd missed. Six, seven, eight. These would take my mind off Dad. Thirteen…eighteen, nineteen. Dad wasn't improving as rapidly as his doctors thought he would. Chime, chime, chime. What if Dad never came out of the coma? What would Mom do? What would we all do? Nothing would be the same. Nothing would be right without Dad. Twenty-two messages. So much the better for giving me something concrete to worry about, something I knew how to respond to.

The oldest text message was from Patrick. "Dwight settled in nicely at ours," he texted. "Locked your house. Keep me posted. I love you."

After receiving Falina's call I had raced home, changed clothes, thrown two black skirts, three long-sleeved T-shirts and underwear into my gym bag, grabbed my license and credit card and headed for the airport. Five hours later, I was on a plane headed for Mom and Dad. Patrick was happy to take Dwight. He had been stunned by the news, and although I knew he wanted to do more, looking after Dwight was the biggest help anyone could be to me at this point.

The second oldest text was from Shiloh. I looked at her name in the lineup, and my pulse quickened painfully. What a change from the depressed, tentative beats my heart must have been keeping the past few days. Ouch. Maybe I'd come back to read that text later.

The third oldest text was from Veronica. "Allura, I'm so sorry to hear! Please call me to let me know what I can do!" I'd call Veronica first after I checked the rest of these messages.

The oldest voice mail was from my editor at *The Indelible* saying how much he appreciated the clean, amusing copy I'd sent on the Mini-Marquee—a personalized door sign that writers, or others who often found themselves behind closed doors, could update via their computers to let others on the flipside of their closed doors know what they were up to. I'd imagined messages such as, "Mommy will be done at 2:35. Eat peanut butter and jelly sandwiches for lunch" or "Killing off antagonist while instant messaging my secret lover." What would my Mini-Marquee say? MIA while hoping Dad wakes up? I toyed with my amethyst beads and bit the inside of my lower lip to quell the tears.

The next two messages were from Shiloh. Skip, skip. Later, I told myself. Later. Or maybe never. Watching my mom worry and fade these past five days had made me realize how hard loving someone could be. We really have no control over what happens to the people to whom we give our hearts. And with that being the case, it was best not to give your heart to anyone. I'd decided during the past few days I was not going to let myself get close to her or anyone else. It wasn't worth the risk of losing someone. I had thought this before, but now Dad and Mom were confirming it for me.

Do what ye will and harm none. The ancient Pagan rule could be best accomplished by not complicating matters with a love relationship. Love just increased the likelihood that a person would harm another. Strangers or people with whom we don't have a close connection rarely harm us. Mom was likely indifferent to the plight of every other patient in this hospital, but the condition of the man whom she spent her life loving, well, that was killing her right now. We were all afraid he'd never come out of the coma, but we were going on with the business of living, for the most part. Mom hadn't been able to eat much or to sleep for more than twenty minutes at a shot for fear of waking to find Dad gone. My own selfish fears of Dad dying were compounded by the fear of Mom losing Dad. That would annihilate her. They had been best friends and partners for decades.

What business did any of us have going out, meeting another person and allowing that person to get attached to us? What business did others have in allowing us to fall in love with them? None. That was bad business. There was more room to harm others that way. Would I have been hurt by Shiloh's reaction to the "Oh Goddess" if she'd only been a one-night stand? Doubt it. I'd have said, "It's been lovely; thanks for the orgasm. Let's not do this again." But since I did care—care deeply—unfortunately, Shiloh's question and the subsequent conversation gnawed at me.

I contemplated deleting Shiloh's messages. Best-case scenario, Shiloh sent words that would make me feel better, but that would also be the worst-case scenario because when we eventually had our inevitable parting, we'd have shared that much more of ourselves with each other. It would hurt that much more. Best to leave it now, after just a few months. A few months? Was that all it had been? Yes, a few months. What was I doing comparing my and Shiloh's relationship to my parents' relationship? Apples and oranges. I'd never allow myself to get that attached to someone.

Even so, I couldn't bring myself to delete Shiloh's messages. I scrolled down to the next message, a voice mail from Davidoff Academy. A man named Boz Green, the Davidoff principal, was offering me an interview. I was supposed to call him back. Hm. I'd have to think about that one later. How tangled a web did I want to spin for myself?

My phone vibrated in my hand. It was Falina… and Dad was slipping. I raced back into the hospital.

* * *

My throat was dry and tight, so I couldn't answer Mom's question. We were sitting on a bench in the Intensive Care Unit hallway. I was slumped back against the wall but Mom was sitting straight up, alert. Her energy was livelier than it had been since I'd arrived.

"You know, don't you, that he's always very proud of you?" she prompted me again.

"Yes," I whispered. I thought of the letter he'd written to my high school principal requesting that she change her mind on same-sex prom dates during the grand march. I thought of the way he'd take me, Falina and Alaina to a cemetery to find the most ragged looking grave to tidy up during our celebration of Higan no Chu-Nichi—the fall equinox. We didn't have any dead relatives in nearby cemeteries, but Dad had always been drawn to autumn, death and dying. He had loved the celebration because it represented the beginning of death in the earth's cycle. He had read the obituaries every day.

I smiled as I remembered the joke question I'd heard him ask more often than any other—do Jews get buried in a *matzoh*leum? Dad had used this question the way some people use the question—do bears shit in the woods? Every time he asked it, he'd slap something across his thigh—usually the rolled up obituary section—and guffaw until Mom told him that was enough. Ouch. Double whammy. Thinking of this made me ache for Dad and for Shiloh both. She'd laugh at that one, I'd bet. I smiled again and then shot a glance at Mom, but she was also smiling.

"You know," she said, "regardless of how this turns out for Benji, I don't regret the choice we made to roam the United States with Gladys. If he pulls through, I will be very happy. If he doesn't make it, I will still be happy that we did what we did and that I loved him."

This wouldn't have happened if they'd stayed home though. I waited for her to say more. I wondered if she'd cry. The only time I had seen her cry since the accident had been that night she had recounted the story of the crash. After the first five days of extreme sadness, it was if she had it all out of her system and had moved on with making sure Dad had the best care. I could never be that calm in her shoes.

She was washed out though. Her now silvery pale red hair and paler skin showed her stress. Hollows had formed under her cheekbones and even her freckles looked faint. Her eyes, however, were bright with memories.

"Allura, we've had such fun! We needed this change of scenery to keep us going, to energize us and to let us play again. I know things might never be the same, but I do not regret going for it, going for our little pipe dream. Even now, I don't regret anything." She leaned forward and patted the back of my hand. Her palm was warm, soft and papery. I had to work hard to not cry at her touch.

I heard what she was saying, but didn't know how to process it. She would trade those good times for her husband? For my father? Is that really what she meant? Was she telling me this because she knew my own new relationship had squealed to an abrupt halt? We waited in silence. Dad was in his room, having been back from his second surgery for a little over an hour. His blood pressure had taken a dive during the operation, but was more stable now. The doctors remained hopeful that this surgery would allow him to come out of the sedation responsive and awake. I had doubts.

I whiled away the minutes thinking about how genuine and how certain Mom was with her words. She'd really rather have loved Dad well and lost him in the end, than…than what? Than to never have known or loved him? My conclusion seemed ridiculous to me now. Of course she was right. Had she not loved him, I would not be sitting here. Falina wouldn't be waiting in Dad's room for him to wake. Alaina wouldn't be at the other end of the hallway staring out the window. For her entire life, Mom would have felt like a jigsaw puzzle that was missing a piece. Thank Goddess she had been brave enough to fall in love and roll with it. I covered Mom's hand with my own and squeezed it.

"Everything will be okay, Allura," she said. "Everything will be okay."

A nurse wheeled an IV stand and an empty wheelchair past us with an empathetic smile on her lips. She looked kindly at us until she realized someone was coming at a quick clip in her direction. The nurse swerved over to the edge of the corridor as my sister careened in stocking feet around the corner.

"Mom! Allura, come!" Falina skidded down the hallway, looking like a girl version of Dad. "He's awake!" She was yelling and crying. "Dad's awake!"

CHAPTER THIRTY-FIVE

Homecoming

"Lilfella, lilfella, lilfella!"

Tears squeezed past my closed eyes as I cuddled Dwight and he crooned to me. I put my lips to the top of his head and crooned back, "Hi Dwight...Hi buddy."

"Lilfella, lilfella." I felt his muscles contract in his neck as he tried to bob his head under my maternal smooches. I let him up for air and laughed aloud over the joy of seeing him. He clenched tighter to my wrist and kept on bobbing as I held him at arm's length to admire his glossy black feathers.

"Dwight, my little man, you are looking good!"

"Lilfella, lilfella, lilfella," he said more quietly this time.

Patrick had taken good care of Dwight. Dwight's cage was clean, he had a variety of interesting playthings on top of his jungle gym and, most importantly, Dwight had not plucked out any of the new feathers he'd grown. There was no reminder of his naked, pink belly to be seen at all. I had worried about how badly the separation would stress him. It appeared that it had stressed him very little. Dwight was the best greeting committee

I could ask for, and it was good to be home. Seeing him again made up for the fact that I'd had to cross paths with the stalker cat to get to my front door. The handsome cat was becoming a permanent fixture, it seemed.

Surveying the usual pens, papers, style books and magazines piled on the corners of my desk and surrounding my laptop like an audience in an amphitheater, my fingers flexed with longing. Was I really happy to see the debris of my *job*? I was! I was *that* happy to be home.

I dug into my writing with a newfound zeal. I wrote two articles in the time it normally took me to start one. On most days I procrastinated by dealing with the laundry that begged for attention, making phone calls to friends to see what they were up to, playing a few games with Dwight, pinching back the herb garden and discovering a couple other tasks so dire they just couldn't wait. I contemplated starting a third article, but decided against pushing my luck. I'd check voice mails instead.

There was one from Mom with an update on Dad, one from Patrick inviting me over and asking me to check in with him when I arrived and the old one from Davidoff Academy offering me an interview. I hadn't yet called Davidoff back. I wasn't sure if the sudden rekindling of my passion for writing would last, or if it were just giddiness from returning home, so I called Davidoff first.

"There must be a mistake. I was called and told to schedule an interview for the writing teacher position." I waited for the secretary on the other end of the phone to double-check her files.

"No…" She cleared her throat nervously. She sounded familiar to me. "No, there's nothing here in the list of applicants about your being accepted for an interview." I could hear the shushing of papers. "Perhaps you were sent the letter in error."

"It was a voice mail." I tried to keep my disappointment from being audible. Even in the midst of Dad's hospital stay, I had been looking forward to interviewing at Davidoff. I may have even counted on the job as a sure thing based on Madame DuVaulle's words. If she were wrong about this, what else might she be wrong about? And then I caught myself…gentle fear and disappointment seeped through my veins as I realized I had been hoping all of Madame DuVaulle's predictions would come true. And if the one about teaching wasn't going to come true, perhaps the one about Shiloh wasn't going to either.

"Okay then, sorry about that." The secretary's voice sounded muffled on the other end of the call.

"Are you sure?" My voice sounded small.

"Yes, I am sure. In fact, the writing teacher position has already been filled."

"Okay, thank you." I ended the call and sat with the phone in my hand, my head hung low. The position was already filled? That fast? I wanted to teach there. I wanted the challenge, and I wanted to be inspired by kids who were overcoming obstacles. I also wanted, if I were to be honest with myself, to be near Shiloh. I listened to my internal whining and complaining and realized maybe I wanted it for all the wrong reasons. It was not about me. Maybe this was the universe telling me I didn't have the right stuff to offer the kids.

"Damn it." I tossed the phone onto my desk.

"Damn it," Dwight echoed as he tossed a half-destroyed peanut onto the floor of his cage. "Damn it."

My phone rang before I had a chance to talk to Dwight about impolite words. I picked it up and was greeted by Trisha's bright voice.

"Allura! I'm so glad to hear your dad is doing okay!"

"Hi Trisha, thanks," I said. She asked me a few questions about his prognosis and about how my mom was doing. She listened to my answers with patience and care. She told me how they enjoyed having Dwight at their house and how sullen Patrick was to drop him off this morning before my return. There was a short silence before the pace of the conversation sped up.

"Okay, before I change my mind about interfering," she blurted, "I need to ask you to consider seeing Mickey in order to clean things up."

"Clean things up?"

"Well, yes," she said more slowly now. "You need to move on, Allura and so does Mickey, but she can't because she…well, she hasn't."

"I don't know," I said, even though I knew she was right. There was no chance Mickey and I would ever work. It wasn't a matter of choosing Shiloh or Mickey, which was how it felt a while ago. Now it was just a matter of not being compatible with Mickey. We hadn't been able to stick together. It was not going to work.

Trisha didn't say anything as I kicked thoughts around in my head.

"You're right, Trisha, thank you," I said. "Any advice?"

"Well, I guess I'd advise meeting face-to-face rather than talking about it on the phone or email. And maybe you want to tell her about Shiloh…"

"Shiloh's done," I said.

"Really?

"I don't know. I think so."

"Allura, you have strong feelings for Shiloh, right?" She didn't give me time to answer. "You don't know if it's over with her. And the fact that you started something with her, and it was *real*, well, that might be what Mickey needs to hear to move on."

"Again, you are right." I smiled as I said this. I felt relief begin to loosen my shoulders, which I hadn't even noticed were tight. It would feel good to tie up the dangling ends with Mickey.

"I know!" she laughed into the phone.

"And thank you for being such a good friend," I told her, "to both me and Mickey. Thank you."

"You're welcome. I love you both. And this is kind of a weird place to be with you two, but…well, I love you guys, so I don't want things to drag on. I think you're both being hurt by…I don't know…by not finishing, I guess."

We said our good byes and as I spun back to attack my writing, I was both fuller and lighter than I had been before Trisha's call.

Four hours and two additional articles later, my phone rang and this time I didn't recognize the number.

"This is Allura," I sing-songed, high on my renewed lust for writing.

"Good afternoon, Allura, this is Boz Green from Davidoff Academy. I left you a message a short while back, but I wonder if you received it because I haven't heard back from you. I'd like to offer you an interview for the writing teacher position, unless you have already taken a position elsewhere."

Happiness, confusion and the fact that he'd said all that without taking a breath battled for my attention. "Oh! Hello, Mr. Green, I did return your call, just today, actually, but your secretary said there had been a mistake."

"Oh?"

"She said the position already had been filled," I explained.

There was silence on the other end, followed by what sounded like the slapping of a folder or paperwork on a desktop. Boz Green cleared his throat.

"I am sorry about that. Beth must have made a mistake. The position is definitely not filled, and we'd really like to interview you. I do apologize. Things usually go very smoothly around here. I, uh...I can find out what happened..." Embarrassment tinged his words.

"Don't worry. I'd really like an interview." I sounded too eager in my own ears, but I didn't care how I sounded in Boz's ears because I was pretty sure he was mulling over the mix-up.

"Are you able to come in anytime tomorrow?"

We made the arrangements, ended the call, and Dwight and I danced around like a pair of buffoons until I worked the excitement out of myself. I pumped my arms out in front of me and did my white-men-can't-dance dance. Dwight strutted around saying, "Damn it." I had an interview with Davidoff! Thank you, Goddess, Mother Earth, and God! Maybe I did have what the kids needed after all.

CHAPTER THIRTY-SIX

Closure, Shmosure

The short bursts of wind whipped my hair across my face and brought tears to my eyes. It was cold when the wind blew, but the hesitant warmth of the early spring sun tempered the gusts. The oversized spoon that balanced a shining cherry on its business end would look out of place anywhere but here in the Walker Art Museum's sculpture garden.

"I'm sorry for calling you judgmental when you told me to get help for my drinking issue, Al," Mickey said, facing the enormous spoon sculpture rather than looking at me. Her short salt-and-pepper hair created tiny spikes like upside-down icicles, and her cold ears almost matched the red of her coat.

"It's no problem," I answered, "maybe I was judgmental, am judgmental."

"Yeah, but I think it's the helpful kind of judgment," she said, turning to look at me and then turning back to the spoon. I didn't answer because every sentiment that crossed my mind did indeed sound judgmental to me. I thought of telling her it's only a helpful criticism if positive change occurs because of it.

So far she hadn't mentioned stopping, or even cutting back on drinking. I thought of asking her what her plan was, but I felt it was none of my business. I decided against tinkering in my mind with various options for her to address her alcoholism because, emotionally, I needed a rest from that kind of involvement. This was Mickey's issue now; I couldn't get re-involved with it. But at the same time, I *did* care what happened to her. I still cared for her but not in the way I had when we were together.

"Mickey, I hope everything works out the way you want it to with…with your drinking." I looked at her, bundled up in a bright red parka that matched the cherry resting atop the spoon. Her face in profile was softer than I had seen it in what seemed like years. This made me ache for what we might have had, who we might have been together had the alcohol not taken my place in the relationship. But the ache subsided quickly as I realized that we were both in exactly the right places now.

"I have to do this without you, don't I?" she asked me, finally turning to look at me fully. Her eyes were sad, but I could sense her strength and determination. She took my hands in hers, our mittens big and clumsy making us have to push our hands together rather than allowing us to really hold each other.

"Yes, I think so," I started, but then I had to add, "I mean, I'll be here, but…not like, not like before."

She nodded. I felt that she knew what I meant, even though I hadn't been able to fully express what was in my mind and heart. We stood that way for a few moments, and she didn't break eye contact for what seemed like the longest time in our recorded history together. Was she finally able to hold my gaze for more than a few seconds because she had nothing to hide or to lose now? Whatever the reason, I felt closer to her than I had in years. It was a nice way to say goodbye.

We walked around the gardens full of cold, whimsical metal art. Her thumb encased in my hand, my hand enclosed in her palm, separated by inches of the woolen insulation of our mittens. She asked how my father was doing, how my mother was doing and how I was doing. I talked to her more than I had talked to anyone else, including Falina and Patrick, since my dad's accident. I told her how scared I had been, how my mom had handled things and how I had questioned my perception of the risk involved with loving mere mortals. We laughed together, another thing she hadn't been able to do much with me in our last years together. It felt so good to experience Mickey's lightened energy. She felt happier in a way that was somehow *tangible* to me as I walked beside her.

I wanted to tell her about Shiloh, but didn't want to ruin what might be the last time she and I really connected. If this was goodbye as lovers and partners, and I wasn't sure there'd be a hello as friends, I thought it best to not speak of Shiloh. That might ruin the moment. Of course, if I didn't tell her of Shiloh, she wouldn't know that I was fully, truly moving on, even if it wasn't with Shiloh. Not telling Mickey may not be fair because she might harbor a hope of rekindling with me. I didn't have to ponder long because, as people who have spent years together often do, she seemed to read my mind.

"Trisha and Patrick tell me you've been seeing someone," she said, making the end of the statement sound like a question.

"Umm," I intoned through closed lips. What was I supposed to say now? Give her the whole story or only its sad ending?

"It's okay, if you want to tell me about her. I...well, I've had time to come to terms with it, so you can talk about it...I think." She laughed a little as she said the last bit. I glanced at her beside me, trying to read her face, but she wasn't looking at me. I could only hope the tears running sideways from her eyes to her hairline were tears brought out by the chill of the winds.

"You sure?"

"No, but I think I need to hear you tell me about her," she answered as she dropped my hand to pull up her hood. She turned like an over-bundled little kid to locate my hand again. As we walked with the knot of our held hands swinging between us, I told her about Shiloh, gently and honestly.

By the end of our moments together, we had both cried and laughed. I had no idea how necessary this ending, this healing, had been. I felt more complete than I had in ages.

I was pretty certain The Funk had left the building for good. People speak of closure as if it is a joke. Shoot, I had even made fun of "closure." But here we were, mending the hurts we had caused each other as we separated further apart as lovers and came closer together as humans. I did not expect that. On an almighty strong, cold gust of wind, I sent out a silent thank you to the Goddess.

CHAPTER THIRTY-SEVEN

Edgier

March twenty-third found me at Patrick and Trisha's front door for our hybrid celebration of Spring Equinox and Passion week: Spring Equipassion. I had gotten ready in a heady rush after receiving word from a Ms. Cranst, not "Beth," at Davidoff Academy that I'd be teaching writing beginning April nineteenth. I'd accepted the position thinking that at least one thing in my life should go well, and if it couldn't be my love life, well, it would have to be my career. Or possibly both of my careers, since I was still on a writer's high. I'd deal with running into Shiloh at the academy when the opportunity presented itself. Until then, I would try not to worry about it.

I would also deal with the fact that the secretary who had made the "mistake" was Elizabeth. Her brown eyes had revealed her surprise as I walked into the office where she was planted behind a computer monitor and a huge bouquet of ferns and baby's breath. Funny that there were no real flowers in the vase. The baby's breath stunk. Elizabeth was dressed as usual in an overly formal purple silk jacket and a pristine white silk blouse.

At her neck was a huge amethyst pendant firmly clasped in its gold filigree setting. I had started to greet her with a smile, but as her eyes sliced away from mine, I knew what had happened. She hadn't wanted me to get the job. I had said nothing to her before Boz Green opened his office door, strode out across the small space, shook my hand with warmth and unspoken apology and ushered me into his office for the interview. When I left, after what was an easy, uplifting conversation, Elizabeth was nowhere to be seen in the office.

There was a card taped to the front door of Patrick and Trisha's house, bringing me out of my reverie. My name was scrawled across the envelope. I pulled it off and opened it. The front of the card held a depiction of the Lovers Tarot card, only the artwork showed two women entwined. Where did they find this? I opened the card and read Veronica's handwriting inside.

"Allura, we interfered. We had to. We couldn't watch your fear get the best of you. You deserve better than you are giving yourself. So does Shiloh."

What the hell? How would they know what Shiloh deserved?

I continued to read, "So, after introducing ourselves...we think you should now open yourself to your very first celebration of Spring EquipassionOVER."

What? To whom had they introduced themselves? What the hell was EquipassionOVER? That was not right, so I read it again. Did they mean the passion was over? Duh. I knew that. But why would they refer to that? Where were they?

I opened the front door without knocking. I could have fallen over dead when I saw Shiloh sitting in the big armchair. She stood when she heard the door open.

"Shiloh," I breathed.

"Hi, Allura."

I glanced around the room, but no one else was here.

"Why, and how, are you here?"

She held out her hand, and me being me, I had no choice but to walk over and take it. I wanted to press her hand to my heart, to my mouth, to my eyes, to everything, but I just held it.

"Shiloh," I breathed again.

"I'm an idiot," she said.

I thought I should refute this, but she started talking again. "I have missed you so much. And I have been so stupid to think that this couldn't work out just because…"

What was she going to say? Was she going to bring up the God-Goddess debate? I wanted to kiss her so badly. Let her have her God, that'd be fine; let her try to convert me, I could handle that—I just knew that I couldn't handle not having her by me, not seeing her. Just looking at her was wrenching my soul in two.

Screw my resolve.

I pulled her close and pressed my mouth to hers. For a millisecond, I worried she might not want me to do this, but then she returned my kiss so fervently, that my heart and my knees went soft. Her lips tasted like the peach tea I had drunk the night I'd blindfolded myself all those weeks ago.

"Allura," she murmured into my mouth. My knees went even softer at the feel of her lips and tongue saying my name into me.

"Allura." This time she said my name into the air as she let a fraction of space come between our faces. "Allura, I am so sorry."

"Me, too," was all I could say back. I *was* sorry, even though it was hard to remember that, buoyed as I was by the joy of seeing her here in Patrick and Trisha's living room. Why was she *here*? Who cares? I kissed her again until she spoke.

"Allura, I need to tell you something," she tried.

But I didn't want to talk. I didn't want to listen. I just wanted to hold her and kiss her. She figured this out and kissed me back until I had had my temporary fill and needed to breathe normally for fear of asphyxiating on lust.

"Can we talk?" Shiloh asked, her smile looking somewhat swollen.

"Yes, now we can talk," I answered. I didn't know what to say, but had the feeling she had plenty on her mind. Over the past weeks, I'd given her so much thought, but nothing else. I hadn't returned her messages; I hadn't even read or listened to them. I had myself convinced that time would help me get over this desire I had to see her and laugh with her again. I could feel now, with her here, that I had been wrong.

She asked if we could sit together, and I remembered that she was in a place that was new to her. Or was it? What was she doing here? We sat knee to knee on the couch. She did not let go of my hands once we were seated, but I feared she might, so I gripped her back not caring what she thought of it.

"Allura, I want you to know that this was Patrick and Veronica's idea," she began, "but I also want you to know that I wouldn't be here if I didn't want to be—for myself."

"Okay," I said. I knew she had more to say.

"I wish I could start over with our last night together," she said.

"Mmm, I'd gladly relive that!" I laughed, not knowing if it was appropriate or not to do so.

Shiloh laughed, too. "No, not like that. I mean," she thought for a second, "yes, like that, but I'd like to take back what I asked you the next day. You are perfect, Allura. And I know what I asked made you feel less than perfect. And I want to take that back." Her voice got quiet and sad.

"Okay," I said, and I meant it. "Okay, you can have that question back." I wished she could see my face so she knew I wasn't being flippant.

"I'm sorry," she said.

"Shiloh, seeing you here, when I opened the door...well, it made me realize I want to be with you. I want...I want you. I don't care if you are narrow-minded and self-righteous." I leaned forward and nuzzled her cheek as I said this in hopes of her knowing I was kind of kidding. Thank my Goddess or thank her God—I didn't care who—she laughed. "I want you," I repeated.

"And I, obviously, want you." She laughed, got to her knees on the couch and pushed herself onto me. We wriggled into the cushions until she was holding me tightly against her chest, with her chin on the top of my head. She told me how Veronica had used *my* cell phone to call her a week ago to ask her if she wanted to get together with Veronica and Patrick to have a "come to our senses" coffee date. How had I not noticed Shiloh's name and number in the lineup of outgoing calls in my phone? I looked at the list of incoming calls, not the outgoing, I guess. Or maybe Veronica had deleted the call from my phone's history. I laughed because it sounded just like Veronica to stage a "come to our senses" talk. She was no-nonsense.

"Are you sure you are here on your own free will and not being forced by my friends?" I asked her, half-joking, half-serious.

"Allura, I am sure. I am not going to let you go." And with this she squeezed me until my rib cage might be damaged.

"I get it. Okay, I get the picture!" I wheezed and laughed.

She kissed the top of my head.

"So what are we going to do?" I asked her. I wondered what her plan was, even though I knew I'd go along with anything she wanted as long as it truly involved not letting me go.

"The real question is what *aren't* we going to do?" she answered.

I liked that answer. Shiloh told me more about her conversation with Patrick and Veronica. Apparently they felt the need to show her that people from different spiritualities could form deep, trusting bonds with one another, as Patrick and I had done with our smash up hybrid holidays. It had been Shiloh's idea to crash, or take over, the Spring Equipassion celebration. It had even been her idea to add her own flavor to the dish—the Passover part.

"Oh! I get it now!" sprang from me as I realized the Equipassionover now held Shiloh's Jewish angle as well as the Catholic and the Pagan angles.

"Is that okay with you?" Shiloh sounded concerned. "I mean, I don't have to barge in on your celebrations, but I just wanted to let you know that I understand you better now. A lot better. I guess I understand myself a lot better, too. At first I thought you'd marginalize me because our religions weren't the same and then realized I had no reason to think that. We're not the same in other areas, and you've never marginalized me. So, is it okay?"

"It's more than okay with me," I reassured her. I was telling the truth; I was honored that she was here, with me, celebrating in this strange and lovely way on Trisha and Patrick's couch. We were to meet up with Patrick, Veronica and Trisha later at Matt's Bar if we wanted to. For now, I just needed to be with Shiloh. She felt the same.

We talked about what went wrong. Shiloh couldn't apologize enough to forgive herself for the weeks that had gone by, but I believed that we needed to have those weeks. I had certainly been mixed up in what I wanted at the time. Patrick and Veronica had not told Shiloh about my dad; they had saved that for me, so I described the accident to Shiloh. I finished by telling her he was healing well. She cried, saying that she was even more mad at herself because she could have been there with me had she not been such an ass about the religion thing.

I disagreed and told her that I needed to go through that alone, or with family, but essentially alone. My mom's words had helped me get clarity on what was most important, even though the full impact of what she'd said hadn't sunk in until I saw Shiloh sitting here today.

We talked about how being in a minority spirituality or religion might possibly make a person hold tighter to her beliefs. How it might make someone more defensive. But we both agreed that a chance at love might trump those beliefs or at least encourage people to "get over their bad selves." Those were the last words Shiloh laughed out before we began making up in earnest. Thankfully, Patrick, Trisha and Veronica stayed out late. We had things other than meeting up with them on our minds.

CHAPTER THIRTY-EIGHT

Laughing Down the Moon

Plucking the postcard from the pile of mail, I noted the bright Florida sun beating on feathery palm trees and smiled. I turned it over and read:

> Dear Allura,
> Dad and I have arrived at Aunt Ana's charming retirement community. He's loving life poolside, sipping drinks and ogling the women (who insist on waiting on him and babying him after he shares his near-death experience with them). I have a question for you. Dad asked me to ask you: how do you avoid running over a blind deer with your RV? I have no ideer. No eye deer. Get it? Anyway, I hope your spring has sprung.
> Love, Mom

I chuckled as I placed the card on the plate rail. Seriously though, who jokes about a no-eyed deer after almost dying because you hit a deer? My father was an odd gem. I trailed my fingertips across the wooden rail. The dust reminded me of velvet, it was so thick. Velvet. I decided to make good on that gorgeous cloak and intriguing *Drawing Down the Moon* book Veronica had given me months ago on our All Samhain celebration. I ran upstairs to tuck Dwight in for the night.

"Good night, Little Fella," I said to him.

"Lilfella," he said back, bobbing his head.

I turned off the light and half-closed his door, went to my bedroom and pulled my cloak from the back of the chair. I grabbed the book from my nightstand where it had donned its own cloak of sorts. Shameful to allow dust to gather on the plate rail, but on the bedside table as well? I laughed quietly. Quite honestly, I hadn't been reading much in bed lately.

Tonight was the perfect night to finally draw down the moon and invite the Goddess's energy into myself. I'd also enjoy the deep gratitude I felt for, oddly enough, the recent shake-ups in my life. The ritual would be supported by the magic of the luminous, fat full moon. I took the book and the cloak downstairs where I laid them out on the table. The luxurious green velvet of the cloak looked even richer atop the wooden table. The book, however, seemed to not fit the picture. I picked the book up and rifled through its pages. The history of Paganism, Wiccan heritage and the stories of various witches would not be of much help tonight.

I knew I had all the answers inside of me already. And I already knew how to do the ritual of drawing down the moon, so I carried the book to the shelf in the corner of the living room, beside the fainting couch and filed it between *Bearheart* and *Twinsight*, a very good place to be filed, as these were two of my favorite books. I knelt there for a few minutes looking at all of the books not relegated to the office upstairs. The living room bookshelf housed those that were dearest to me. I wanted to keep them close and not move them into the business area of my office. Not that I had any intention of rereading them. In fact, most of them had hit me so profoundly that complete passages from each had permanently imprinted on my soul; there'd be no need of a second reading with any of them.

Kneeling before the bookcase, I leaned back on my heels and let my eyes gloss over all the book spines. I wasn't sure *Drawing Down the Moon* belonged here on this shelf. I'd decide after tonight.

I got up to gather the necessary items: wine and sea salt from the kitchen, the chalice and incense from the little wooden box under the dining room window, a bundle of dried sage and my wand from the windowsill above the wooden box. All I needed was to find an appropriate Goddess image for the night and to take a cleansing shower before I began.

The night was warmer than most early spring nights, but I planned on a shower so hot that the heat would stay with me. I'd go sky-clad under the cloak. Since it had no closures, any warmth that lingered with me after the shower would be more than welcome. The southwest corner of my backyard always offered the perfect place for solitary rituals. There were three mature pines that stood like sentinels and made a delicious little alcove that protected any open flames from the wind and me from the prying eyes of neighbors. Not that they'd be interested in whatever it was I was doing out there, but one never knows for certain.

Flames. I almost forgot candles. I went back into the kitchen after depositing everything on the dining room table beside the cloak. I opened the cupboard. A wonderful, high-pitched squeak resounded throughout the kitchen. I knew that if it weren't so late, Dwight would have answered the cupboard door with a mimicking squeak of his own. He, for some reason—probably left over in his brain from days when his ancestors had to be wary of predators—never made noise this late at night, unless it was quiet little bedtime talk in response to my wishing him sweet dreams.

I looked at the selection of candles. I needed a color that signified the beginning of a new journey. Red...no, too full of willpower. Willpower might very well be what got me to The Funk in the first place. Wanting to control everything and then panicking when things didn't go my way. I had even panicked when things *did* go my way. Black would be perfect for banishing negativity, but again that seemed too controlling tonight, too judgmental. I wanted a color that would allow me to enjoy the flow that life was offering.

I didn't see any white candles...how the hell could I not have white? White would have been perfect for representing a new beginning. It had been a long time since I had gone shopping, I had to admit. Okay. My eyes rested on the perfect, most appropriate color, even better than white. I drew two long indigo tapers from their box. Beautiful. Indigo was for life changes. Nothing would suit me better tonight. I would anoint them with oil right before lighting them outside. First, a shower.

I padded up the stairs, went to my bedroom to grab the lavender oil from my dresser and then into the bathroom. I didn't turn on the light because the glow of the full moon outside was streaming in, blurred by the patterned glass in my bathroom window. The hot water cascaded over my shoulders, breasts, hips and thighs. I leaned my head back under the spray, appreciating the heat and then abruptly snapped my head forward. Shit! I should have kept my hair dry. It was unseasonably warm outside, but probably not warm enough to be prancing about out there with wet hair. Damn. I could wait for it to dry, but that'd take too long. Well, I'd just have to pull on a ski cap. The one with the big green and blue pom-pom on top would complement the greens of the cloak quite well. Okay, no worries then. I let my head fall back under the hot stream.

Worrying was the last thing anyone was supposed to do in the cleansing bath or shower prior to a ritual. The shower washed away negative thoughts and concerns so that a person came clean and positive to the ritual. I laughed out loud as I pictured the worry of wet hair on a cool night taking physical form and spiraling around the tub's floor a couple of times before washing down the drain.

Okay, wash-wash, suds-suds, goodbye worries and negative thoughts and hello lavender oil. I was done.

In less than ten minutes, I found myself outside between the cedar fence and the three pine trees, dressed in a green velvet cloak, a blue and green pom-pom'd ski hat and my black cowboy boots. I had walked outside barefoot and then realized that I hadn't swept up out here yet this spring. All the little branches, pine cones and stones that somehow materialized after the snow melted were just waiting to puncture the winter-soft soles of my feet. I had dashed inside to get my boots—and here I was—fashion police be damned.

I looked up at the moon, directly above me now. Elation coursed through me like a swollen river, jumping its banks and cleansing everything in its path. There is nothing like the first full moon of spring. Chunky, serious-looking clouds roamed the sky, but none threatened the light of this fat, glowing moon. I felt lucky and warm. I sent a silent thank-you to the moon for everything and nothing in particular. I knelt to set up the altar at the middle of the tiny clearing. I had chosen one of Dwight's big glossy black feathers for the Goddess symbol. He was actually looking pretty good these days, with his feathers grown back in. He had so many new ones that he was even starting to go through a molt, which I learned from my Humane Society connection was a regular happening for most birds. I laid his feather between the two candles. In the light of the moon, Dwight's feather almost matched their indigo.

I cast a circle and addressed each of the four directions with gratitude and honor. I knelt and lit the candles, thanking the flames and asking that they guide me. I was about ninety-nine percent sure how the ritual was done, and I knew my intentions, so I wasn't worried. The best part of being a solitary practitioner is that as long as you are respectful and your intentions are defined and kind, you can't go wrong. According to me, at least. There are others who would argue this point and say that ritual is only real ritual if it is performed in accordance to tradition. I seemed to be completely alone, so I'd do it my way. I looked over my shoulders to make sure of it and laughed as the pom-pom atop my head wobbled to the left when I looked right and to the right when I looked left. I'd do whatever I wanted to do.

I was ready to bring some Goddess energy into myself, let go of The Funk and move on into the unknown—no matter how frightening that was. All around me, people were doing that very same thing—moving into the unknown. My parents, after decades of unchanging creature comforts, had decided to break free of their old lives. It had brought what seemed like insurmountable challenges, but they were healing. They were staying with Aunt Ana for a few months and were getting stronger every day.

Mickey was letting go of one of her creature comforts as well. She had recently told me, albeit hesitantly, of a first date she had had with a woman she met at her Alcoholics Anonymous meetings. I had listened to Mickey's words with one ear and had listened for any reaction in my heart with my other ear. The only reaction my heart had was to be genuinely happy for Mickey. I didn't expect to have another reaction because I knew I was in the right place with the right person now, but a part of my mind felt fear that I'd experience at least a twinge of jealousy when I heard Mickey was dating again. Nope, not a twinge. I was relieved but not surprised. I hoped for the best for Mickey.

And then there was Heather who was venturing into the mysteries of motherhood. Was she afraid? Maybe, but she wasn't so afraid that she stopped herself and Julia from pursuing a pregnancy.

Falina was starting something serious with Brian. She was the last person in the world who'd mis-button her shirt, yet here she was, putting herself out there in ways that were out of her comfort zone in order to strengthen the connection with him.

All those kids in Cami's classes…they were going into the unknown every day, weren't they? Really, who knew what each day would bring when you were sixteen or seventeen? Of course, you *were* more used to embarrassing demoralization at that age, I reminded myself. That was pretty much the theme of the teen years, unfortunately.

My new students at Davidoff Academy brought me into their unknown every day with their stories and their questions. I had never felt more honored than when I was listening to a student who had never had sight share his or her vision with me. How wonderfully well they could see the world. There was Joy, the older sister of triplet brothers who identified each brother by his scent—according to her one smelled of Doritos, one of laundry soap and one of wood. There was Miranda who refused to learn Braille because she was certain that her vision was going to be restored soon. She couldn't explain how she knew, but she *knew*, and I believed her. Then there was Walter, the King of Practical Jokes, whom I'd kill with my own bare hands if he weren't so good at providing me with amusing anecdotes to share at social gatherings. I couldn't begin to guess at the unknown my students faced every day.

And then there was Veronica. She was moving into the unknown, too. She had purchased an old filling station on the corner of Nokomis and 43rd and had her business plan drawn up for her garden shop.

I thought of my upcoming trip to the Boundary Waters with Shiloh, said "Egads," aloud and then started laughing. I was moving forward, no more second-guessing. Shiloh was willing to move forward with me. Whatever would happen would happen; I knew we'd be together.

Speaking of moving into the unknown and speaking of Shiloh, was there anyone out there who moved more into the unknown than she did every day? Not that I could think of. Every morning, Shiloh had to get up and face what life had to offer without even being able to see it. The unknown was comprised of everything for her, wasn't it? It didn't get more unknown than being unseeing.

And there I had it. I could make this decision to go for it in my love life and on my career, right? So what if I had had a little breakup and shake-up in my life? People around me were setting prime examples of moving on. I would move on, too. Even Dwight with his new, "Oh God, Oh Goddess, Oh God" routine, which horrified me but made Shiloh laugh until she couldn't breathe, even Dwight was moving into the unknown, trusting me and his new life enough to stop tearing his feathers out and learn some new tricks, or new phrases at least. I smiled as I thought of how ridiculous it was that I hadn't yet been able to look him in the eye as he imitated my and Shiloh's throes of passion. And recently, with the windows open for spring,

Dwight had begun to meow in response to the polite meows of the stalker cat—whom I'd patted twice on the head in the past week. Who knew Dwight would become such a funny little guy? Who knew a cat would begin to grow on me? Perhaps the persistent feline was Shiloh's familiar. After all, they'd showed up in my life at about the same time. Fear and love. Were they always this impossibly intertwined?

My laughter began low and easy and continued until I felt tears pushing at the corners of my crinkled-up eyes. I laughed with my whole being, until I tasted the pine and the night and the silvery light within me. I craned my neck to see the moon, right above me and realized that like the moon, I was full. I had gotten my edges back and was no longer just sliding through life. I'd been caught. Life had me in its wonderful snare.

Bella Books, Inc.

Women. Books. Even Better Together.

P.O. Box 10543
Tallahassee, FL 32302

Phone: 800-729-4992
www.bellabooks.com